DATE DUE

TIME
EXPIRED

Also by Susan Dunlap

TIME EXPIRED

A Jill Smith Mystery

SUSAN DUNLAP

Delacorte Press

Published by
Delacorte Press
Bantam Doubleday Dell Publishing Group, Inc.
1540 Broadway
New York, New York 10036

The trademark Delacorte Press® is registered in the U.S. Patent and Trademark Office.

ISBN 0-385-30444-7

Manufactured in the United States of America

For Kathy Steingroot

Acknowledgments

A great deal of research is necessary for a book like this, and the author is indebted to the generosity of:

Sergeant Michael Holland of the Berkeley Police Department Hostage Negotiations Team, who gave of his time and knowledge. The highly regarded HNT has careful and specific personnel and guidelines to protect everyone involved in every hostage situation. It was not possible to include them all in this work of fiction;

Sergeant Kay Lantow of the Berkeley Police Hostage Negotiations Team for her gracious, forthright, and clear explanations;

Officer Karan Alveraz of the Albany Police, for her never-failing goodwill and her ability to track down information that I needed right away;

Berkeley Senior Parking Enforcement Representative Vickie Frasier, one of life's true diplomats;

Dr. Elise Blumenfeld, LCSW, for her insights into motivation and behavior;

Dr. Robert Stebbins, for his expertise on canyons and their inhabitants—four-legged, two-legged, and rooted;

Jennie Arndt, for her unique perspective.

Although some characters in this book have jobs or positions which do exist in real life, all the characters are entirely fictional.

CHAPTER 1

□

He dragged her right down there, into the canyon. Her legs were all swelled up, like old lady's legs. She was kicking."

"Fighting him, Mr. Jenkins?" I demanded, trying to get an accurate picture of the victim. "Was she yelling at him, too?"

"No, not kicking that way. Kicking like she was swimming. You know, up and down. If she was saying anything, I couldn't hear. But, it's real noisy, now, with Sunday evening traffic and all." He looked up at Arlington Avenue above the canyon. He was half shouting above the roar of engines as buses hauled themselves up the steep grade to the uphill lane ten feet higher than the downhill one. Patrol had closed the lower lane to civilians as Hostage Negotiation Team members raced in from their regular assignments and squealed to stops there. The air was thick with exhaust fumes.

"You're going to get her out." Jenkins's statement was half question, half hope. "It's only a tiny canyon down there."

"The more you can tell us, the better we'll—*I'll*—be able to negotiate with the hostage taker." As primary negotiator I would be the one dealing with him.

"But I didn't see any more than the guy's rifle barrel and the woman's legs. They were so swollen, like she was already sick, you know?"

I tried not to picture it, not to get caught in envisioning an old woman down in the cold, wet canyon controlled by some kind of pervert, a pervert for whom we had no ID, no description, nothing. I couldn't let myself think about the victim, wonder if she was shivering down there, terrified, or if the perp was holding a cigarette lighter to her fingers, or . . . *Don't let yourself get stuck on the victim,* they tell you in Hostage Negotiation classes, *your job is to get the facts that will save her.* But it was a battle; even when we role-played in training, it was hard not to get caught up in caring. And now . . . those legs bouncing up and down were a bad sign. If Jenkins, who had been within forty feet of her was right, the victim's legs were just bouncing up and down from the jolts of being dragged. I swallowed and said, "Describe her."

"I already told the patrol officer, I couldn't really see her exactly. Just her legs, I mean from the knee down, and the bottom of her skirt."

Dammit, why couldn't he have *observed*? He couldn't even swear the victim was old. Thick legs? She could have been a young muscular soccer player. I needed an idea of how desperate the situation was, how much slack I'd have—if any. Hostage negotiating made Homicide Detail seem like slow motion. "What kind of shoes was the victim wearing?"

"Black. Lace up. Oxfords like old ladies wear. When I spotted her the guy was already in the field here, by the chute—that's what we called it when we were kids, the chute down into the canyon. That house over there"—he pointed to a wooden building fifty yards south—"that used to be right here, above the chute. But the land's real unstable, one good shake like the last quake and that house would have been down there in the canyon. They had to move it."

It had been over an hour since his call. Half an hour since the patrol officer verified his claim that he'd seen a man with a rifle dragging a body down the chute—the rocky gorge cut by Cerrito Creek—into the canyon. A woman who had been walking a spaniel had seen it, too.

Normally the dispatcher alerted all members of the Hostage Negotiation Team to report to the operations command at the station downtown. But with this situation, with the perp in a canyon the neighborhood kids used as a playground, with a perimeter we could never adequately secure, there was no time for that. It was already dusk; half an hour and it'd be night. Fog was blowing in across San Francisco Bay, settling on trees up here like birds nesting for the night. The dispatcher had rolled the mobile station; we'd set up on the Arlington.

Now patrol officers from district 1A were ringing the canyon, waiting for the Tac Team to relieve them. On the Arlington the guys from the Tac Team were running for the mobile van. They'd crowd in there, eyeing as much of a map of the canyon as we had. The high ground observers would be looking for places to get out over the canyon unseen, on roofs of cottages that clung to the canyon wall, or perched on a live oak branch. They'd crouch there and wait, for as many hours as it took.

This finger canyon, so named because it resembled the space between open fingers, was seven acres, flush in the middle of one of the wealthiest Berkeley hills neighborhoods, high walls at this end, petering out to nothing at the other. Houses stood shoulder to shoulder all around it, blocking sight of it so thoroughly most people didn't know it existed. But down there among the dense oak and bay trees there were deer, possums, skunks, lots of wild blackberries, and enough poison oak to have the whole department scratching. The remains of a quarry office was fifty yards or so downstream, Jenkins had said—it had been little more than a cement floor when he was a child thirty years ago—and a lean-to was closer to the chute. Chances were the perp and the victim were in one of them. But the trees and shrubs, and the fog, were too thick to let us get a good view into the canyon, even with night glasses. There was enough underbrush to camouflage an arsenal. And a hundred routes of escape, a thousand places to hide. A hostage situation in here was a nightmare.

Another car squealed to a stop. I turned around, spotting Inspector Doyle, the field commander. His graying red hair was fluttering in the wind. His white shirt was rumpled, and his skin, as always, hung too loose from his bones. His appearance said: major surgery; inadequate recovery time. But he always looked like that. Today he'd spent a hard Sunday he should have had off, knocking his head against Homicide-Felony Assault's pain-in-the-ass case of the month—the meter maid assaults. I'd worked a lot of homicides under Inspector Doyle; at the best of times he was brusque.

"What do we have on the perp, Smith?"

"Zilch. No suspicious strangers reported, no weird hermits living nearby. Not a damn thing to start negotiating with," I added before he could.

"Victim?"

"Could be old, sick. Witness can't be sure."

"Someone checking cars?"

I nodded. Maybe a license plate would give us a lead to the perp. I needed something, some edge to start negotiations.

Without comment Doyle strode to the van. He looked ready to snap, but he was no more on edge than I was. When I made contact with the perp I had to know what kind of carrot to dangle, what shape stick to threaten with. If I made one wrong guess, the woman down there could be dead.

Doyle was setting up an inner perimeter inside the canyon around the perp and his hostage, making it as small as he could. Patrol would ring an outer perimeter line around that and clear the space between the inner and outer perimeters. No one would get past their line without an ID. As soon as they were set, I'd try for contact with the perp.

The mobile van doors opened. Twelve officers hurried out. A couple were still in street clothes. The rest were already in the all-black uniforms they'd be wearing if and when they came in for a rescue. Doyle motioned one of them over to Jenkins. Behind them, beyond the outer perimeter, neighbors holding cocktail glasses or coffee cups grouped together, reporters leaned forward, cameramen balanced equipment on shoulders.

At dusk any other cold foggy November day houselights would ring the canyon. Warm glows from those cottages halfway down the canyon wall would twinkle up behind the live oak and bay trees. Now I watched the houselights go off one after another, till only a few were left. Without them the tiny canyon loomed larger, blacker, and deep as a well. I looked around for Murakawa, my secondary negotiator—probably still caught in crosstown traffic. Doyle was standing beside the van, foot tapping irritably as he conferred with the Tac Team commander. He kicked a clump of dry weeds, nodded, and strode toward me like he'd been given a shot of caffeine. "Contain's in place."

I aimed the loudspeaker toward the canyon and stood momentarily looking out into the unmapped dark. I hated negotiating with a perp who could be a teenager flipped out from drugs, hormones, and an F on a history test, or a con who'd spent half his life in Q, or one of our homegrown crazies directed by voices telling him to kill at the mention of "hamburger" or "sidewalk." It was like tossing pennies in a bottomless wishing well. Except now a woman's life depended on those wishes coming true.

I couldn't wait any longer. I turned on the speaker: "This is the police. We have you surrounded. We know you're down there. If you have a flashlight, turn the beam upward. Now!"

I stared down into the deep gray mass. Did something flicker in the middle? No. I repeated the command, word for word. We keep it as simple as possible. The perps shouldn't have to think, just obey.

No change. Not a ripple in the dark.

Murakawa came toward me double time. As my secondary negotiator he'd be the liaison between me and the rest of the team. I briefed him. Then I lifted the loudspeaker and repeated the command again. "This is the police. You are surrounded. If you have a flashlight, turn the beam upward. Now!"

"Smith!"

"There!"

We were both pointing to the middle of the canyon. A light had flashed. Murakawa motioned to Grayson, head of the Tac Team. "He may be coming up. Get everyone back. Give him room."

"Take position," Grayson called to the Tac Team. "He may be coming up."

Black-uniformed officers jumped the two steps to the ground, landing as lifeless as beanbags. With a perp who was walking out on his own, odds were nothing would happen, but they had to play the low percentage. Later they would find out about the victim, be glad her ordeal ended so soon. But now . . . Hostage negotiation was an adrenaline junkie's dream. Going cold turkey like this was hell.

I moved onto the sidewalk. Grayson's team flashed their lights across the field toward the trees by the path down to the creek. They stood, weapons poised, listening for footsteps.

Squeals of brakes and staccato bursts from patrol car radios mixed with calls from onlookers, pleas from the news guys jostling for the best spot, and the low groans of foghorns across the bay. The team wouldn't be able to hear the perp till he'd climbed up the rocky canyon wall and swung around the live oak at the entrance to the stream. But when he did, the first target he'd spot would be the team.

My black windbreaker flapped and the nylon that was supposed to keep out the wind had turned icy. I stood by the van with Murakawa and Doyle and waited.

"He's not coming out," Bates, one of the reporters, yelled.

Too soon to know, I assured myself. The perp had around fifty yards of path to cover. Maybe carrying the victim. I couldn't take the chance of spooking him. Blood pounded in my neck and my stomach; I could have run the length of the outer perimeter and still been too tense to stand here and wait.

"Hey, Smith, he's taking you guys for a big ride," Bates yelled. I drummed my fingers on the loudspeaker. Was Bates right? Had we hallucinated the light, from our hopes? Was the perp sitting down in the canyon laughing at us? Pulling out the victim's fingernails? I pushed away the thought. Behind me I could feel the crowd pressing at the perimeter line. I'd wait another minute.

"Smith, he could be in San Francisco now, ordering dinner at the St. Francis," Bates called.

Ignoring Bates, I counted down the seconds. After everything was over we'd front up a press officer; that was the agreement, and reporters knew it.

"Hey, Smith, the guy's suckered you," Bates yelled just as my count got to sixty.

Picking up the loudspeaker, I strode angrily into the inner perimeter to the edge of the canyon. "This is the police. Turn on your flashlight and leave the beam on."

Nothing.

I gave him two minutes, then repeated the call. We give the perp every chance to come out freely. A successful hostage operation is one where no one—neither hostage, cop, nor perp—is injured. He hadn't been using his flashlight; the battery wouldn't have gone dead. Still I gave him an alternative. "Yell as loud as you can. Yell 'Hello.' "

No light; no sound.

"Murakawa, find Doyle; tell him we're getting nothing here. Time for Plan B."

He nodded and walked up toward the street. I kept my gaze on the path down to the stream, but I had role-played breakdown of negotiations enough times to know that Doyle would be stepping into the van to call the operations commander. The O.P. would huddle with Chief Larkin. Maybe Larkin would give the okay to go with Plan B. Probably not.

Nothing in Berkeley wasn't political. Of the 120,000 residents probably 110,000 of them had opinions on every move we made. Most of those opinions weren't positive. We had a top-notch force, but the aura of the sixties still surrounded us. And decisions like this one were rarely decided by the operations commander or even the chief, much less the primary negotiator. There was too much flak potential. Probably the city manager would decide.

When the word came down, Doyle would tell Grayson. Grayson would alert the Tac Team. As often as I'd practiced coaxing the hostage taker to come out for a sandwich or a talk with his wife, they had practiced storming a house, setting off diversionary flares, breaking through all the doors and windows simultaneously, making instantaneous threat assessment, and if the perp was not doing what they told him—if he was heading to endanger the hostages, moving fast—they opened fire. And they kept firing till the threat was gone, till the perp was down. All that in less than a minute.

Doyle strode toward me. "Too soon. C.M. says to wait."

"Too soon!" I snapped. "We've got an injured hostage down there. She's probably old, terrified, fragile. She could be bleeding to death."

"Tell that to the city manager's office."

"City manager's not going to call and tell her family she died because he couldn't get off his ass."

"Smith, run for mayor and you can make the rules." He smacked his fist against the van. "No hotdogging, the C.M. says. Too dark, too dangerous, too many people around. Can't have half the force tramping around in there with guns out. Could be kids down there. Or anyone. Could endanger the victim. C.M.'s got to think of the bigger picture. You know that, Smith." The loose skin on his cheeks twitched with anger. He'd picked up the loudspeaker and was squeezing the handle like it was the C.M.'s neck. Or the perp's. Or mine.

"Here's the bigger real picture, Inspector. How much longer can we keep the contain? We've got kids coming home; they're going to take it as a challenge to sneak past our lines. We've got half the neighborhood out here behind us, watching us do nothing but keep them from dinner. You can bet they'll be on the horn to the city manager first thing tomorrow. Tell him that!"

Doyle glared at me, then at the canyon. "What's that light?" he growled to one of his team who'd just walked up.

"Nursing home, sir. They couldn't evacuate."

"What?" he growled. "A building the size of a nursing home hanging off the edge of the canyon?"

"Private place. Converted house. Just a few patients, sir."

I turned to Doyle. Sweat coated my forehead; it ran down my back. But my voice sounded dead calm. "Perfect spot for a hostage taker to commandeer."

Doyle nodded and grabbed the phone. He wouldn't remind the operations commander of the potential flak; the O.P. wouldn't think of reminding the chief or the C.M., but we could all see the headlines if that happened.

The canyon was black as a well now. Fog cloaked the trees. The wind rustled oak leaves and scraped branches of bay trees against each other. It had been nearly half an hour since I'd seen the light flash down there. The hostage taker could be gone by now. And the hostage dead.

Doyle put down the phone and motioned Grayson over. "Tac Team'll set up a diversion and go in."

"No! Not with a perp we know nothing about and a victim who . . . we can't take that chance."

Doyle stared at me. "Smith, you're the one—"

"Sir," I said, lowering my voice. The press was too far away to hear, but still I didn't want to take the chance. "There's only one kind of diversion that'll work."

Doyle's eyes narrowed. He knew what I was going to say. He didn't like it, but he didn't object.

"The only thing we can count on to hold his attention and not spook him is what he's used to: the negotiation. From here we don't know how much he can hear down there. We need to be down there to be sure." I waited till he gave his nod of reluctant agreement. "I'll take the loudspeaker and go down there."

CHAPTER 2

□

It was against all our procedure. The rule is the negotiator makes sure that when the perp surrenders, he gives up to weaponry. He emerges not face-to-face with the negotiator, but face-to-barrel with the Tac Team's guns. The negotiator never gives up her gun, never gives up herself, never puts herself in the immediate danger zone.

But when you're dealing with an armed perp and a hostage in as bad shape as our victim could be, you don't have the luxury of following regulations. Besides, breaking the rule *is* the rule in the city of Berkeley.

The level footing of the canyon rim fell off by the live oaks above the streambed. From there it would be a matter of my hanging on to branches and bracing on rocks, maneuvering down the crevice.

Berkeley is striped with streams, but most have been covered over. This one, Cerrito Creek, runs under the Arlington and out for a while before it goes back underground at the other end of the canyon. In November there isn't much water down there. Just enough to make the rocks slippery. The local kids didn't call this the chute for nothing.

An icy Pacific wind was blowing up the canyon, rustling live oak leaves and teasing us all with the homey smell of bay leaves. End-of-the-weekend traffic had subsided; the Arlington had shifted back from main thoroughfare to mere hillside conduit. Cars still squealed to halts spewing out off-duty sworn officers, crisis groupies, and a Super Bowl's worth of camcorders, toted by a passel of news photographers and three or four passels' worth of civilians. My descent into the canyon would be better documented than

The Catch that gave the 49ers the 1981 championship. By midnight I'd be a star in living rooms, family rooms, entertainment centers, and bedrooms all over Berkeley.

Doyle and Murakawa came up behind me. I glanced at Murakawa. He was one of the patrol officers I felt most at ease with, a tall, thin guy, with a spray of brown hair that fell boyishly over his wide forehead. With minimal provocation he'd tell you he was just doing police work till he applied to chiropractic school. But we'd all heard that tale for five years; now Murakawa was the only one left who believed it. In Berkeley few of us want to admit that whatever we're doing is our ultimate job; most of us secretly believe there's something more on the horizon, for when we grow up. So we can't afford not to be gentle with the chimeras of our friends. Whatever Murakawa's future, now he was thorough and almost compulsively reliable—just the guy I wanted to back me up in the canyon. As primary negotiator I'd do the talking, bond with the hostage taker. As my secondary, he'd be in my ear every moment, listening to that bond form, and making sure that when the transference linked us, it pulled the hostage taker into me, not the other way around. The intimacy between the negotiator and the hostage taker can overwhelm everything we've learned. It can turn on you, and draw you in too deep. Negotiators have trusted too much, and they've died. It would be Murakawa's job to see that I stayed out of the line of fire.

"You ready, Smith?" Inspector Doyle asked.

"Ready, sir."

"Smith—"

I had the feeling he'd been about to pat me on the butt and tell me the whole game was riding on my throwing arm. And that he'd thought better of the pat. "Get him to talk, Smith. We don't want half the team going in there blind."

I started down the creek crevice, hanging on to a live oak branch, bracing my feet against the rocks. I wanted to move silently. I'd clipped the loudspeaker to my belt. But I couldn't keep it from banging sharply into my thigh and loudly against the rock. The flashlight next to it rattled. I sounded like the entire offensive line rushing down the cement hall to the dressing room. Murakawa, behind me, sounded like the rest of the team. I just hoped the perp wasn't near enough to hear.

All around the canyon the Tac Team would be inching their way down, eyeing the dark terrain around them for signs that the perp had been there, trying to discern drag marks of the victim.

The stream gurgled anemically. In the distance I could hear a rubbing noise. The perp? Or a deer? There was supposed to be a herd of deer in the canyon, fat, happy deer who moved from garden to garden devouring rosebuds. Deer, and raccoons, possums, and skunks. And snakes. Critters a city cop shouldn't have to deal with.

Above, the cars still had to be idling in first gear waiting to move to the upper level of the Arlington, the radios still spraying calls, brakes still screeching. But I couldn't hear any of it. It was as if I were in a swimming pool and someone had pulled the canvas cover over it.

Murakawa eased down onto the rock behind him. I started forward, pushing a branch out of the way, holding it till I could feel Murakawa take it. In the dark I could make out a narrow path, but I couldn't see more than a yard on either side. And that nursing home light that might have been a landmark wasn't visible at all.

The cold nipped at my face, but under the black coverall I was sweating. The ground was mushy. Down here the pungent aromas of bay and eucalyptus leaves were muffled by the smell of mud. I stopped, listening. There was no sound but indistinguishable rustling. Wind in the leaves?

The Tac Team would stop halfway down the hill. They didn't want to spook the perp. They couldn't take him out before they knew the status of the hostage.

I moved forward slowly, making a visual sweep of the area on either side with every few steps. The fog was sinking into the canyon like sludge. If the perp wasn't moving, he could be a yard away and I wouldn't spot him. But he wouldn't be on this entry path, not unless he'd abandoned the hostage, and one of the things I'd learned was that hostage takers understand the value of their hostages; they know that without them they're dead.

I almost fell over the lean-to—the kids' clubhouse. Lean-to was too grand a word for this rotting door propped on cement bricks. One side backed in toward the canyon wall. I crouched down under the door and looked around at a stash of soda cans, a clutter of magazines—I couldn't read the print but I could make out the naked female bodies. Some things never changed. Stuffed in the back was a blanket. The stench of wet wool battled the smell of mold. Even skunks wouldn't have bedded down on it. And just beyond the far edge of the roof was a small three-legged pot, probably about a quart. I pointed it out to Murakawa. "A caldron. Maybe we've got a community center here, horny adolescents Tuesdays, witches Wednesdays."

Moving carefully on the slippery ground, Murakawa edged around me to look at the caldron. I squatted down and unhooked the loudspeaker from my belt. The lean-to wasn't much but it was as good a setup spot as we were likely to find for the moment.

Still bending over, Murakawa turned back to me. He was holding a black running shoe. A woman's shoe with mud caked on the back of the heel. He squatted and eyed the ground. "Looks like drag marks."

"There's supposed to be a quarry office, or remains of one, farther into the canyon."

"How far?"

"Thirty yards, maybe. Grayson was trying to round up a kid who'd been down here recently." We both knew we couldn't wait to see whether Grayson succeeded.

The perp could be in the quarry office remains, or not. But I had to play it as if he were in spitting range. I clicked on the speaker. "This is the police. We've got you surrounded. Give us your location. Call out, and flash your flashlight."

No answer.

Murakawa had his hand on my shoulder. "You see anything?" he whispered.

"Nothing. We wait." I had a palm on the ground for balance. We squatted, stone still. The wind rasped the leaves. The stream sounded like Niagara Falls. I could have sworn I heard the thump of feet, but I knew that adrenaline had magnified everything, and those feet, if they even were feet, belonged to nothing larger than a squirrel.

"This is the police . . ." I repeated the instructions. "Can you make out any movement, Murakawa?"

"Nothing."

I lowered the speaker. "We'll give John another minute."

We called the perp John, the most innocuous name. He hadn't given us a name, and we knew not to make up another one, one to which we'd unconsciously attach attributes. No tough guy we'd overestimate or weenie we'd take too lightly. I'd heard a tale about guys who'd labeled their perp Twinkie, flubbed and called him that on the line, and blew the whole scene.

Behind me I could hear Murakawa talking softly into his mike.

"Anything from up top?" I asked, even though I knew he'd tell me if there were.

"*Nada.* Doyle's checking back with the city manager."

I lifted the speaker. "This is the police. Signal us, now. Flash a light. Make noise. We want to work *with* you. Give us a sign."

The sudden silence told me Murakawa was holding his breath. When he started breathing it sounded like someone turned on the air-conditioner.

The Tac Team would be in place for the final assault by now. From the look of the overhanging branches, the high ground observers could be right over the perp—if they could spot him. I opened the mike one more time and repeated the call, expecting no reply and getting none. To Murakawa I said, "Tell the inspector we're getting no response."

I leaned forward and moved my feet out to the sides. There was no decent position in here. The damp rose up from the ground. Already my butt felt icy. I thought of the hostage. Most likely she'd be lying on the bare ground. She'd been dragged down the chute. That descent was jarring on foot. To get down there and haul her, the perp had to be in good shape. I wished it were light enough to look at the trail to see if he'd had to stop to adjust his burden, or if we were dealing with someone strong enough to carry the body over the hard spots. Whichever, by the time he got here he'd been dragging her. And when her shoe came off, he'd have been banging her stockinged foot along the ground. Farther along the path the mud would have pulled off the sock, the rocks would have scraped her heel raw, and now, was that heel lying bloody in the mud?

"Any word, Murakawa?" I whispered.

"Doyle can't get an answer."

"We got a hostage here who could have broken bones, infected wounds; she's probably terrified and freezing. She could be dying while they test the wind."

Murakawa nodded. "Inspector," he said, softly, "Smith says to ask them to consider the state of the hostage." Part of the liaison's job was interpreting.

"So, Murakawa?" I knew I was pushing him, but I couldn't keep quiet.

"Doyle's waiting."

"John could be cooking the hostage by now. Ask him how that'd play in the papers: 'Kidnapper cooks woman while cops wait for dinner invite.' Tell him, Murakawa."

"Inspector, the perp could be up to anything."

I stood up and bent over. My lower back felt cold and brittle as ice.

Murakawa's radio crackled. "Inspector says the manager's office is trying to get the mayor."

"Shit! What about the city council? We wait, we lose what we've done. Tell him this is it!"

I could hear Murakawa calling Doyle as I said into the speaker, "This is the police. This is your last chance. Signal us now!"

Time stopped. The rustling of the leaves, the scraping of the underbrush seemed deafening. My chest shook with each heartbeat, and the thump seemed to echo off the canyon walls. I stared into the charcoal-brown fog around me. No light flickered. Only leaves moved, or so it looked in the dark. No sound broke the rhythm of my heartbeat and Murakawa's breathing.

I wanted to push Murakawa, make him goose Doyle, goose the O.C., the chief, the city manager sitting on his padded chair in his heated room in City Hall, thinking not of the sludge and jungle down here, of every moment when a sudden noise could loose a trigger, not thinking of the terrified victim, but of the vast and ambiguous larger picture.

"What are they saying, Murakawa?"

"Nothing. Same as a minute ago."

I wanted to grab his mike, to yell "To hell with public relations!" My legs screamed their need to pace, my feet yearned to kick ass.

"If we're just going to sit here, we might as well drive down to City Hall and do it with them." I didn't expect Murakawa to call that in.

It was a minute before he said, "Okay, Smith. Prepare for Plan C."

"Tell them we don't know what we're dealing with here. John could walk a yard in front of us and we wouldn't spot him. Tac Team will be banging into each other. Keep on the horn while they move in."

Murakawa reaffirmed our location, and translated my instructions into phrases more pleasing to an inspector's ear. Then we waited.

"Okay, Smith," Murakawa said. "Count three and make the last call."

I forced myself to count slowly, listening to the silence between each number. "This is the police." I let another second pass. "We know you're in here." I repeated, "We know you're in here." I had to make my diversion last long enough for the Tac Team to get a bead on him, figure a path in behind him, and move in quietly. The lead guys would have night glasses, but I didn't know how good they'd be in dark, fog, and underbrush. "There's no way out, you know that, don't you?"

Tac Team's trained for negotiations to break down, to have the scene mapped out, hours of planning the entry behind them, and a picture of the perp etched into their brains. They're ready to run in with weapons drawn, assess the threat, and, if necessary, take out the perp. Adrenaline just about busts the skin then. It's all go. But this, creeping into unknown territory in the dark, not daring to shoot, not knowing what they'd find—all that adrenaline would be pounding back on themselves.

"Let's talk about what you want here. Let's talk."

Ahead a light flickered. I could feel Murakawa's hand tighten on my shoulder.

I murmured, "You can never guess—"

"Smith," Murakawa said, "Doyle says Tac Team's got the hostage."

I squeezed my lips together to keep from yelling "O—kay!" My heart thumped against my ribs. I was grinning and squeezing my hands so hard into fists my skin hurt. "They've rescued the hostage? What shape is she in? And John, what about him?"

"No sign of him."

"Where's the hostage?"

Murakawa relayed my question. After a few seconds he said, "Quarry office."

The light flickered again. It looked to be twenty yards ahead, as much as I could figure in the dark. "Tac, that you up there?"

The light flashed five times—the signal.

"We're coming on."

Murakawa grabbed my shoulder. "What do you think you're doing? John could be halfway there. He could be anywhere."

Murakawa was right. The negotiator never puts himself in the immediate danger zone, I knew that. Still, I insisted, "He's not there."

"Let Tac secure the path," he insisted.

The adrenaline surged against my skin. I wanted to run forward, to see the victim, to know she was all right. Instead I waited while he called.

"Ask them how she is, Murakawa."

It was a moment before he said, "Grayson says she's depressed, seems a bit deflated, but she can be patched up fine."

"Sounds pretty good."

Murakawa nodded. His radio crackled. "Okay, now we can move."

The light stayed on ahead. I flashed my own light on the path and pushed through the underbrush. Suddenly I couldn't wait to see the woman, to know for myself she was going to make it. The quarry floor would probably be no bigger than an eight-by-ten-foot room. My light caught the edge of the raised cement floor. In front of it was enough firepower to subdue a small nation. The black-suited Tac guys stepped back off the path as I neared the cement floor. The first thing I spotted there was the other black running shoe.

It was a moment before I noted the leg it was attached to—or what remained of it. I stared in disbelief—and rage. The legs were plastic— blow-up dummy legs. It looked like a blow-up dummy like the kind you get from the sex catalogs. But I couldn't be sure because all the air was gone. In the harsh beams of the flashlight the too-blue eyes, cherry-red lips, and pink cheeks looked garish and the deflated body unbelievably old.

"A dummy," I muttered. My neck was so tight the words were barely audible; my head throbbed. I wanted to kick something, some*one*, the perp, till he was as lifeless as the dummy. "Shit! Shit! Shit! We're the dummies."

The Tac Team guys were grumbling and shaking their heads. "At least, Smith," Murakawa said, "you got us down here now. We could have spent half the night up top waiting to liberate these plastic legs."

I nodded. I hoped the city manager's officer and Inspector Doyle saw it that way.

The remains of the old quarry office and the ground around it were bright as day. Every one of the Tac Team, plus Murakawa and I, had our flashlights out. We were all spraying the lights, looking for something to save the situation.

It was Murakawa who spotted the wooden box under the overhang against the hillside. It was covered with papers. Envelopes, official forms.

"Here's the final irony," one of the guys said. "An extra load of paperwork."

"Hey," another said, "add that to your report. You can check it out in your spare time."

Groans came from all around. Hostage Negotiation Team work was extra—the exercise and the follow-up. Everyone would get home late tonight and spend tomorrow trying to squeeze in writing the report.

"Look at this!" Murakawa held up a form.

"Parking ticket?" someone asked.

"Right." He turned back to the box. "The whole batch are parking tickets. Christ, there must be hundreds of them."

We all made for the pile and grabbed. There were plenty to go around.

One of the Tac Team, Samson from traffic, was the first to say "Oh, hell! Parking tickets! And they've all got different license numbers."

"From different cars," someone said.

I picked up one. "This is dated five months ago."

"This one's yesterday," Murakawa put in.

"I don't believe it!" Samson said. "This bastard's been lifting parking tickets from windshields for months. All over town people have been thinking they've gotten away with not feeding the meters. They haven't paid their tickets because they didn't know they got them."

"And if this hits the newspapers, no one in town is going to pay a ticket. They're all going to say theirs got lost," Murakawa predicted.

"And the people who have paid are really going to be pissed," I said. It would be the big brouhaha of the year, the kind of fuss that Berkeley was famous for. "It'll make a great companion piece to the main story for all those reporters who've wasted their Sunday night here: Hostage Negotiation Team outwitted by dummy."

"You think this is the work of our meter maid vandal?" Samson asked hesitantly.

No one answered, but I would have put money on the same thought filling thirty heads: a news photo of the deflated dummy with a caption TICKETED TO DEATH. I'd have upped the ante to cover thirty minds sure that the Berkeley Hostage Negotiation Team was going to be the laughingstock of the Bay Area, and the press was going to make the whole department a circus until we found the perp who'd collected this load of parking tickets and the perp (maybe one and the same) who'd been staging pranks on parking enforcement carts all over the city.

Bugging meter maids was one thing, but this prank was something else. I couldn't have said if it seemed that way because this time it was I who'd been had, or if, in fact, it signalled a turn from the playful to the malicious. And indicated a mind that couldn't see the difference.

CHAPTER 3

□

If there had been any way to avoid it, we certainly would have. But the field operations center was at the Arlington. We had to come back there. And thus, there was no way to avoid having the entire Negotiation and Tac teams emerge from the canyon debacle up the chute, person by hostage-less person, with the regularity of baseballs from an automatic batting machine. After the dark of the canyon, as each one of us hit the blinding lights of four TV crews, we stopped, blinked, and looked like rabbits stunned by headlights.

The adrenaline rush was gone. Now I felt drained and had one of those dull caffeine-hangover headaches that only throb sporadically—as if to remind me that I'd let myself get too caught up in this operation. Every guy on the team looked worn-out and surly; I was willing to bet that at some point in the last hour every one of them had thought that the "victim" was a woman like his aunt or mother or grandmother. But I was the only one on the team who'd thought the "victim" was someone like me.

"What's the story down there?" Alison Saunders, one of the reporters, shouted leaning far across the second line of tape—the outer perimeter. Behind her cars were still gunning motors for the sharp uphill spurt to the upper lanes of the Arlington. Brakes squealed in the distance as gawkers, drawn by news bulletins, filled the curbs on the far side of the Arlington and doubtless all the streets that fed into it. The crowd had quadrupled in the hour I'd been in the canyon. Earlier it had been mostly neighbors who'd wandered out with glasses of wine. By now some of them had gone home and retrieved the bottles. And there were the crisis junkies who'd grabbed windbreakers and helmets and hopped on bikes, plus the normal array of Berkeleyans: bejeaned ponytailed guys in old flannel shirts and down vests, college girls with used rabbit coats and bare feet in Birkenstocks, shoppers from the stores a block up the Arlington still clutching grocery bags. Clearly our operation was the social occasion of the day.

"Hey, Smith, what went on down there?" Saunders insisted.

Ignoring her, I huddled with Inspector Doyle and McKinley, the field press officer liaison. They'd be the up-front officers with the press. Grayson moved in next to McKinley.

"So you lost him, Grayson," Doyle muttered.

"Not us, sir. He was probably gone long before we got the go-ahead. The only flashlight signal Smith *thinks* she saw was over an hour ago. And she's not sure about that. For all we know, the perp plopped the dummy down there and was home in time for the six o'clock news."

"And he'll have a good laugh when he sees you guys on at ten," Doyle said.

I restrained a smile at Doyle's support. Grayson made no secret about not liking working with a woman. The woman he most resented was me.

"Sir—" McKinley began.

"Do I take it, Grayson, you've got no indication at all where he went? Your Tac Team surrounded the whole canyon and he just walked off?"

"Like I said, sir, he could have been gone before we got here, while the focus was in the hands of Negotiation."

"Or he could have crept up the hillside while you were coming down."

I had been around Inspector Doyle a lot more than Grayson had. Doyle had had his own hesitations about a woman in Homicide Detail, but we'd worked through most of them. Now, I said nothing to draw attention to myself, or remove Grayson from the line of fire.

"We've got deadlines, you know!" Saunders called.

"Put a sock in it, Saunders. We'll get to you," McKinley yelled. To me, he said, "So, Smith. Is there a connection to the meter mangler?"

"Good chance," I said, "not that that's much help. As far as I know, there's no decent lead on those cases either."

In a remarkably ill-conceived effort to reduce traffic by making driving more difficult for its citizenry, the city fathers had installed cement-roadblock flower pots at intersections and parking meters at every commercial site in the city. Rapidly three things became apparent: First, there were no fewer cars on the streets. Second, it was not an iota easier to find a parking place. But third, there was lots more money in the city coffers.

The city's reaction had been to raise the parking meter rates to the highest in the area. The citizens' reactions had been to grumble about meter maids (of both sexes) lying in wait for the meter to run out, meter maids ticketing when the meter had run out but another quarter had been added, meter maids in general.

So when a vandal began stealing chalking wands from carts, slashing meter cart tires, chaining meter carts to meters, he became an instant hero. When he hijacked a cart, stranded it in a mudhole, and left an ersatz ticket in its windshield, he moved to All-Star. And when he deposited one in a pile of fresh manure, he became Most Valuable Player.

Until this week the meter maid cases had been considered pranks and given low priority. Sworn officers, who'd gotten their share of tickets in the two-hour zones around the station, hadn't fallen over one another to be first to remove the burr from the butt of parking enforcement. It was only last Wednesday that Doyle had told us that the chief figured it was a matter of time till the pranks became assaults. He was leaning toward assigning the case to one of us in Homicide-Felony Assault Detail. As one, Jackson, "Eggs" Eggenburger, and I had inched back in our chairs. But lying low isn't easy in a small room.

"Well, Smith," Doyle said now, "clear up what you're doing and make this meter maid thing your priority."

I wasn't about to give Grayson the pleasure of hearing me sigh. Before the Tac Team head had a chance to catch my eye and savor his triumph, Doyle added, "And while you're at it, Smith, you can take the paper on this operation."

So much for the joy of Doyle's support. I nodded, and deliberately ignored Grayson, who probably wouldn't be able to resist a grin of satisfaction at the thought of me rounding up reports from every one of the team members involved. Doyle's assignment also meant that he was entrusting me with the assistant field commander's—lieutenant's—work. In a successful case, that would have been a coup for me. In this case it just meant work. And the danger of being swamped by the flashiest disaster in years.

For Grayson it provided a virtually risk-free chance to sabotage me by letting word out that there was no rush on reports. If the paper wasn't in on time, only I would look bad. It was the type of subtle harassment women dealt with in departments across the country.

"So, sir, what's the official line?" McKinley asked.

"No hostage," Doyle snapped. "The witnesses were mistaken. We found shoes, but no hostage, no hostage taker. We don't want to speculate what the witnesses saw. But we've searched the canyon and we've got a team checking every house on the canyon rim. And, McKinley, no mention of the meter maid business. Press'll make that connection soon enough without our help."

McKinley nodded. When he turned to the reporters, he wouldn't be saying the perp could be hiding in any of those houses, he'd be couching our search in terms of reassuring homeowners.

"Grayson," I said before he could leave, "your guys have any ideas on the perp's likely route out of the canyon?"

Grayson hesitated. Maybe he would have shot back a retort if Doyle hadn't been there, maybe not. As it was, he said, "That nursing home was lit up. In panic these guys either head for the darkest spot or the brightest."

I shrugged. "We've got seven acres of dark. I'll give the light a try." If I was going to be taking the paper on this operation, I needed to have as broad a view as possible.

The traffic on the Arlington was still diverted to the top of the embankment. Even though the word that the negotiation was over had spread, the crowd of neighbors hadn't dispersed yet. I rolled the patrol car and headed to San Antonio, the first downhill street in Berkeley. It was dark now; on the north side streetlights cast odd solitary islands of light that faded into the thick fog between. On any other night lamps in windows would have taken up the slack. Then the fog would have smoothed the corners of houses and softened the lights and given the street the aura of a candlelit restaurant. Normally all the houses would look as inviting as linen-clothed tables with Chardonnay already uncorked. But tonight the houses that backed the canyon were dark; behind the thickening fog they stood like medieval castles with walls, thick and forbidding. The only lights were the flashers from patrol cars bleeding into the fog. Homeowners had been evacuated from their houses; they stood in groups across the street behind the outer perimeter line. As they spotted my patrol car, they started toward me, clearly hoping for word that their discomfort had been rewarded with a spectacular collar. I kept moving.

Across from the nursing home the contain officer gave me a thumbs-up.

If it hadn't been for him and its lights, I would have had a hard time picking out the nursing home. It looked like just another house on the canyon rim—pale stucco, door in the middle, and two windows on either side. Originally the door would have led in to a foyer between the living room and study. But when I walked up on the stoop I could see that the study had become an office. I had barely pressed the bell when the door opened.

The man in the doorway looked to be about twenty with dark hair cut short for Berkeley where ponytails are still in fashion. By Berkeley standards he was well dressed: fresh plaid cotton shirt and newish jeans with creases pressed in. By any standards he was pissed off. I'd barely introduced myself when he said, "You've made a mess of our schedule. We've got sick people in here. By dinnertime they're tired. It's all they can do to watch the news or talk to a friend if one calls. They don't have the *strength* to tell them to call at a sensible time. *I* have to do that—when I can."

"You've had what?—one?—visit from a police officer?" I asked, careful to sound more amazed than irritated. Public relations is a big part of police work—sometimes the hardest part. "And you didn't have to turn your lights off like everyone else did."

"And where do you think the neighbors wanted to go in the dark? Two or three of them marched right up here and leaned on the bell, like we were a drive-in movie for the show you guys put on in the canyon. Like our residents' lives were so meaningless that it didn't matter who marched through their rooms to stare out their windows. They would have walked right over me if they could."

I found that accusation of callousness hard to believe in an old, settled neighborhood. "Your next-door neighbors?"

"Right. Both sides."

"People who know the owners here? And maybe the patients?"

"People who had no business trying to get in here after dinner. I told them that. Our residents need their rest."

We were still standing in the doorway. Inside I could see the office—dark wood, red Oriental carpet, the promise of warmth. The dark-haired man didn't seem to notice the chill, but after my hour in the canyon I felt like it had migrated into my spine. "I need to ask you a few questions. Inside?"

"Can't they wait—"

"Look, we've had a dangerous situation down in the canyon. We need your help. I'd like to ask those questions inside," I said so as not to give him grounds for saying I'd forced my way in.

The first thing that struck me inside was the smell of orange. It took me a moment to recall that odors I usually associated with nursing homes were of urine and defeat. I'd assumed that after a point there was no way to vanquish them. Clearly I'd been wrong. I looked down at the sparkling linoleum and wondered if the orange was in the wax. From somewhere in the back came muffled sounds of a newscast.

What I had taken to be the office turned out to be part office and part sitting room. But it wasn't a place where visitors waited for patients or vice versa. The one padded chair faced the windows. Next to it was a table and next to that was space for a wheelchair. "It provides a change of view for our residents."

"The patients?"

"The *residents*. This isn't some shabby nursing home where people warehouse their maiden aunts, you know."

It occurred to me that that was how I viewed all nursing homes:

warehouses for the commodities the undertaker couldn't get to yet. I had visited my grandmother in one, and then only once, when I was eleven. I hadn't liked her beforehand, and an hour with her complaining, next to a bedridden woman who moaned constantly, by a hallway that seemed like a moving exhibit of the possibilities of human deterioration, had stamped the feelings so deeply in my brain that I had become physically sick the remaining few times my family had visited.

"Canyonview isn't a nursing home at all, in the official sense," he continued. "It's a co-op. The residents are owners."

"And when they die?"

"Their heirs get a financial settlement and the right to the room reverts to Delia. Delia's the manager."

"And you are?"

"Michael Wennerhaver. Look, I have a lot to do," he added, maintaining his pique. I'd taken him to be no more than twenty, but now I realized he was older. It was the pouty quality in his voice and his wide flat cheeks and small, full-lipped mouth that gave him the air of a boy not used to being told no.

I settled in the chair and took out my notepad. From one of the rooms I could hear low sounds of music. Not television background, the tempo was wrong for that. Maybe from a radio. "Your address?"

"I've got a room downstairs. I take care of the grounds, too, so I have to be here. Can we make this quick?" He propped his bottom on the desk and stared at me, opening and closing his right hand as if squeezing the excess water from a sheet.

"What's the rest of your job?"

"LVN, licensed vocational nurse. Look, I have to check on the residents. I don't want them unnerved knowing the cops are in here."

I found myself writing the three letters of his job title down slowly. For a guy on the edge of a hostage negotiations operation, Michael Wennerhaver was remarkably uninterested. Most people would be dying to know the details, and even the least curious would ask whether the perp was still on the loose, possibly in their own backyard. Careful not to change my tone, I asked, "And where were you for the last hour?"

"Here in the office."

"Who was with you?"

"No one. I *told* you the residents are tired by this hour." He was still squeezing and releasing his hand, his skin reddening and paling with the movement. "I did take a couple calls. You want to know who I talked to? Their phone numbers? So you can verify I was here, is that it?"

I tore off a page from my pad and held it out to him.

He grabbed it, smacked it on the table, and began flipping through the Rolodex.

I made a note to myself: I hadn't considered Wennerhaver a suspect, and still would stick him at the bottom of the list. But he was making such an effort to move up.

I took the paper from him. "So, in the last two hours, did you hear anything like someone walking up around the house? Or see anyone unusual on the street?"

"No!"

I could have pressed him, made him sit and pretend to think. But I'd seen this kind of response often enough to know that nothing but circuitous coaxing would elicit anything. And right now that was more of an effort than I could bring myself to make. I didn't even ask the question foremost in my mind: What's a reasonably bright, middle-class guy who clearly is not a social charmer doing working as an LVN? He could have made more money, a lot more, sweeping streets. And Michael Wennerhaver didn't seem the type to opt for the helping professions. More suitable to him was work as a guard dog; not a Doberman, though—too sullen for that. Or, I thought, glancing at his closing hand, maybe a milker at a farm that mistreated their cows.

I stood up. "I need to check with the people who had views of the canyon. Are they awake?"

"No," he said automatically.

"None of them?"

"No."

"Then maybe you should turn off the radio back there," I said walking into the hallway that divided the street side of the house from the canyon rooms.

On the far side I'd expected to find two residents' rooms, with windows facing into the canyon. Instead I found myself in a large dining room and looking through the doorway into the kitchen—just like a regular house. "Where are the residents?"

"Upstairs. There's an elevator. When they feel up to it they can come down, like they did in their own houses. Almost like going home." He blushed and suddenly looked twelve years old. "It can never be like home, we all know that. It was dumb of me to say."

I shrugged, searching for something to say to alleviate his discomfort. But when I looked back at him, he was an adult again. The transformation was so complete that if I hadn't trained myself to observe witnesses so carefully, I would have wondered if I'd imagined that blush. With him I had the sense of dealing with an adolescent who hadn't learned to control his impulses and whose threads of personality hadn't yet woven into one cloth.

"The thing is that if you can't be alone, this is the best possible place. I mean, other places talk about homelike atmospheres, call themselves family. But here we really are. I know. The residents can be here a long time. So I get to know them, like family." He laughed. "Better than family. Claire," he said nodding toward the back of the building, "is just like one of my teachers when I was a kid. It's nice here."

"Who all lives here, besides you and Claire?"

"Edgar and James. But there's no point in bothering them. They're both very old and on medication."

"Who else?"

"Stan, but he can't talk. He's recovering from surgery. And the fourth room upstairs is empty."

I sighed. For all the use I was getting from this place, they might have had the windows bricked up. "Michael, I'm looking for a suspect who was in the canyon. Who could *still* be in the canyon. I only need to know if anyone saw him go down or come back up."

Michael's pursed mouth relaxed. "Sorry. None of them is in any condition to be looking out the window."

"What about Claire?"

"I pull her blinds after dinner when I give her her night pill. She doesn't like the idea of anyone looking in at her; she's very old school, proper. Only Madeleine leaves her blinds up."

"Madeleine?" I added her name to the growing list, feeling like I was dealing with the stationary equivalent to the Toonerville Trolley. "So Madeleine is likely to be awake and looking out her window. Which way does it face?"

"She's not strong. She doesn't have the energy to be dealing with people like you."

"It's not an interrogation," I snapped. "We're only asking for help. I'd think you would be concerned about who's running through your canyon."

"Well . . ."

"Or is it you who have some problem with the police?"

When he didn't answer I pulled out my pad again. "Give me your full name and your birth date."

"Hey, what is this?" His voice rose.

"Shh. I know you don't want to wake the guests. Middle name? Date of birth?"

"Mike?" a female voice called on an intercom. The voice was shaky, but still one that you'd ignore at your peril.

As I took down the information from Mike's driver's license, he leaned over the intercom. "Just a question about the search in the canyon, Madeleine."

"Madeleine . . . ?" I asked when he turned back to me.

"Madeleine Riordan."

"The lawyer?"

"Right."

Madeleine Riordan, the lawyer. No wonder Michael was behaving like a guard dog. No wonder he thought my presence would disturb her. If history was any indicator, having a police officer trot into her room would elicit scathing sarcasm. To the unwary she had invariably seemed like a quiet, attractive, lawyer dressed in a better-than-Berkeley suit. The unwary one settled in the courtroom and forgot about her. Then, in one of those voices so low that everyone stops and listens, she'd skewer you.

There was a time when Madeleine Riordan's picture had made it to the dart board in the station men's locker room. It had only been up there half an hour when Chief Larkin heard about it and pulled it down. But the word I got was that it was so full of holes by then that there was next to nothing left.

She knew about the dart board—everyone knew. If her house were burglarized, we would, of course, send out a patrol officer, but not before we all had a good long laugh. She could have figured that out, too.

My first thought was that the feeling of disdain was mutual. But I realized that although I had known Madeleine Riordan well enough to pass a word in the courthouse or comment on the hors d'oeuvres at a bailiff's farewell party, I really had no idea at all what was beneath her thick dark hair, behind those better-than-Berkeley suits.

But one thing I did know was that when she had needed investigative help for a client, she chose Herman Ott, the most antipolice private eye in town. And that connection alone was sufficient to remind me I'd have to do some fast talking to convince Madeleine Riordan that our suspect was less desirable than we were.

CHAPTER 4

□

Madeleine's out back," Michael said.

"Out back?" I almost asked: Just how nontraditional a not-nursing home is this? Did the halt, lame, and elderly wait to meet their Maker in tents?

"She and Claire are in the cottage suites—two rooms connected by a companionway. I'll call and see if she can see you."

"No, you'll call and tell her I'm on my way."

His mouth pursed, and he seemed to consider a moment before saying, "Very well, I'll tell her. But I should warn you it won't put her in the best of moods."

I nodded. I understood only too well.

Madeleine Riordan was with a law firm that did a fair amount of pro bono work. The cases that paid the rent were routine civil matters. It was her pro bono work that brought her into contact with us, at trials, and most annoying to us, at police review commission hearings. I don't know exactly what she'd done to other officers—they tended to be closed-mouthed about their encounters with her. I suspect their encounters were like mine, and mine I never mentioned freely. Mine, the Coco Arnero case.

I could still see Arnero sitting by Madeleine Riordan at the next table, in a ratty chocolate sweater with a silver chain around his neck, his thin, straggly mane a contrast to her thick, shiny auburn hair. Arnero had protested during one of the Peoples' Park demonstrations that had erupted every couple years since the 1969 riots. The demonstrations were usually in response to the university's attempts to construct dorms, parking lots, or sports facilities in the park, the only open space near Telegraph Avenue. Pro-park people faced off against BPD, or in more serious cases, a line of BPD interspersed with the university force and the county sheriff's department BPD had called in. Some years bottles were thrown and wooden bullets shot; other years it was just passive resistance and a line of patrol standing guard.

The Arnero incident came after a rocks-and-wooden-bullets day. Protesters were chanting, screaming. Bursts from our radios cut the air; brakes squealed, sirens whined ever closer. Camera flashes stung our eyes. Reporters were yelling. Officers shouted at onlookers to clear the area. The whole place smelled of dirt and sweat and fear. I'd been on the force less than a year; in riot gear, shoulder to shoulder with the sheriff's deputies less than an hour. Until the first rock hit, my sympathies had been all with the demonstrators. Officer of the peace. But rocks can dent objectivity. The commander repeated the order to disperse. A yard in front of me Coco Arnero plopped himself down, cross-legged in the street, smiling. A deputy sheriff swung his baton and shoved it into Arnero's stomach. Arnero doubled over. The deputy hit him in the back. Arnero screamed in pain but didn't move. Behind me the commander yelled at us, "Don't break the line." The deputy stepped back. Arnero's friend dragged him away.

That experience made me question my career. How much violence—how many batons, how many rocks—was I willing to accept to be an officer of the *peace*? Was I too "Berkeley" to be a police officer? If so, was I writing off the whole profession, deciding it wasn't possible to both uphold the law and treat our citizens decently? It was as close as I've come to quitting.

Weeks later, when I got the notice of the fair-hearing complaint, I wasn't surprised. I expected the hearing to be for show. Whatever qualms I had about the incident, they weren't that I had broken the law.

The hearing was in a shabby upstairs room in some city building—I've blocked out just which one. My then-husband and some of his university colleagues were in the audience. The night was warm for Berkeley; I was sweating under my uniform. Madeleine Riordan presented Arnero's complaint—that the Berkeley Police Department, and I in particular, should have recognized and respected the ground rules of passive resistance, arrested Arnero when he sat down in the street as the unspoken covenant of passive resistance decrees, and failing that, at least protected him from the assault of the county sheriff's deputies, the deputies whom BPD had called to the scene. I struggled to keep my face impassive, to reveal neither my own qualms nor the comfort I found in Berkeleyans' expecting their police department to adhere to a more humane standard than the norm. Sweat was running down my back, but outwardly I looked as controlled as Madeleine Riordan. Or I did until Arnero said, "I can't describe any reaction to that billy club hitting me. In situations of conflict like that I make a habit of leaving my body."

All my tension bubbled over. I laughed.

But Madeleine Riordan wasn't smiling. "Officer Smith?" she asked with no inflection whatsoever. I remember that distinctly. It was as if no human voice were connected to her words, as if an elemental omniscience were questioning my reaction.

I said, "It just seems excessive that Mr. Arnero would expect the police to be guarding his body when he isn't even in residence."

There was laughter in the room. It came like clumps of clouds from various places. Madeleine Riordan let the laughter subside completely, let the silence sit two beats, and then said, again without any inflection: "So, Officer Smith, what cosmic view must a citizen hold before you feel the need to protect him?"

The laughter that had comforted me turned to questioning murmurs.

"Or," she added almost as an afterthought, "during which moments is his life important enough to deserve respect?"

It was a rhetorical question, and I was thankful for that. I had no answer.

Arnero's complaint failed, as I knew it would. I left the hearing room feeling like I'd been hit harder than Arnero. Maybe it was because I was so young, so new to the force; whatever the reason, Riordan's question kept poking, at the time leaving me awash in questions about my career and my values. I never again judged a suspect quite so automatically. Maybe Madeleine Riordan's poke made me a better person. But it didn't make me like her.

Now Michael Wennerhaver walked back from the phone. "To get to Madeleine's cottage you have to go outside and around the house," he said grudgingly. Pulling open the front door, he added, "And just because Madeleine looks okay and she can get around by herself, don't assume she's strong. She's just come back from a bout of chemo that would have knocked a lesser woman on her ear."

"You mean she was in the hospital?"

"No, she was here when she had it, then home awhile. She's only been back a couple days."

She had gotten married a couple years ago. At the station, there had been ribald speculation about Madeleine and the groom. Allusions to a wrecking ball and demolished structure were among the more gracious. "Is she still married?"

Michael shrugged, then added, "Yeah."

"And she left her husband to come here?"

"Yes," he snapped and headed outside before I could ask more. He didn't comment that the state of her marriage was none of my business, but he could have and been correct.

I followed him out into the fog. It had thinned a bit while I'd been inside, and going around the side of the house and down the walk wasn't difficult despite how steep the path became in the last fifteen feet between the back of the house and the cottage.

We stepped onto the companionway between the rooms. "I need to tell Claire what we're doing here," Michael said, then knocked and pushed open the door to his right. A door, I noted, that was not locked. Many things are casual in Berkeley, but this arrangement was asking for trouble.

I stood shivering in the wind, wondering if Madeleine Riordan still recalled the Coco Arnero incident, or if it had been just one of many similar ones in her career, if there were too many abashed cops for her to recall one from another.

The times I'd passed her since—she, on the way to a trial or hearing—she'd been dressed in those suits that were just a bit better than normal Berkeley garb (much as was Michael's attire). She looked as if she'd taken time from more lucrative work to deal with this case, because, her whole demeanor said, this particular offense was so egregious. I remember one of those times thinking that she could have been pretty—and maybe she was when her eyes and mouth weren't tense with indignation—but she had chosen to override any decorativeness that would have undermined the seriousness of her commitment. Her eyes were a dark no-nonsense blue. And her thick brown hair had one streak of gray, a touch of legitimacy, even back then, nearly ten years ago. But it also shone in the light like a child's hair. I was looking at her hair just before she "got" me in the hearing, absently wondering if it was possible for thick brown hair to have such a shine naturally, or if Madeleine Riordan's hair revealed a soupçon of vanity, if there was more beneath her stiff demeanor than I had assumed.

Michael walked back out onto the companionway and knocked on Madeleine Riordan's door.

"Send her in, Mike."

Michael was halfway in the door when she said, "You don't need to stay." Her voice was softer than my remembered version, but the words were a dismissal nevertheless. He paused as if to say something, then took a quick step back. It took him only a moment to regain control of his face, but in that time it screamed how much he hated being dismissed.

I stepped inside and shut the door. The room was homey in an impersonal way: framed Sierra Club prints, overstuffed chair, lamp and table by the solid wall where no window looked toward the basement of the main house. TV, VCR at the foot of the bed. The piney smell of floor polish mixed with a musky odor of tracked dirt, and dog. I observed all the things professionally looking first this way then that. I was nearly beside her when I looked at Madeleine Riordan.

I didn't gasp, but it took all my control not to.

She was gaunt, icy pale, and her hair was gone. Her face seemed tiny in the ashen expanse of her scalp. She wasn't wearing an institutional nightgown with the opening in the back that leaves patients cold and exposed and reminds them they are at the mercy of whoever sneaks up behind. The one she had on must have been her own—a nightshirt with a *Far Side* cartoon. But somehow that shocked me more. I just caught myself before saying that it wouldn't have occurred to me that she had a sense of humor.

I don't know what I expected—I guess the woman with the shining brown hair in the better-than-Berkeley suit pointing to exhibit A, insisting on justice. Had I walked in and found her naked, I could have dealt with that. I shower in the Albany pool. I see naked bodies every morning. But to walk in and find her bald . . . I should have been prepared. But I wasn't. Nothing makes a woman so naked as a dry, uncovered scalp. So utterly vulnerable.

Awkwardly I met her gaze. Madeleine Riordan was smiling, or, more accurately, silently laughing at my discomfort. *She* didn't appear uncomfortable under her bald scalp.

It was almost as an afterthought that I noticed the chocolate Labrador retriever lying on the bed beside her. Gratefully, I focused on the dog, a big-pawed, wide-faced fellow with a luxurious brown coat that clearly had been brushed today. He was watching me with the detached interest of the well loved. More than once I'd joked that in my next life I was coming back as a retriever and would spend the entire incarnation being petted. I didn't say that now, but the memory seemed to fill my mind and block out any other thought.

I held out a hand toward the dog. He sniffed and cocked his head in acceptance.

When I looked back at Madeleine again, her cheeks had pulled in, her eyes were shut, and her teeth pressed hard together. The hand nearest me she held taut, as if refusing to give in to the pain. Only her left hand betrayed her. With it she clung to the dog's back, pressing her fingers so hard into his fur that it nearly covered them. I expected him to yelp, but he made no sound, and no movement except to lean the side of his head into her leg.

Her hand eased. But it was a moment before the dog moved back to his original position. Frail as she was, I was amazed she'd had the strength to grab the dog so fiercely. She cleared her throat and spoke as if her throat was raw and it was an effort to force each word through that rough passage, "This is Coco. He accepts tribute, but he's much too spoiled to acknowledge it."

My breath caught. I would have given a lot to avoid asking, but I couldn't, "Coco? For Arnero?"

She smiled. "Not many people get that connection." She said it in the same neutral voice I remembered so well. There was no way to tell whether there was anything beneath her statement, or if she even recalled my connection to that one incident in Arnero's life.

No point in pursuing it; I'd ask my questions about the canyon perp and get out. I reached across and scratched the brown retriever's head. Briefly he looked at me, then glanced back at Madeleine Riordan. I said, "I'm Jill Smith, Homicide Detail."

"Homicide?"

"Yes . . . but I'm here with the Hostage Negotiation Team. You probably know we had a situation in the canyon—"

"Did you free the hostage?" she asked in that raw voice.

"It turned out there wasn't a hostage," I said. "The original witness was mistaken."

"No hostage? Then no hostage negotiation." I could hear the wagging finger in her voice, but I wondered if that was just because I recalled it from the past. She was asking if we'd been hotdogging. It was, I recalled, a charge she'd made in the Arnero hearing.

"The perpetrator himself can be the hostage if he's in danger of harming himself. And we had reports he had a gun."

"So you could break into anyone's house . . ."

"No. You of all people know that." Before she could respond I said, "Look, I know you don't want to waste your strength talking to me. We're concerned that our perpetrator could be creating a dangerous situation down in the canyon. We need to know how he's getting in and out of there. Have you seen anyone moving around down there?" Madeleine Riordan wasn't one to give the police information. When the Arnero hearing ended, Arnero had turned his anger on her. I heard him threaten her, but she refused to press charges, and the next time he was arrested she defended him again. Now I wouldn't have been surprised if she'd refused to answer my questions altogether.

"I'd have to have my snout pressed against the glass to see down in the canyon."

From anyone else I would have taken that as a slap of dismissal. But Madeleine Riordan's dismissals didn't veer in from the side like that. I took a chance. "And have you?"

A hint of a smile flashed and was gone. "It can be very boring here.

You don't sleep much when you're in pain, unless you're drugged up, and I'm not about to spend my last weeks that way. Oh, friends come, but it's so goddamned awkward for them that I'd rather they sent cards. They stumble for words. Some of them say they know how I feel, which was bullshit even before I was dying. They couldn't know what this is like unless they spent the hours I have learning about the rules of dying."

"Rules?"

She was looking out the window at the dark canyon, not at me. "Rules, the lawyer's life. We think that the law is the rule for all society. We know that there are plenty of people who break the rules, even among those who swear to uphold them," she said with a small snort—of disgust, admission, what? Now she did look at me, her blue eyes large, demanding, shining against the pale dryness of her skin.

"They tell us if we stay in our lane we'll be safe. So we do. You follow all the rules society insists on, you lock your doors, you cover your ankles, you don't sleep around, you protect your sacred hymen, and what happens? You end up here wearing a piece of cloth slit up the back with your ass bare to whoever comes in. . . ."

She glanced at me and stopped. I hadn't been monitoring my reaction like I do interviewing witnesses. I'd been thinking what an odd old-fashioned slant that was for Madeleine Riordan—not sleeping around. "But they haven't made you wear a hospital gown."

"They don't dare. My body may be weak but I've still got my tongue. I've heard tell I can raise welts with it." She flashed a suggestion of a smile.

"I've seen some."

She motioned me to sit on the bed. Another time I would have pondered the unprecedented acceptance that her offer indicated, but now I sat and said, "So what have you seen out the window?"

She raised her hand as if to run it through her hair. I remembered that movement from the hearing, when she'd been considering whether to speak. Now she stopped the hand halfway up and let it fall back to the covers. "I haven't observed much. You can't see down under the trees. There are kids down there during the day, they tell me, but I never see them. Coco barked a bit the first time I was here. But he was just put out to find potential sources of attention who were ignoring him." She gave his head a rub.

I nodded. The live oaks and the bays made a carpet twenty feet above the canyon floor. Even for someone with spyglasses it'd be a trick to see movement beneath them. Of course she hadn't observed anything down there. I braced my hands to push myself back up and leave.

"I used to sit outside when I was here before." Her voice was higher, more anxious. "Down there on the walk. In the summer the sun would get that far in the afternoons. I could walk down there by myself then. We didn't have many sunny days this summer. Maybe one every three or four. I'd go out, but each time it was a little harder. You see, the body becomes the enemy. When you're healthy, you don't realize. It inconveniences you, it hurts you, it waits to kill you. By the time you understand it's an object that you can't control and they can do whatever they want with, well . . ." She looked up, suddenly flushing. "You watch your control growing narrower and narrower, like water circling down the drain."

I didn't know what to say; the chasm between us was so great, much wider than at the police review commission when we were merely defending police officer and prosecuting attorney. Now we were the living and the dispossessed. Despite the bed large enough to accommodate Coco, the woodsy prints on the wall, the deep red clearly authentic Persian rug, I was struck by her absolute poverty. When you have no future, you have no power. And if you have no control, you have nothing.

Equally, I could feel my own fear of contagion, that somehow if her hand touched mine she would grip it in a death vise and yank me with her across the Styx. It was all I could do not to pull back.

And yet I couldn't possibly have moved.

She rubbed Coco's head. As if reading my thoughts, she said, "I'm fortunate to have a place like this, not like the awful nursing home my mother died in. Here I can have Coco with me, and have Mike to take care of him. And"—she forced a laugh,—"even Claire."

She was trying to keep me from leaving: me, a cop. Anything to keep out the dark that echoed pain and let fear race unchecked? Or was there something she couldn't quite bring herself to tell me, tell the police? I swallowed hard. "Claire?"

"The woman in the other room. She really doesn't like dogs, but she'd never say that to my face. She's one of those traditional ladies, trained to be polite, remain pure, and never create unpleasantness. A product of the days when purity was all." The scorn was clear in her voice. I wouldn't have expected otherwise from a woman who had spent years representing those who marched and demonstrated, who slept in doorways on Telegraph Avenue, those who wouldn't or couldn't conform.

"If Claire doesn't like dogs, why did she choose to share this cottage with you and Coco?"

"I promised to keep him out of her room." Madeleine half smiled. "That lasted almost a day. I was sure once she knew him she'd see what a sweetheart he is." She rubbed his head, her forefinger running down the ridge between his eyes.

"And did she?"

"She asked Mike to keep the door shut. Said she was worried about fleas. And germs, when Coco licked her hand. You know how those clean, clean ladies are."

I smiled, recalling the horrified reaction an aunt by marriage had had to our family Great Pyrenees. At eleven months and well over a hundred pounds he'd jumped on her lap. And we, less than perfect hosts, had laughed. "What happened with Claire?"

"Coco took the door as a challenge. I went in after him one day and found Claire huddled in the far corner of her bed and Coco stretching his neck as far across the bed as it would go. It was clear it wasn't the first time they'd come to this standoff." She smiled, just as my family had.

"And Claire never complained?"

"She isn't that type of woman. Besides, everyone on the staff here loves Coco. No one would take her complaints very seriously. I knew she'd come around. I sat in there with Coco every afternoon until she could pat his head without shrinking back."

"And now she's comfortable with him?" I asked, ready to disbelieve the answer. We pet lovers have raised self-deception to an art.

"Now she's not in enough control to . . ." Her hand moved down to wrap around the big dog's chest. She turned toward the window, but it showed nothing of the dark fog-filled canyon beyond. The glass reflected her bald head and the bony hollows of her face, and in it, I suspected, she could see herself in a few weeks no different from Claire.

I said, "About our suspect in the canyon—"

"Even when I sat outside I didn't see anyone escaping from there."

I stood up. Coco stretched his head toward me for a final scratch. Careful to avoid Madeleine's hand still on his neck, I scratched behind his ears. Having satisfied himself of my place in the herd, he looked away.

"Let me think overnight," Madeleine said slowly. "Maybe there's something I'll recall that will help you."

"Fine," I said.

"You can come back tomorrow, can't you?"

"Yes." My voice was barely audible.

"About this time, eight-thirty." Desperation didn't come through in her voice; she still had that under control.

I nodded. I wanted to reach out to her. But the moment had passed; she would have looked at me as if I were crazy. I held out my business card to her. "If you do think of anything beforehand, give me a call."

"Do you need anything, Madeleine? Mike and I are right here." A woman with a spray of red frizzy hair stood in the doorway.

"The detective's just about to leave. If you can wait a minute, I'll go to the bathroom."

"Sure, I'll be right here." She moved out of the doorway, leaving only her elbow to indicate she was waiting outside.

Madeleine reached for my card. Glancing at it she nodded. "Sometimes I think I'd be better off if I let them dope me up. Maybe keeping your mind clear enough to be appalled every time you can't maneuver in the bathroom without help isn't such a boon." She emitted a noise somewhere between a snort and a laugh. "But nothing's forever."

Now I did reach toward her hand. Automatically she lifted it as if to shake. Our hands came together at the wrong angles, intentions unclear on both sides, and ended in an awkward touch that was neither a squeeze nor a handshake.

"Till tomorrow," she said so softly I wouldn't have recognized the words had I not understood. But, in fact, I heard in them the request that I come back, that there was something she wanted me to know but couldn't bring herself to say now. I could feel how much it cost her, a woman who never let herself ask an indulgence from a police officer, particularly one she'd viewed with the scorn she'd shown in the Arnero trial. I let go of her hand and left, making my way up the hillside path, wondering with each step what was so important that it had moved Madeleine Riordan to breach her own wall of reserve.

CHAPTER 5

□

I circled back to the top of the can-
yon. Traffic moved normally now. The mobile unit was gone, and all but
one patrol car had coasted on to other things. The officers from that car
would be interviewing people at the edge of the canyon. I hadn't realized
how long I'd spent with Madeleine Riordan. It was almost nine o'clock
already. I checked in with Inspector Doyle, then headed back to the station
for the Immediate Incident Debriefing. It would be a somber affair; no one
wanted to spend his Sunday night reporting on his contribution to a failure.
Doyle would announce I was taking paper—all the reports on the hostage
operation. Maybe he'd authorize another call to witnesses and potential
witnesses—every resident on the canyon rim—and an early-morning
sweep through the canyon itself to see what daylight illuminated. Beyond
that there wasn't much he could do; you can't put out an APB on an
unknown perp.

The meeting ended at ten forty-five. Still wired, I headed back to my
office. If I was taking paper, it wouldn't hurt to get my own report done.
Grayson would be responsible for rounding up the reports from the Tac
Team. I could assign Murakawa to prod patrol for theirs. Knowing him,
he'd be first in with his own. The major hassle would be checking through
all those reports before they went on to Chief Larkin, the city manager, and
the mayor. And, no doubt, the police review commission. With thirty officers involved, chances were some citizen would file a complaint about

something. I should just be glad none of those complaints would be handled by Madeleine Riordan.

I shuddered at my thought, then reminded myself that had I said it aloud in her room, Riordan would have laughed. Maybe.

I sat staring at my notes. In a minute, or maybe it was ten minutes, I realized that I wasn't looking at the pad. I was running my fingers through my hair, absently tugging; at a level way below thought I was reassuring myself it wasn't I who was dying.

I closed my pad, got up, walked to the clerk's desk, and left a request for background checks on Michael Wennerhaver and on Madeleine Riordan. Then I drove home. If the rest of the guys involved were having as much trouble getting down their reports as I was, it'd be a long time before the mayor saw anything on this operation.

Down here in the flatlands, the fog had closed in. We don't get many like this. Most of our fogs are Pacific fogs—thin gray roofs that block out the sun. But tonight's was a land fog, the type they have back east, that separates each individual, encases him in an icy gray capsule, and creates a treacherous illusion of soft edges.

Howard's house was an elderly brown shingle on Hillegass Avenue a mile south of Peoples' Park. In that mile Berkeley changes from the off-campus lair of students, sidewalk vendors, and street people begging for change that hasn't been spare in over a decade to a neighborhood of comfortable Victorians shaded by tall oaks and magnolias. Many of the homes have been repainted or reshingled, the yards landscaped. Almost all of them are in better condition than Howard's.

Howard has to keep five tenants, including me, to pay the rent. He tries to fix up the house. But his manual dexterity just isn't in the hammer-and-nail department. Since I moved in we've argued about the house, and what Howard terms his interest and I call his fixation with it. I felt so claustrophobic I almost moved back out. But fears don't come from outside the skin. And I'm too much of an adrenaline junkie to care much about where I live; home is only a place to eat food from white bags and plastic containers, and wait for my pager to go off. And to snuggle into the familiar ridges and hollows of Howard's long, sinewy body. A bond connects us, like the vibration of cello strings beneath all the other sounds of the orchestra. It's not just knowing about unreliable hours, investigations that bulldoze plans, auto chases that rev you up like nothing else; it's laughing at the same thing, in the same key, that shows me I'm not alone. Not like Madeleine Riordan. For that, for now, I can put up with an irritating violin or piccolo in the orchestra.

The violin that grates on my nerves is Howard's never-ending sanding, painting, dismantling sinks and showers. The piccolos are the array of tenants necessary for the rent. There's almost always a tenant in the living room anxious to talk, or more like it, complain about the piccolos, the violin, or me. Or I come home to a fire in the fireplace and grunts and sucking sounds coming from the sofa. But tonight the whole house was dark. And, I noticed when I walked in, cold. The place never gets warm. It can be 80 degrees outside and it's still sweater weather in here. And Berkeley sees 80 degrees maybe two days a year. Oboes.

I made my way through the living room, up the stairs to the balcony, and around to Howard's door. I could hear the ebb and flow of his breath. It comforted me, that reassurance of life, the communal rhythm I could slip into. I took off my clothes and left them on the floor. The cold air seared my skin. I needed a steaming bath. I'd never go to sleep shivering like this. My arms were shaking against my sides. I pressed my hands against my legs but I couldn't stop the shaking. And somehow I couldn't deal with the linear procedure of running the tub water, climbing in, washing . . .

Howard and I don't wake each other up when we come in late. We'd never get enough sleep if we did. But tonight I climbed into bed and pressed my icy body against his, feeling the warmth of his skin against mine. It didn't cut the cold of my own flesh. I wrapped my arms around his back and pressed my face into the notch of his neck and felt him breathe, and felt myself breathing. And when he was awake enough to respond, he ran his lips across my cheek to my mouth. I opened my mouth and felt his tongue pushing in and I sucked hard, going with it till the passion blotted out my thoughts, blocked the awareness of his breathing, and mine, and ours, till I wasn't even reminding myself that I was alive.

"You're still shivering," Howard said afterward.

"Don't take it personally," I said, laughing.

"Wrong! Shows how little you know about men."

"Oh, no, not the California State Authority on Testostoral Behavior again. I—"

"See, Jill, what you don't realize is about St. Peter and fooling around."

"Howard, even I know enough about religion to be sure St. Peter didn't, at all."

"Perhaps not," he said dismissively. Nothing so organized as religion had entered Howard's childhood. "But all guys understand what the saint is talking about when he asks at the pearly gates, 'How did you do?' And you, Jill, could be responsible for damnation."

"At least you'll be warm." My tone of voice was off. I'd wanted to keep up the banter, to talk a little and let him go back to sleep. Six o'clock comes early, a lot earlier than the sun in November.

"Jeez, you're really freezing." He wrapped his arms tighter around me, but that only made my shivering more noticeable.

"What happened?"

I chose to answer that on the more superficial level. "We got down to the canyon floor and the asshole was gone." Howard, of course, would have heard about the hostage operation; he'd want all the details. Normally I loved that. Getting into the meat of each other's cases was almost as important as laughing in the same key. I could handle the details of the operation tonight. The deeper level I didn't know that I could put into words. But I would talk to Howard for the same reason Madeleine Riordan kept me with her. I shivered again and desperately wished I could brace my cold feet against Madeleine's desolation and push myself away. Instead I heard myself saying, "You know Madeleine Riordan?"

Howard laughed. "No wonder you're shivering if you've had a run-in with her."

"She's dying," I said before he could add something he'd feel awkward about later. "Her window overlooks the canyon. I was hunting for a witness. It happened she was it. Fortunately, she doesn't seem to remember me from the Coco Arnero trial."

"Jill, that was nearly ten years ago. She's punctured half the force since then."

I gave his hand a squeeze.

Howard intertwined his fingers with mine. "I'll bet you, Jill, there's not one guy in the department who's escaped her. They wouldn't care if she weren't so good at getting them."

"Hey, you're supposed to be comforting me, not praising my erstwhile oppresser."

"Oops. Well, for what comfort it is, every guy I talked to, when they were willing to talk, said he came out of a hearing with her feeling like he'd been led down the garden path and knocked cold with a daisy. Never saw it coming; couldn't believe it afterward. They'd say they were walking down from the stand shaking their heads and the judge and jury were still laughing. Make you feel better?" he asked, circling his arms around my ribs and pulling me back against his chest. "And the worse of it was they couldn't say anything to a woman who was limping off with a cane."

I groaned. "You know, I'd forgotten about her needing a cane. Somehow it makes her dying seem even worse. Like she didn't get enough life, and now even what she had wasn't up to par. What happened to her? Did she injure her leg?"

"Dunno if it was her leg or hip or some combination. Whatever, it was from an auto accident way before I came on the force."

He laughed.

I pulled loose and turned to face him. "You're amused by car crashes?

Or that there was life before the department was graced with your presence?"

Howard pushed himself up, leaned against the wall (where a headboard might have been)—his settling-in-for-a-talk position. I wriggled up next to him.

"I'll bet, Jill"—the grin returned to his lantern jaw—"Madeleine wasn't much help once she realized your canyon perp might be the same one who's hassling meter maids."

"I didn't get around to telling her that."

"Damn good thing."

"Why? Why would she care, Howard?"

"Because, Jill, before they had blue curbs and handicapped stickers, Madeleine Riordan got her car towed so often she almost sold it. She said taking cabs would be a whole lot cheaper than supporting a car, an insurance company, and the city, too. She said she'd use the money she saved to have a life-size picture made and sent to Elgin Tiress, since he'd become accustomed to seeing her so often."

Elgin Tiress, vulture of the expired meter. "Or, more accurately, seeing her car?"

"Yeah."

"Is there one citizen in all of Berkeley's driving population that Tiress hasn't swooped down on? For the amount I've paid in tickets outside the station—all from Tiress—I could get a new car."

He laughed. "Jill, prices have gone up a bit since you bought your bug. Maybe you could get a new driver's seat."

"Maybe."

Howard reached over and draped his right arm over my shoulder, and with the left caught the blankets before they fell. It was a good save, but then we sat talking like this three or four nights a week, and Howard had had a fair amount of experience. "You know, Jill, I'll really be sorry to see her go. She pulled some great saves. I would have loved to know the mind that created them."

"But you didn't?"

"No way. She was hardly a woman you'd invite out for a beer and shoptalk." He brushed his chin against the top of my head. "Not like some."

Beer and shoptalk had sustained us during the tense year of my divorce and several increasingly tense years afterward while we both tried to avoid the dangers of an affair with the person who shared an office. We had discussed cases so long and in such minute detail we could have applied to be Department historians. Sublimation in crime! There are cases I'll never remember without thinking about Howard's long firm thighs.

I leaned into his body, feeling the warmth of his skin, willing that warmth into my own. And seeing Madeleine Riordan, clutching the back of her dog. She had a house, a husband; what could have made her leave them for a place like Canyonview where she was so alone? "Howard, she kept me there tonight—because she didn't want to be alone."

His hand tightened on my arm but he didn't say anything.

"She asked me to come back tomorrow night. I had the feeling she was deciding whether to tell me something about the hostage operation. You think?"

He drummed a finger on my arm for a minute before saying, "She's caused us a lot of problems over the years. She got me more than once. But she was the best at it, the subtle sting. I just . . . well . . . I hate to see her sunk so low she'd sell out for half an hour of company."

I nodded.

He squeezed me to him playfully. "But one thing you can count on: if Madeleine Riordan does give you something, it'll be damned good. You better make sure you've got a cell waiting. By this time tomorrow night you'll have your perp looking out through the bars."

CHAPTER 6

□

A good start to the week is getting up at six fifteen, having a cup of Peet's Coffee, Viennese Blend, with Howard, and then whipping through a mile of Albany Pool water like a yellowfin heading for open seas. An average Monday begins closer to seven o'clock. A sip from Howard's mug. Five eighths of a mile with the speed of a sea turtle in danger of becoming soup. This Monday's entrance came at closer to seven twenty. No time for coffee. No swim. No movement faster than a clam's. No sight of Howard at all.

I left my car—parked illegally on the street—and raced through the front door of the station. Before I was halfway up the steps to reception, I heard a low rumble from the second floor. It sounded like the distant rumble you hear seconds before an earthquake. Before you realize what it is, the earth is shaking like crazy.

"Behind me," Sabek at reception said. "You'll love it, Smith."

I raced through the double doors and around the corner to Records and almost smacked into Clayton Jackson, my fellow homicide detective. Jackson was at the back of half a dozen guys crowded into the hallway. He was looking ahead, grinning. When he spotted me, he stepped aside.

I elbowed my way past Murakawa, Al "Eggs" Eggenburger, the third homicide detective, and wedged in next to Pereira before I could see the cause of the shouting and realize why the guys had been such utter gentlemen letting me move to the front. They were all enjoying the scene, but it was true no one was going to get the kick out of it I was. There, barrel chest to barrel chest, were my two least-favorite colleagues. Grayson stood, his dark shaggy eyebrows shaking, that thick droopy moustache that had been unchanged for as long as I'd known him, unable to conceal the snarl lines of that hidden mouth beneath. "The hostage negotiation, last night, in Cerrito Canyon. Maybe you heard of it?" Sarcasm dripped from Grayson's voice. Down onto the red-tufted top of the head of Elgin Tiress.

"Your car was outside here." Tiress wasn't shouting. I'd never heard him raise his whiny voice. He stood, arms crossed, stocky little body braced like a fireplug waiting to be parked in front of, or, more likely, pissed on. Either way he would win—there'd be a violation for him to ticket.

"Of course my car was here," Grayson shouted. "You don't drive across Berkeley without lights and siren, not if you want to move. If I'd taken my own car, I'd still be sitting in traffic." It was something of an exaggeration, but not so great a one it caused any of the onlookers to protest.

"You left your car by a green curb." Elgin Tiress's voice was like a jabbing finger. Tiress was a head shorter than Grayson, but that voice of his was jabbing right in Grayson's face.

"A hostage could have died, Tiress."

"Green curb means twenty minutes. Your car was there three hours and fifty minutes." Elgin Tiress was not known as Tight Ass for nothing. "You're lucky I only gave you one ticket."

Grayson's hand tightened into a fist. "Can't you get it through your head, you . . . I was out on a life or death case!"

Tiress puffed up his small, rounded chest, looked directly ahead—at Grayson's chin—and said, "Tell it to the judge."

"Too big for your fucking little britches," Grayson muttered as Tiress made—in small but rapid steps—for the door.

The rest of us headed for the meeting room and slid into chairs just as Chief Larkin walked in. The chief attended Morning Meeting only sporadically. His presence was rarely a good sign. I figured things couldn't get worse.

Jackson pushed me a cup of coffee. "I don't know if this'll do it, bad as you're looking, Smith," he muttered. "It's good, but it doesn't resurrect." A couple years ago I'd made a deal with Jackson's son: swim lessons for morning coffee. Darnell was away at college now, but during the swap days Jackson had gotten hooked on Peet's, and now he filled a thermos every morning. It was a practice I wasn't about to question.

Now the chief settled into his chair directly across from me, his gray suit and signature red tie looking crisper than anything in the room but his own self. Irritably fingering a clutch of messages, he waited while the hot car list circulated, and representatives of the various details reported the last twenty-four hours' activities: tools stolen on Parker Street, stereos on

Sixty-second, Hopkins, Fairview, Sixty-seventh, and Mabel; assaults with gun, stick, feet, bottle, metal pipe, and a water balloon; commercial burglaries: telephone from an auto sales shop, fax machine from a copy shop, and from a cleaner, cash and every suede item in the store.

Chief Larkin listened, pensively rubbing his messages between thumb and forefinger. I began to doubt the words would survive long enough for him to read them. I should have been so lucky.

When the regular daily business was over, Larkin leaned forward and said, "The Berkeley Police force is becoming a laughingstock. It's bad enough we have some crazy fixated on Parking Enforcement. This one loony's running all over town stealing marking wands out of the Cushmans like they were free samples."

Cushmans, the little golf-cartlike vehicles Parking Enforcement used, had metal roofs and zip-up sides. Meter minders like Elgin Tiress were too busy popping out and depositing tickets to fasten the siding each time. We all knew that; no one felt called upon to remind the chief.

Larkin went on. "He's crashing into the Cushmans. He's stealing them. He's rolling one into a pile of manure, depositing another in a Dumpster—we had to get a crane to get that one back out!—and now stealing traffic tickets and helmets."

I'd been around long enough not to interrupt his tirade. Howard had too, but as a Vice and Substance Abuse detective he knew he wasn't going to be mashed with the fallout from this. He said, "Helmets?"

"Stole a helmet right out of the meter vehicle. Left the officer in violation of the law!" City governments across the state had applauded a new state law mandating helmets on motorcyclists. They'd been less pleased to discover that meter cart drivers came under the same classification. And downright distressed when informed they couldn't send out those drivers to check on meters, much less generate new revenue when those meters expired, until the drivers were legally helmeted. "Meter maid had to borrow a helmet from a Cycle Patrol guy on vacation. Thing was so big it floated on her head. Took us a week to replace hers." Chief Larkin's face wasn't the color of his blood-red tie, not yet.

Celia Eckey from Parking Enforcement glared. She was a short, comfortably plump gray-haired woman who made you think of Mom. Usually it was Mom with cookies and milk, or Mom who wanted to hug you and make you well. There was a reason Parking Enforcement sent her to Morning Meeting rather than the more senior Elgin Tiress. Parking Enforcement was aware of the odious Tiress's reputation.

Eckey stood up to her full five feet three, placed both hands on hipbones, and announced, "This shit can't go on!"

Police officers are not shocked by much, and certainly not by common four-letter words. But from Celia Eckey no one expected more than a "Pshaw."

Eckey glared around the table. "We get more shit than the rest of you put together. The citizens of this town, they think we make up all these rules: If you live in Area D, you can't park outside your house unless you pay for an Area D permit. Your parents come to visit and they can't park there unless they get a permit. You get them a temporary permit and put it on their car and still they get a ticket because you forgot to write in the year; you've just got the month and day. What do you do? You scream at Parking Enforcement: 'Hey you idiot, we all know what year this is! Do you have a quota? Do you get a bonus for stupid tickets!' " She fanned another glare around the table, daring anyone to take her on. I felt like a four-year-old caught with cookie dough on her hand.

But Howard, whose charm had insulated him from normal rebuke, stretched his long arms forward. He was grinning. "So, Eckey, what do you tell him? Why do you insist on the year?"

"We do it for little boys like you, Howard. College boys think it's a big joke to save their temporary stickers for an entire year so they can use them again."

"Or sell them," Howard said. "Remember the black market the under-grads were running with them? Good little profit maker until they made them the prize in a Homecoming Weekend lottery. The gift for someone who's got everything, and no place to park it!"

We, who get no more mercy than any other citizen when it comes to parking in this the tenth most crowded city in the nation, laughed. In an hour some of us would be running out to move our cars from their two-hour spots here in Preferential Parking Area C, in which we were neither the blessed residents nor commercial tenants. Organized officers like "Eggs" and Acosta worked in pairs, swapping their spots. The rest of us hunted and grumbled. And, as Eckey would have been glad to announce, bitched at Parking Enforcement. Berkeley is not a city prone to offer its public employees special privileges.

Eckey was not laughing. "Permits are all yellowed; edges are curling with age; and these kids think we're not going to catch on!" She shook her head. "I'd like to send every one of them to his room without supper."

Everyone laughed harder, and even Eckey joined in. Until Chief Larkin's cough brought us back to business. "Eckey, how long has the perp been operating?"

"No way to say, sir. Much harassment as we get, it's hard to spot a new strain." The captain started to speak but Eckey was not to be denied. "Accuse a guy of murder and he says he didn't do it. But you stick a ticket under his wiper and you get a bunch of excuses that would shame a politician."

"Eckey—"

"You ticket a Californian's automobile; it's the next thing to spitting in his hot tub." Before Chief Larkin could try again, Eckey said, "We've seen it all, sir. And there's no way to tell how long this perp has been doing penny-ante stuff. Eight marking wands have been stolen in the last month.

"In the last three weeks," Eckey went on, "we've had keys stolen from one vehicle, wipers from another twisted in knots, another one he stole the keys and left it parked going west on Shattuck."

It took everyone two beats to register that Shattuck was a north–south thoroughfare.

"We've had the Cushman in the manure, the Cushman in the Dumpster, and at five to six last Friday, with five goddamned minutes to go before the weekend, Glassborough jumped back into his Cushman and landed on a bag of fresh fecal canine matter."

"Even the dogs are after you, huh, Eckey?"

Eckey glared at Jackson.

Neither Eckey nor Chief Larkin mentioned the overriding indignity to the Department. All of his acts might have been added up to a minor nuisance if the perp had committed his vile deeds in secret. He hadn't. He'd done his damage on main streets, and worse yet, he'd alerted the media. Before Parking Enforcement arrived at the scene, a reporter from *The Daily Californian* was already there. Then it was the *Daily Cal* and the East Bay *Express*. Next he included KPFA radio. Then a TV station.

Chief Larkin held up this morning's *San Francisco Chronicle*. A page 3 headline announced: THE BABE RUTH OF THE METER GAME. "Listen to this," the chief began. " 'He tips his hat to a meter truck and before befuddled police can find him, he's created Coq au Cart. Only in Berkeley,' it goes on . . .' " The chief was shaking the paper. "What it goes on to is to announce how he made monkeys of thirty officers last night by luring our Hostage Negotiation Team into Cerrito Canyon to find the kind of dummy you can order from catalogs you wouldn't show your wife, stolen shoes, and half the city's parking tickets!" By now Larkin's tie looked pale in comparison to his face. He glared across at me. "The perp's a goddamned folk hero. Our Parking Enforcement officers get enough hassles without the whole town rooting for their enemy. They can't be citing vehicles if they're watching their rears all day."

"If we don't stop this," Eckey insisted, "we'll have half the citizens in Berkeley trotting off with their meters empty, hoping the perp swipes their ticket so they can look at the nightly news and say, 'Hey, man, there's my car!' "

Larkin turned to the inspector. "Doyle, you were in charge of the hostage negotiation. Smith's taking paper on it."

Doyle moved his head so infinitesimally that only the loose flesh under his chin nodded. "She'll be doing the follow-up."

I didn't realize I had groaned aloud until I heard the laughter around me.

Diplomacy kept me from asking Chief Larkin who had been heading up the Parking Enforcement investigation so far. If there were no centralized command, that would reflect poorly on the Department, i.e., on the chief himself. I didn't want to be the one to bring that oversight to his attention. But if there had been an officer in charge, *formerly* in charge, I didn't want to flag his inadequacy, particularly since his attitude could mean the difference between taking over the investigation and moving forward, or starting from scratch, interviewing the same witnesses and victims, who'd be even less pleased to answer the same questions again, questions asked by a police force they would have now labeled incompetent.

So it wasn't till the end of the meeting that one of the guys in Traffic Detail took me aside to tell me that my predecessor on what had become known as the Traffic Control Caper was none other than Grayson.

When I looked around for Grayson, he was stalking out of the room. And before I could call to him, Inspector Doyle came up. "Smith, how're you doing on the hostage reports?" Doyle's graying red hair was grayer than red. His skin was battleship gray, and the circles under his eyes charcoal. He looked like he'd been up not just as late as most of us, but the entire night, which meant that he looked slightly more exhausted than normal.

"The hostage reports," I said, giving myself time. "They're not all in."

Doyle nodded. He'd been around long enough to know "not all in" meant "not *any* in." "City manager wants 'em on his desk first thing tomorrow. Get 'em to me by the end of the day."

"This afternoon? The assignment didn't end till after midnight! Guys had to be back here at quarter to eight this morning. When does the city manager think they had time to dictate or type their reports? Is the C.M. out of touch with reality?"

"He's manager of *Berkeley*, Smith. That's pretty much an oxymoron."

I didn't want to laugh, but I did. Indeed, what could possess a sane individual to take a job managing 120,000 people who resent rules? "Right, Inspector, for job frustration, city manager's right up there with meter maid."

"But a damned sight better paid." We both nodded at that. Howard, who'd come up behind Doyle, nodded, too. Doyle went on, "The C.M. is going to be keeping close tabs on this meter maid business. Him, the mayor, the media. You know, Smith, that this is exactly the type of 'only in Berkeley' article they just love to run in *The New York Times.*"

"Look at the bright side, Jill," Howard said. "Your family'll get to see your name in the paper." My parents had moved to Florida, but I still had cousins and aunts and uncles in Jersey to read about my tripping over a mound of parking tickets. Wisely, Howard moved on before I could comment.

"For now, Smith," Doyle said, "just get me the hostage reports before you leave."

"Right." No one would have thought about a report yet. An operation like that one where everyone comes up feeling dumb is the hardest to get paper on. Guys just want to forget it. The second to last thing they want to do is resurrect the event so they can make a report. The last thing they want is to type it from their handwritten—their angry, pinched, nearly illegible handwritten—copy. The power of the officer in charge was reduced to begging, cajoling, and threatening. At the best of times none of the thirty participants would even begin writing till I made the first round to nag them.

It was after noon before I'd nabbed twenty-six of them and given them the bad news that not only would they have to do their reports now, but they'd have to type them up themselves. No way could two clerks handle all of them. Of the remaining three officers, one was Doyle, one was off today, and the last, Grayson, was in Contra Costa County to the north picking up a prisoner, who, it seemed to me, could have been escorted here by a CoCo County officer. I went back to my office to assemble my own report. When this day started, I'd thought the worst part would be seeing Madeleine Riordan again. Now that was looking pretty good.

On the computer I called up Michael Wennerhaver on Records Management System and was a bit surprised to find he'd had no contacts at all with us. No detains, no complains. Likewise Madeleine Riordan. My first thought was to be surprised she hadn't been arrested in any of the more recent Peoples' Park demonstrations. Then I recalled her limp. No complains either. I would have pegged Riordan for a woman who'd call us when someone blocked her driveway or left his dog tied out in the sun. But maybe when the urge to call us had arisen, she'd thought of her picture on our dartboard, realized the kind of service a complaint from her would get, and put down the phone. *So, Officer Smith, what cosmic view must a citizen hold before you feel the need to protect him? During which moments is his life important enough to merit your attention?* Apparently there'd been no moments in recent years she'd found a citizen sufficiently in need of our attention.

I exited Records Management and sat, taken aback at how clearly I recalled Madeleine's words to me so many years ago, and how they still pissed me off.

By five o'clock I had twenty-nine reports, all of which tried to make the affair look better than it had been. But the form doesn't allow for much editorializing, and from the impression I had at the end of the twenty-ninth, none of the Hostage Negotiation guys had much of a future in fiction.

I glanced through the report from Tim, the D.D. clerk. He'd run both Madeleine Riordan and Michael Alan Wennerhaver through CORPUS, for countywide arrest data, the Police Information Network (PIN) for statewide warrants, NCIC (Nationwide PIN) and CLETS to check for stolen property. Both came up clean. It looked like the only infractions either of them had were Madeleine's parking tickets, and she'd have gotten them too long ago to be on file.

At five twenty Grayson's report was still outstanding. I made my way past reception to Grayson's desk.

I was surprised to find him there. "Grayson, I left you a message." I could have been more diplomatic.

"I was out." Him, too.

"I need your report."

He glanced at his watch. "Not possible. I'll get it to you tomorrow morning. I—"

"Now, Grayson. Doyle needs it today."

"Smith, it's nearly five thirty."

"Twenty-nine of the thirty are done."

Grayson, a whiz at bureaucratic politics, understood the implication of that. He looked up, his forehead shirred with anger he couldn't unleash. "I'll dictate it. Get the D.D. clerk to type it up in the morning."

I let a moment pass, in part to control my own anger, mostly to tacitly remind him that sergeants don't give orders to detectives. "Tim's got his own work. Make what arrangements you need, Grayson, but have the report to me by seven-thirty."

As I started to turn, he muttered something.

Slowly, I turned back. "I'm sorry, I didn't quite make that out."

"Nothing."

I glared down and said softly, "It wasn't nothing, Grayson. I've dealt with adolescents. I've seen this routine. And I know that you're planning to do the report and to keep me waiting. So, let me tell you now, I have to leave at seven forty-five to get back to that nursing home on the canyon ridge to see a woman who is dying. I don't plan to wait around while you sulk over this." Grayson's eyes widened and his whole face—color and expression—faded. "If your report's not in by then, the file goes without it."

"I'll call you if—"

"I won't be back till quarter after." I headed to the parking lot, congratulating myself on neither stalking angrily away nor slamming anything, and on leaving myself plenty of time to handle a last-minute surprise from Grayson and still make my eight-thirty appointment with Madeleine Riordan. It wasn't till I hit the night air that I realized I'd sauntered out without a jacket. The night air cooled the heat of victory.

I met Howard for dinner at DaNang, the Vietnamese place on San Pablo with the wonderful prawn satay. If it hadn't been for Grayson I could have gone straight on to the nursing home instead of driving across town. It was close to eight o'clock when I got back to the station. I didn't bother to put my purse down in the office—just checked my IN box. No report. I pulled out the cover sheet for the Hostage Negotiation file and penciled in Grayson's name under Reports Outstanding, and headed for Doyle's office.

At the top of the stairs I saw Grayson walking away from Doyle's office. I walked into the empty anteroom. Grayson's report was on top of the IN box.

Grayson had indeed stretched the deadline even longer than I had expected. But two can be adolescent. Without changing the cover sheet, I plopped the file on top of his report.

Then I headed down to the patrol car and drove to see Madeleine Riordan.

CHAPTER 7

□

I would have liked to drive up to the Kensington shopping area and down by the top of Cerrito Canyon to survey the hostage scene from last night. But I was already late for my appointment with Madeleine Riordan. She wasn't going anywhere, but she also wasn't one to overlook delinquency in arrival time. I've lived in Berkeley too long to be put out by lateness (twenty minutes late is de rigueur here), but every so often I find a trace of my stiff-backed grandmother coming out in me. *She* had no tolerance for tardiness (or much else, for that matter). It's something of a cosmic joke that the traits I hated most in her have woven their way into my own fibers. For the month after I first discovered this errant thread in my weave, I was no less than half an hour late for everything but work. At the end of that month Howard made a point of telling me how taxing personal evolution is to friends and lover.

I turned down San Antonio Road and made my way along the narrow winding street between parked cars, wondering if this trip would be worth the hassle. Surely Madeleine Riordan would not come up empty. Pride would force her to honor her part of the bargain. (Even my grandmother never invited anyone in without offering them a piece of cake, albeit the driest confection they might ever have forced down.) What would Madeleine's dry slice be? A lecture on the proper conduct of the police force in the investigation? Too blatant. Grandma wouldn't have thrown the cake at a visitor. No, Madeleine's slice of information could be a coterie of kids she'd seen in the canyon (who would probably know nothing and take up gobs of our time). Or perhaps she'd offer an observation on meter maid ritual she'd had during the period she had amassed all those tickets. In fact, my guess was that when she asked me to come tonight, she hadn't had anything more in mind than warding off the demons of isolation. For most of us demons wave their banners of fear in the middle of the night. The Four Horsemen of four A.M. Maybe when you're dying and alone they ride all the time.

The wind had picked up with the setting of the sun. Now at ten after nine it snapped the fronds of the fan palms in front of the Mediterranean-looking pink stucco building. Light from Michael's office windows hung above the path illuminating the top of the shrubs at the property line but making the footing not much clearer. Madeleine's cottage was no more than fifteen feet beyond, as the crow swoops, but the grade was so steep that the roof was below my line of vision.

The wood cottage had the look of a Bernard Maybeck house, a little gem tossed playfully out of sight of the road. More accurately, it was two rough-shingled studios joined by a red Japanese temple gate arch that crested the companionway.

I made my way down the sloping cement path to the companionway and stood a moment. The doors to both rooms were shut. Beyond, in the canyon, oak and bay and eucalyptus leaves rustled and the smell of pine wafted up. Or maybe that was Madeleine's floor wax from inside. I was about to knock when Coco ran toward me, tail wagging, a yard-long gray dowel in his mouth. Dropping his stick he poked me, demanding to be petted.

"So you remember me, do you? Or is this how you greet all Madeleine's . . . friends?" Even though I was alone with the dog, my voice caught at the designation of "friend." Not right, but not altogether wrong, either. And a silly point to get caught on.

"Maybe," I said to him, "you've discovered something down there in the canyon and brought me up a clue, huh? Maybe that's what Madeleine's going to tell me."

The big dog shoved in front of me, thrusting his nose against the door. I knocked. I couldn't hear an answer. I hesitated. In care facilities like this a knock was merely a formality; the right to keep people out was one patients forfeited. There were practical reasons, of course, but suddenly it seemed so demeaning to have people invading your privacy at will. I knocked again, louder. When she didn't answer, I put aside my just-defined principles and turned the knob.

I barely had the door open when Coco pushed in and ran around Madeleine's bed. I heard him bound up. The room was dark. She must have been asleep. She'd forgotten all about my coming. Or she'd taken pain medication. Or . . . I gave Madeleine a moment to wake up and adjust to

Coco. Vaguely, I wondered if there would come a time when she was too delicate to be bounced around like that.

"Madeleine, it's Jill Smith."

She gave a soft groan. Or was that Coco?

"It's Jill Smith, from the police. Do you want me to come back another time?"

When she didn't answer I said, "I'm going to turn on the light."

I felt for the switch, flipped it on, and walked in. It took a moment for my eyes to adjust to the light, for me to see Madeleine's deep blue eyes staring blankly, her bare hairless head hung uncomfortably to the right, her translucently pale skin drooping over her cheekbones like a shroud. I watched Coco push at a hand that didn't move, then roll in against legs that would no longer feel the comfort of his presence.

She was dead; I'd seen enough of death to recognize it. But I couldn't believe *Madeleine* was dead, not now, not when we were going to talk, not . . . I turned away, squeezing my eyes shut, tightening my muscles till my neck was so tight I couldn't swallow. I had to give my head a sharp shake to force myself out of the shock.

The bowels evacuate with the relaxation of death. Now I could smell the effects, slight but evident even over the pine wax smell. Bypassing her wrist, I pressed my fingers against Madeleine's carotid artery. Nothing. I knew there would be no pulse, but I had to try. Her skin was clammy, but not noticeably cold. Now I looked more carefully at her face. Her skin was not merely translucently pale, but blue—cyanotic. And around those dark blue irises were red dots—petechial hemorrhages from broken blood vessels. Both could be the result of asphyxia.

The end of her pillow was shoved in behind her head, but most of it hung to this side. In the middle of the pillowcase were marks of fluid that looked like saliva and blood, marks just where they would be if someone pressed that pillow over her face until she stopped breathing.

I stared angrily. How could anyone . . . Coco was pushing in harder against her, poking her leg with his snout. He was disturbing the scene. I should have moved him, but I couldn't bring myself to order him off the bed, not while he was nestled next to her as if she were still alive.

Her body was still warm. She couldn't have been dead long. Not over an hour or two. "No!" I said, wanting to disbelieve what I saw and what I knew. But it was true: If I had arrived an hour or two earlier, Madeleine would have been alive. Maybe she would still be alive now. I felt like I'd been hit in the stomach. Madeleine was going to tell me something— probably. Was that why she was dead? If I had insisted she tell me last night . . . But no, surely not. The parking perp was a prankster. He wouldn't suddenly kill a woman to avoid being arrested for crimes for which he'd be a local hero, maybe even a national star. Not a man who called the media with every prank he pulled. That conclusion comforted me a bit. But still, if I had . . .

No! I couldn't play that game. I'd seen survivors run that script for years, over and over and over. No. Madeleine was dead. Maybe she suspected she would be killed. Maybe that was the reason she wanted me to come back now—because I was a homicide detective. Maybe she wanted me to find her killer.

Illogically I wanted to call the paramedics, have them pump a miracle into her veins. But I had seen too many bodies over the years to fool myself. They could do nothing for her and they'd ruin the evidence of her death in the process. Pulling a tissue from the bedside box, I lifted the receiver and called the dispatcher to have him notify Doyle and send Raksen, the lab tech, and the rest of a death scene team. He didn't mention the coroner; neither did I. When the coroner comes, he doesn't wait around. He takes the body and leaves. Later, when Raksen had taken every photograph, when he had bagged every fiber and dusted for every print, when we were done with the scene and the body, then I would call the coroner.

Coco was whining now, not a panicked whine, but merely a confused call for the attention that had never been denied him. I scratched his head and took one more look at Madeleine Riordan. It would be my last look at the woman I had just begun to know. After this she would have to be "the deceased," "the body."

Her head was hanging almost to her shoulder. I wanted to lift it up, to ease the pain she no longer felt, to make it okay. Amid the halo of her bare head her face seemed much too small. Her eyes were still drawn and deep pin lines slashed down into her upper lip. Most faces relax in death, but hers hadn't. She looked like she couldn't believe it had all ended like this.

I turned away, squeezed my eyes against tears. *This wasn't the time for that!* And I wasn't the person to grieve; *surely* she had closer friends than me. I stood like that longer than I'd intended, in silent good-bye. And somehow it seemed a fitting farewell to Madeleine Riordan: one lone person fighting desperately not to give in to emotion.

I gave my head another quick shake and turned back to the body. The mouth was open, but there was no sign of obstruction, nothing to suggest choking. I checked her hands but didn't move them. If she had scratched her attacker, particles of skin or hair could still be embedded under her nails. The lab tech would bag her hands before moving her. In ten days to two weeks we'd get a report back on those particles. I scanned the arms. On the insides bruises had begun to form. She'd have been reaching up, flailing at her killer. And he'd smacked her arms away like dead limbs of an old plant. Then he'd pushed the pillow tighter over her nose and mouth. She didn't look panicked now, but how could she not have been?

I swallowed hard and took a last look at her. It wouldn't have taken a big man to smother her; a child could have done it. Her arms were so emaciated she couldn't have fought off anyone. Her skin hung loose like . . . All the tears I'd fought back gushed out. I sobbed and ground the heels of my hands into my eyes as hard as I could. My whole body was shaking. What Madeleine looked like was the deflated dummy in the canyon last night, the dummy left there as a joke. What I was feeling now, I told myself, was all the anger and frustration I hadn't had a chance to vent then. I knew there was more to it, but I concentrated on that, wiped my eyes, reminded myself that Doyle and Raksen would be here any moment. And I couldn't let them see me like this. Not about any death, but especially not for Madeleine Riordan.

The dog whined and burrowed in closer to the dead woman's legs. I stepped back against the wall and began taking notes: Bed, cherry bedside table, Shaker ladder-back chair, and Shaker rocker. They must have been her own. Too hard for a nursing home. Type of thing a woman with back or hip problems uses. Today's *Examiner* on the floor. Between the chairs a floor lamp. Red carpet looked undisturbed. Framed Sierra Club prints still hanging straight. Bedside table held phone, tissue box, clock, bottle—probably containing water—empty.

Using the tissue, I pulled open the bedside table drawer. Inside was a mirror, a bottle of Visine, hand lotion, several closed small plastic containers I didn't touch, and one book—a copy of *Final Exit*, a book on suicide. The book didn't surprise me. If I had found Madeleine dead by her own hand, I wouldn't have been taken aback. I would have assumed she'd decided to forgo another month of pain and boredom and loneliness. God, why hadn't she, instead of dying like this?

The door opened. Raksen, the lab tech, waited for me to give him the okay to come in. Behind him were the woman with the wild red hair I'd seen here last night and the young man who'd been at the desk, Michael Wennerhaver.

"What's going on?" Michael demanded, trying to skirt around Raksen. I moved into the doorway. The woman grabbed my arm, "You can't—"

"Madeleine's dead."

"She can't be dead!" she said. "She was walking around this afternoon. She ate dinner at five. Liver and bacon. Bacon, for chrissakes. You don't eat bacon and die."

"What is your connection with Madeleine?" I asked her.

"I'm Delia McElhenny. I own Canyonview."

Michael's eyes were wide open. I wondered if he was in shock. His hands dangled at his sides and he seemed to have lost connection with his body.

Inside the room the dog growled.

To Raksen I said, "I haven't finished there. But the dog's on the bed next to the deceased."

He nodded and took a step toward the door.

"Raksen, the dead woman is Madeleine Riordan." A stranger wouldn't have caught Raksen's reaction. His face froze an instant, just long enough to tell me he had known Madeleine. I'd ask him about it later. Now my concern was the dog on the bed. We had to get him out of there. But there could be particles or fibers adhering to Coco's stomach or legs, evidence of the killer that had fallen on the bed. Raksen would know that. He wouldn't let Coco go without a vacuuming worthy of spring cleaning.

But Raksen couldn't do it by himself. Someone would need to hold Coco for him. Me? I couldn't leave the two witnesses alone. Raksen's helper would have to be one of the staff here whom Coco would trust. Michael?

But as soon as I turned to him, he let out a sob. "How can it . . ." Struggling for control, he rubbed his sleeve across his eyes. It was a move utterly out of place. Michael, in his freshly laundered oxford-cloth shirt and jeans, looked like he would perish before letting cloth near mucous membrane. He grabbed my arm. "She can't be dead. She just can't."

"I'm afraid—"

"Why her? How could she die? It's not fair. It's just not fair!"

The woman put a hand on his arm, causing him to release mine. "Mike, you know she didn't have long, only a month or two at best."

"She didn't have to die now. Not *now!*" He smashed his fists against his legs.

The woman shook her head. In a soft voice, she said, "Look, Mike, I know you're going to miss her. She's done a lot for you."

Coco wasn't going to stay on the bed indefinitely. When he moved, he could be dispersing the possible evidence on his fur anywhere in the room, to say nothing of tromping, slurping on, or knocking over other evidence. I was just about to ask Raksen to put in another call for patrol assistance when Connie Pereira and Paul Murakawa came down the path.

As if cured by the surplus of possible help, Michael now seemed together enough to handle the dog. But in case that was too optimistic a prognosis, I sent Murakawa in with him and Raksen. Pereira and I moved a couple steps off the companionway while I briefed her. The woman, dressed in what looked like tie-dyed long johns, stood still, her long red hair skimming on the night wind like a kite.

The door opened. Michael emerged, pulling Coco by the collar. And when the door shut, the dog flung himself against it, and let out a high piercing whine.

That whine cut through me. I scrunched my shoulders and hardened my ears against it. In Homicide we get training and plenty of advice on how to toughen up at the sight of dead people; but with moaning dogs we're on our own.

The dog quieted, the dog named for Coco Arnero. I thought back to the Arnero hearing. Even if I hadn't lobbed up the ball for her to spike, Madeleine still would have won the match. All she and Arnero wanted was an airing of his position, a hearing that would garner enough press coverage, create sufficient citizen pressure to make BPD think twice before calling in outside forces and ceding control to them. The Department had a videotape of the baton incident. Madeleine had uncovered three more. She'd come up with five witnesses, every one of them more believable than Arnero. One was a law professor visiting from Santa Cruz. At the end of the hearing, had I not been left stunned by her retort, her research would have left me speechless. I've seen my share of review commission hearings since, but none planned out and stage-managed like that.

How had a woman so competent, so in control allowed herself to be murdered? How had she let herself be as helpless as the deflated dummy in the canyon? I should have been able to accept her murder. Eighteen or twenty people are murdered every year in Berkeley. But there was no indication of theft, nothing to suggest the break-in that could so easily have taken place through her unlocked door. I couldn't believe that she just happened to be killed, not right before a Homicide detective is due to arrive.

Before *she scheduled* a Homicide detective's arrival! Could she have stage-managed the timing of her own murder so I would find her body? With anyone else I would have dismissed the idea as ridiculous. But Madeleine Riordan . . . she knew how quickly a trail gets cold. Had she somehow arranged to give me a jump start? Or was I merely imagining I was a key player, psyching myself up to focus on the case and escape "if I'd only come earlier"?

I walked back into the room. Raksen was poised at the foot of the bed, Nikon aimed. The flash went off.

The light made Madeleine—the body—look bluer, frailer.

"You finished with the bed, Raksen?"

"Just a couple more."

I hadn't even hoped for a yes. Raksen never wanted to admit he had enough shots. But my question hurried him along.

When he turned to the bedside table, I pulled the cover down to check the body for wounds, bruises, any other suspicious marks. Her legs were thin, but on the right one the skin hung from the bone with barely a sign of muscle. I recalled seeing her leaning lightly on the cane with her right hand. Lightly, which meant she had had muscle tone back in those days in court. But now it looked like the disease had sucked the life out of the weakest limb first. I was surprised she'd been able to walk at all yesterday.

Not she, *the body!* But it was too late. I'd lost the distance. And as I pulled up her nightshirt to check for marks, I flushed with the full sense of violation I would have had if she had been alive. As many bodies as I have investigated, never before had I felt so strongly the continuum between life and death. It was too soon for Madeleine Riordan to become merely an object of investigation. I had come to talk to her; how could she be . . .

Gently I replaced her clothes and covers. I looked at Madeleine's back, not expecting to find anything, and was not surprised. Then I laid her down and called the dispatcher to notify the coroner.

As Raksen worked, I checked the closet—nothing but a couple pairs of sweats, and a single dress. I went over the room again. And when the coroner arrived, I stepped outside and stood staring into the canyon, thinking of the woman I had visited last night, who'd told me how awkward it was to talk to friends. Now I saw her as I'd seen her then, taut from a spasm of pain, her fingers digging with all her strength into the dog's coat for support, for comfort.

And I thought of someone coming in through that unlocked door and smothering her with her own pillow, and I could imagine her fear, her fury fighting back with arms too weak to do more than prolong her fear—no, not fear, to prolong her outrage.

Suddenly I laughed. "Bullshit!" she would have said at the arrogance of my thinking I knew what she felt. I swallowed hard, trying to force down emotions and deal just with the investigation. I pictured her body as a Homicide officer does. And the question that left me was, *Why?* She was going to die in a month or so. She had a book on suicide in her drawer, so chances were she might have killed herself sooner. All her killer had to do was wait. Why had she/he bothered to kill her now? Just like Michael Wennerhaver had demanded: Why now?

And if Madeleine had called me here because she suspected she would be killed—if I was not making that up out of the cloth of my own need—I would never know. But I would damned well find her killer.

CHAPTER 8

□

From the patrol car I called the dispatcher. He had informed the Evening Watch commander, Lieutenant Davis. Doyle was on his way to the station. He would coordinate the investigation from there, dealing with the hospital, and the coroner once he finished here. Soon we'd have enough manpower to secure the scene around Madeleine's room, do preliminary interviews with witnesses, and canvass the neighbors, and a scene supervisor to keep track of it all.

I hurried back down around the house to the cottage companionway. Pereira was standing with Michael and the frizzle-haired woman, Delia McElhenny. Raksen was inside Madeleine's room setting up his camera stand. "Take one shot of the window to the canyon, Raksen, then pull the shade back down. We don't want to have everyone on the far rim calling the Kensington station."

Outside, on the companionway, Michael's pager buzzed. A red light came on at the edge of the roof.

Michael looked from the light to the closed door beside him. "Claire! God, she must be terrified."

Delia caught his arm. "You stay with Coco. I'll see to Claire."

"No. She'll be expecting me. She'll be—"

"Michael," Delia said with authority, "I can handle this."

Clearly, he had no choice. "Make sure she knows that I'll still be around for her. I'll be in and out of her room every time she needs something."

She squeezed his arm before releasing it. "Of course, Mike. I'm sure she knows that, but she'll be comforted to hear it anyway." She knocked perfunctorily, opened the door, and walked inside. I motioned Pereira in after her. In delicate situations like that we don't like to intrude, but we're not about to leave two witnesses alone together before we've interviewed them.

I remembered Madeleine mentioning Claire, scornfully describing her as "one of those traditional ladies, trained to be polite, remain pure, and never create unpleasantness. A product of the days when purity was all." No doubt Claire would be frightened. Anyone would in her position, alone in a nursing home, never knowing when staff would come in, or in her case never sure when a large dog would bound in. She was completely dependent on the staff for her care. And now they had let a younger, more vibrant woman die. I wondered what Delia would tell her. There had to be a standard line; it was a situation nursing home personnel faced all the time. And at least here, the dead woman hadn't breathed her last in the next bed as would have been the case in many places.

The door to Claire's room shut. Michael released the dog's collar and brushed the dog hairs off his freshly pressed jeans. That compulsive neatness (or what those of us familiar with dogs think of as compulsive behavior in the undoggy) was something I would have expected of Madeleine Riordan. Before I'd seen her with Coco sprawled on her bed, I would have pictured her living in cold beige rooms, furnished with hard chairs and not many of them, and all of it spotlessly clean. Sterile. I would never have imagined her opening her door to a carrier of fleas and loose hairs.

To Michael I said, "The residents can call you anywhere on the grounds here?"

He nodded.

"Then let's use your room to talk in." Before he could protest, I added, "It'll be quicker for you to get back here in case Claire needs you." And I would get a clearer picture of him as he reacted to his own place while he talked to me—and a better sense if there was anything hidden in there.

He unlocked a burglar's special—one of those doors with the glass on top—by the path and led me into a basement room. It might once have been a tool space or wine cellar for one-glass-with-dinner people. Mostly what it looked like was a college dorm room. I cataloged it in my mind as if I were taking notes. Narrow bed covered by green plaid spread next to the inside wall. Reading light over pillow. Bookshelf high on the wall over the bed—an invitation to maiming in earthquake country. Three drawer dresser with peeling black paint against back wall; on it were statues of the Virgin Mary in flowing robes and Parvati, consort to the Hindu god Siva, in belly dancer garb and stance.

"An unusual pairing," I said to Michael.

A smirk crept onto his face. "The old nuns at St. Sadists gave me the Mary when I graduated, because I'd been such a *good* boy, which meant because they'd taught me to cower and grovel so well. Parvati I got on my own."

"Because they'd be so appalled?"

Michael giggled. "They'd flip their habits if they knew their prize boy ever thought of women like that."

I continued my survey. Next to the dresser stood a slanted wire bookcase with shaving kit, change, hair dryer on top. And a bottle of prescription medication, for poison oak. Beyond that was a desk with a pile of textlike books on the nearest side. The six-by-twelve cell ended with a wooden door in the far wall, with a latch locked.

"What's in there?" I asked lightly, turning the desk chair around to sit down.

"Bathroom. I share it with Delia."

"You keep the bathroom door locked?"

He shrugged. "Delia's an old hippie. Her view of private property is hazy." He winced, and I had the feeling the line he'd just given me was one he'd used before when describing Delia to his friends, and that it had flashed on him it wouldn't get as good a reaction from the police. "It's not that she'd *steal* anything important, but if I left the door open I could never count on having a pencil or"—he shuddered—"even my toothbrush." He was wearing those five-dollar Chinese black cotton shoes with the thin rubber soles. He sat on the bed and wiggled his feet to slip off the shoes. They stuck. His round face scrunched into a look of exasperation as he bent and yanked them off, then pulled his legs up to sit cross-legged. There was an awkwardness about his movements, as if he were still an adolescent who hadn't adjusted to his latest spurt of growth. I looked at his hands but there was no sign of poison oak.

"Michael," I asked, "were you close to Madeleine?"

He leaned forward and absently pulled the bedspread up around his socked toes. I was expecting him to answer "Yes." He had told me he cared about all the patients here and in the nursing homes he'd worked before. But I wasn't prepared for him to stare down at the bunched bedspread, press his knuckles into the fabric, and mutter, "I don't know how I'm going to get along without her. She—" His voice caught. He swallowed. "Sorry. It's just that Madeleine is the first person who thought I was something special, someone with a future. She was my sponsor."

I waited, letting him talk at his own pace. The room was cold. He had a space heater next to the desk. It didn't look like it would do much.

He let go of the bedspread and leaned back against the wall that doubled as headboard. "You've probably heard about the Professional Coalition Scholarship?"

I had, vaguely, but I decided to let him explain.

"It's a full scholarship to graduate school. The Professional Coalition— they have a hundred members in Berkeley, each one of them has a different profession—and they give this scholarship each year. Madeleine"—he shut his eyes and took a deep breath—"Madeleine nominated me. She shepherded my application through the whole process. She told them how I had worked at nursing homes all through college, even when I could have gotten better-paying jobs. How I did it because I cared that someone should be there for people who don't have anyone else. She convinced them it was something special, that *I* was special, and that I would make a difference as a doctor."

"How many candidates were there?" I wondered just how big a commitment this shepherding of Madeleine's had been.

"A lot. I was astonished when I won. I mean some of the guys were really good. Madeleine really went out on a limb for me. I don't know what all she did, but I do know that she said that medicine has lost the sense of what it should be. Doctors are too interested in exotic research or just plain wealth." He looked up at me, a watery smile playing on his face. "She said if your dog is old and in pain you can get the vet to come out and put him to sleep; you can hold his head in your lap while he slips away. 'You'll never get anything that humane yourself,' she said. I guess they believed her; her husband is a vet."

Madeleine was one to know; *she* hadn't gotten that kind of treatment from her husband, the vet. I made a mental note to tell Doyle before he interviewed him. He'd need to find out what exactly made Madeleine leave home and come here to die.

"She told them," Michael continued, "that they owed it to their friends, their children, their country to support a decent student who wanted to be a caring doctor." He shrugged. "She convinced them. So I start medical school next semester."

"Her death won't affect that?"

He glared at me. "Of course it will. My triumph would have been hers. She would have cared about my courses. Discussed them with me. I could have shared everything. She's the only person who ever really thought I was worth something. Now there's no one to care. Oh, I'll go on to school. I owe her that. And, well, I've worked really hard for this chance. Even if I'd had the money, which I no way did, I don't know that any school would have accepted me without her influence. She was the key . . . to everything." He swallowed. "Everything."

"You don't have family?"

He squeezed his eyes shut; he looked like an adolescent fighting the last vestige of childhood and yet desperately wanting to hang on to it. "They're back east. They couldn't help me through college, much less medical school. I've always had to work. Even if you're not taking a full load of classes, it's not easy to spend four nights a week on duty in a nursing home and make respectable grades." He glared at me through watery eyes.

I nodded slowly, using the time to look at him. He was average height, not heavy, but not ever likely to be too thin. His dark hair was parted in the middle, blown back around round cheeks and a full-lipped mouth. There was nothing in his appearance at all similar to tall, slender Madeleine Riordan. I could recall seeing Madeleine a few years ago when she was thinner than normal, when her cheekbones looked like they'd break her skin. Michael Wennerhaver would never have a visible cheekbone. But his tone, or was it his mannerisms, or his choice of words; something about him was just like Madeleine. I wondered if that similarity was what had first attracted her to his potential: a bit of herself for posterity? The son she'd never had? Or had Michael unconsciously mimicked his mentor? Whichever, the bond between them seemed to have been strong enough that she might have revealed her intentions, her fears, whatever made her too dangerous to live. His first reaction to her death was to cry out: "Why now?"

"Michael, did Madeleine ever talk about fearing death?"

"She wouldn't have done it." His face reddened. "She wouldn't kill herself. Not now! Not without talking to me! She's the only person who's cared about me in years. She wouldn't do this to me!" He yanked the bedspread up and wiped it roughly across his eyes. He was sobbing now.

There was nothing I could do. Grief takes its own time. I recalled Michael when I'd first seen him last night, when he was trying to keep me away from Madeleine. Now, knowing her, having heard him, I could understand his fierce protectiveness. Still, it was interesting that he had assumed suicide.

It made me wonder about her husband, the veterinarian. "Did she talk about her husband?"

"You mean problems with him? No. I mean he didn't even bother to bring her here this time. She got someone to drive her over. Her husband hasn't been to see her once. It's like she was a dog he sent to the kennel! No, worse—at least you take your dog there yourself. He didn't even bother to do that."

"So maybe there were problems."

He laughed, a high, awkward croak. "Was she so depressed about him that she killed herself?" he asked mockingly.

"Maybe he wanted her out of the way?"

"Well, she was. She was here."

"Why didn't he visit her?" I insisted.

"Because he's an asshole." He swallowed and said, "Actually, I never met the guy, and Madeleine didn't talk about him, so who knows?"

"Well, did she have any other visitors?"

"None I saw."

I was getting nothing. I'd have to bait the hook. Leaning forward I said, "So in a sense, Michael, you were her closest friend?"

"I guess."

"This isn't going to be public knowledge for a while, and I have to ask you not to tell anybody, *anybody*." I waited till he nodded solemnly as do all but the most jaded witnesses at that invitation into the inner circle. "Madeleine may have been murdered. And we have to treat this like a murder investigation. So, Michael, what could lead to her being killed?"

He fingered the bedspread, slowly shaking his head.

I could have kicked him. Or myself. When that inner circle gambit fails, it bombs. I thought of Madeleine sitting in Claire's room, holding Coco. "Michael, Madeleine spent a lot of time sitting with Claire. Maybe she talked to Claire about something threatening her?"

Michael's eyes widened as if I had suggested something horrifying, or at least, indecent. I had to struggle to keep a straight face. He looked away, and wiped his eyes, this time with his hand rather than the bedspread. The process took longer than it had to—he was camouflaging his reaction. The Michael who'd told me he'd worried whether Claire would make it through the night was not likely to admit he was appalled at the idea of Madeleine's confiding in her. He looked up. "Sorry. I don't know what Madeleine talked to Claire about, of course."

I noted that he viewed their conversations as one-way affairs. "But, do you *think* she would have confided her concerns to Claire?"

Now he looked directly at me. "No. The only thing she talked about that upset her was her mother. Her mother died in a nursing home. Not a place like this, but one of those places that smell of urine, where you hear people down the hall wailing all night."

People we assume will never be ourselves. "Did that make Madeleine afraid?"

"No. Not afraid. Guilty, even though she had no reason to be. She couldn't help. It was right after her car accident. She was in the hospital herself. There was nothing she could do."

Nothing she could do. Like Madeleine's husband, I thought, only his distance was by choice. Maybe. I stood up, and used the moment to check out the bookshelf over the bed. Medical books, anatomy, physiology, some ologies I couldn't place, the type of words you wouldn't want to hear from your own doctor. On top of Gray's *Anatomy*, *Biochemistry II*, and several ringed notebooks was a pile of magazines. I smiled. "So not all hard work here, huh?"

He looked up at the magazines and blushed. "Oh, them. They're just stuff I've taken from some of the old guys' rooms after they died."

I didn't respond.

"No, it's true. I mean their children don't want to think the patriarch, the man who bounced them on his knee, was reading *Playboy*, or *Hustler*, or *Western Gun Digest*."

I said nothing.

"Look, most adult children assume their old parents have no interest in sex. Like everything dries up when they come here. But getting old doesn't make you impotent. Our residents remember what it was like. They have fantasies. Sometimes we even have romances here. That's great for them. They love it."

I turned back to the dresser and picked up the poison oak medication. "The canyon's a bad spot for someone allergic to poison oak." When he didn't answer, I said, "Do you go down there much?"

"No. I'm very allergic."

I let my question lie between us a moment, then asked, "How do you feel about meter maids?"

He stared at me a moment. I couldn't tell whether he was really baffled or just putting on a good act. Then he adjusted his face into a smile that wouldn't have fooled anyone and said, "Actually, I'm grateful to them, or at least to the guy who's after them. One of the men upstairs says he paid so many tickets if he doesn't write checks to the city he feels like his week is wasted. He can't wait to read about the latest meter maid stunt, and talk it over with everyone. They all just love it. Starts them thinking about what they'd like to do. Thinking about new things, planning; it's good for them. I just hope the stunts keep up till baseball season starts again."

Meter maid assaults as an extra nine innings for shut-ins; I figured I wouldn't mention that to Eckey. I gave Michael the usual warnings. I'd have Murakawa take his official statement tomorrow. Maybe a man would get a different angle from him. There was something Michael Wennerhaver was hiding. Lots of witnesses hide things that have nothing to do with the investigation, things we don't care about at all but to them are scarlet *A*'s. Michael probably would have given a lot to keep me from coming across the girlie and gun publications. But what interested me was the poison oak medication. He could, of course, become infected in the yard, or if he touched wet sap on the dog's fur. But if he went into the canyon regularly . . .

I didn't see him setting up meter maids to provide a diversion for the old residents. But loners like Michael Wennerhaver raise suspicions. A loner who resented the narrowness of his life was just the type for our perp. And the old man upstairs with all those parking tickets, did he still drive? Or did someone get those tickets for him?

CHAPTER 9

□

When I stepped back outside into the yard between the main house and the cottage where Madeleine Riordan died, I wondered why I'd bothered telling Raksen to pull Madeleine's shade back down. To avoid drawing attention? Fat chance of that. Lights were clipped on every protruding surface around the backyard and over the path. The place looked like a movie set. Patrol officers were hunched over, eyeing the steep ground for signs of an intruder none of us expected them to find. Too many feet had run down the path and onto the companionway. The best we could hope for would be to find an item the killer dropped— preferably something like a driver's license.

Michael Wennerhaver took one look, hurried down the path, and knocked on Claire's door. He was halfway in before Heling, who had replaced Pereira in there, cautioned him.

Inspector Doyle would be at the station by now, coordinating background checks, talking to the doctor, going over the notes from the preliminary interviews, and taking witnesses' final statements.

Murakawa was on the companionway. Today he was back on patrol, just another patrol officer. But something of the bond between us from last night's hostage operation still held. I wondered if he had seen Madeleine Riordan's body and if he, too, had thought of the deflated dummy in the canyon. If so, he didn't let on. I gave him a summary of my interview with Wennerhaver. "You can take him to the station," I said. "And tell Doyle

Riordan's husband didn't bring her to Canyonview. According to Wennerhaver, someone else brought her, and the husband hasn't visited."

Murakawa nodded. Anyone who didn't know him so well would have missed the slight judgmental pursing of the lips.

"Where is the woman in the sunburst suit?"

"Basement door at the far side of the main house. Right up there." He pointed to a light just beyond the corner.

Pereira met me at the door, with her notes from Delia McElhenny's preliminary statement in hand. She stepped outside and shut the door behind her. "To begin with," Pereira said with an undercurrent of disgust in her voice, "she's not even a nurse. She's picked up some knowledge—well, who wouldn't, running a place like this for five years—but no degree. Says she purposely avoided it—as if nursing degrees arrived at the door like Jehovah's Witnesses and you have to be on the lookout so you don't open up." Pereira, who had gone to school in a district that has since been taken over financially by the state, who'd worked her way to a B.S. in economics, had little patience for . . . well, the truth was, Pereira had little patience, period. Michael Wennerhaver was more sanguine about his hardships than she, but then Michael was headed to medical school, and Connie Pereira might never make it into the elevated realms of finance that so fascinated her. "Seems, Smith, that she owns the place. Seems she inherited it from her parents. Seems," she said, disdain dripping from her words, "she's forty-eight years old and still living in the room she took over when she was fifteen, and probably wearing the same clothes."

I nodded. Suddenly, tie-dyed dresses, skirts, tights, and shirts were for sale all along Telegraph Avenue. Twenty-plus years after it had faded into the sartorial purgatory of bell-bottoms and micro-miniskirts, tie-dye burst into bloom, like plants on a burned-out hillside. What had rekindled the dormant seeds of tie-dye, no one seemed to know. Or what kept the shopkeepers and street vendors displaying it. Despite its massive availability, Delia McElhenny was one of the few people I'd seen actually wearing it.

"Seems like," Pereira went on, "what she's most concerned about with this homicide is liability."

"By which she means financial liability?"

"Right. Not that she has an alibi for the last few hours. Of course she's got no idea who went in or out of Riordan's room, even though lifting her head to look out her window could have shown her. She admits she was around all day. Doing what, you might ask, since she provides none of the care? A little cooking. 'Mostly hanging out'—that's a quote."

I stifled a laugh. In the Pereirian lexicon hanging out was about as acceptable a use for time as shopping for tie-dye.

"The woman has raised irresponsibility to an art form, Smith. Not only does she keep herself too ignorant to provide any care for her people here, but she's even had the cottage windows walled up on this side so she won't know what's going on in their rooms. And the contract the residents sign— they're part owners as long as they live—"

"Like residential term insurance?"

"Sort of. It's all legal, I'm sure. Residents can do whatever they want in their rooms—hire a nurse, or refuse medical care—it's no business of Delia's. And when they croak, she resells the room."

"Any incentive to help them along faster?"

"I assume you want me to check. She must get something, and the way she lives, even a little would help. But the thing is, Smith, you could offer her title to the entire city of Berkeley and it wouldn't get her moving! Even so, she doesn't gain much. Basically what she's got here is the dying making her house payment and supplying her enough to live on if she doesn't have any fancy plans, which, of course, she's too lazy to come up with."

"So, Connie," I said, reaching for the door, "you think she'll still be awake when I get in there?"

"It could take a trained detective to tell."

I stood for a moment, mentally stepping back from Pereira's view of McElhenny. Chances were I would concur with Pereira—she was a good judge of character. She sized up a suspect with the care she gave a stock option or a pork belly future. It was only after she'd made her judgment that she dumped the pork bellies in the pigsty and carried on about the stench.

I knocked on Delia McElhenny's door and walked in.

The room was perfect for the woman Pereira had described; it could have suited any teenager in the sixties. The double bed was jammed against an inside wall and covered with a Madras plaid bedspread that must have spent the past thirty years bleeding out its colors. Now it was a dull orange. On the white block panel walls were splatterings of fingerprints and an Everly Brothers poster so old I was surprised the paper survived. The cement floor (painted black) held an orange rya rug. Delia McElhenny looked up from one of those barrel chairs that were popular only long enough to remind people that barrels are best used to transport liquids.

I introduced myself, decided against a swinging hammock chair in favor of a beanbag, and sat. "Why would Madeleine Riordan have been killed?"

I'd hoped to startle a response, but clearly in the world of the slothlike I was up against a pro. She gave a small shrug. "Got me. I don't even know why she came back here. If she was going to die, why couldn't she have done it in her own house?"

I realized, with a start, that I was the one who was surprised. Despite

Pereira's characterization of McElhenny, I recalled Delia from the firm but gentle way she handled Michael outside Madeleine's room. At some level, I had been prepared to see beneath Pereira's description to find a sensitive, mature woman. But Delia wasn't letting me. Her reaction to Madeleine's death here was a complaint, seemingly aimed at the powers that be. But it was one thing to which Delia McElhenny had allotted thought. "Why *did* she come back here?"

She merely shrugged.

"She was here before this time? When?"

Delia ran a hand through her long wiry red hair, pulling a clump loose from the band that held it. The red, blue, green, purple, and yellow tie-dye she was wearing appeared to be pajamas, but might, in fact, have been her all-occasion wear. "Madeleine bought her room in July. She stayed here through a ten-week bout of chemo, then she went home."

"If you don't offer anything she couldn't arrange at home, why didn't she stay at home?"

"Got me," she said sliding down in the chair.

"No, Delia," I snapped, "not good enough. There has to be some reason people spend a lot of money to live here. You run this place; what's the draw?"

A smile flickered at the corners of her mouth. It seemed a great effort. A myriad of sun wrinkles around her unadorned eyes suggested a long and close acquaintance with the out-of-doors. For someone with more muscle tone I would have guessed long hours spent cycling or hiking; however, from the look of her, her idea of serious exercise was turning over on a beach towel. But then *laid-back* and *well-preserved* are terms rarely used in the same sentence. "A number of residents come here to take control of their lives, and to avoid all the family psychological baggage that gets unpacked when someone's dying."

That sounded like a quote from an oft-given spiel. "But Madeleine—?"

"Who knows? She wasn't profligate with her confidences."

I smiled. Sluglike Delia would have driven her crazy. "Maybe she confided in Claire. She spent a lot of time in Claire's room, right?" The question had worked with Michael; it was worth a try here.

She laughed.

"Why not?" I demanded, exasperated.

But if Delia noted my tone, she showed no reaction. Probably she'd seen exasperation so frequently she assumed it was the norm of conversation. She leaned back, running her fingers through the ends of her red curls and then letting the hair wrap around the fingers. "Madeleine would never have confided in Claire."

"Why not, Delia?"

"Well, the thing is it's probably just political. In the social sense, I mean, rather than political political. I mean, Claire is pretty old school. She was a teacher at Minton before I got to school. She's not one to shake things up."

"You went to Minton?" I should have kept the amazement out of my voice. I failed. Minton was a conservative private girls' high school. Minton girls married doctors, or became corporate lawyers or interior decorators. Minton girls did not spend their lives in basements or run ersatz nursing homes where they might have to listen to patients and, when the staff didn't show up, handle bodily secretions. Minton girls didn't acknowledge the existence of bodily secretions. And above all, they didn't look like Delia McElhenny.

"Yeah, I was a Minton Girl. If you saw my freshman picture, you wouldn't recognize me. But everything changed after we had the Minton Hall demonstration." Anyone else would have leaned forward eagerly, but Delia settled lower in the chair. If memories of the watershed event in her life couldn't animate her, I suspected nothing would. "You probably don't even remember hearing of it. But at Minton it was like the line between B.C. and A.D."

"Actually, I do know about it." It had been well before I'd come to California. When Delia was in high school, I'd have been carrying a little plastic shovel and bucket and making sand castles on the Jersey shore. But it doesn't do to be a Berkeley detective without knowing the city's history. The Minton Hall demonstration was a very minor part of it—an antiwar demonstration, it followed the even less likely event of a group of Minton girls hiding the state government's most sought-after antiwar planner in the Hall. Cisco, the guy was called. A faculty committee called the governor's office. The state police arrived. Students surrounded the building. The standoff lasted less than an hour, but it was enough time for Cisco to escape. "Were you one of the collaborators?"

"I wish I had been. But I didn't even know about it until the cops got there. In fairness, even if I'd had the opportunity, I didn't care enough about the war to be bothered. It wasn't till I saw a friend get clubbed that things changed for me. Until then I thought government was there to protect me." For the first time she looked me right in the eye. "I've never made that mistake again."

"And Claire?"

"She was on the faculty committee."

"Is that the reason why she and Madeleine were at odds—different basic outlooks?"

Delia slumped back in the chair. "It's just an example of it. I'm fond of Claire; she's a sweet woman. When she was a girl, being a teacher was about as assertive as a woman could get. But she taught in a very protected environment; she never had to take a chance. Every decision she's made has been for the status quo. I mean, if she hadn't been the English Chair, I could easily have seen her with flour on her hands and an apron around her waist all day. Except that she's much too timid and prudish to ever have married, much less gotten naked with anyone, man or woman. It's all she can do to let me help her bathe. And even then she's so modest it takes me twice as long as it should. But that's the way she was brought up."

"I'll need to talk to her."

"Not tonight," she said emphatically. "Madeleine's death really shook her up. I gave her a sedative. I mean, she took it; I just suggested it, like anyone would."

I almost laughed. Either Delia was abnormally wary of being sued, or the line that allowed her to run a no-fault non-nursing home was entirely too narrow to walk. I could understand her position here. I could see Michael's, and maybe the rest of the residents, but for someone like Madeleine coming back here just made no sense at all. "Delia, Madeleine moved here when she was apparently well enough to stay home, right?"

Delia nodded.

"She had no visitors, right?"

Again she nodded.

"But she did spend time sitting in Claire's room with Coco. If she wasn't talking about her plans or her fears, if she didn't even like Claire, why was she sitting in there?"

For the first time Delia smiled, the kind of smile I would have hated to see on my own caretaker. "She was torturing Claire. You see, Claire hates dogs."

CHAPTER 10

□

I leaned back in Delia's beanbag chair, shifting my butt to make the beans rewedge themselves enough to provide a decent seat. Delia was smiling, presumably at the thought of Madeleine Riordan sitting with Coco at the end of Claire's bed evening after evening torturing the old woman. I wriggled the concept around like beans in the chair, but it didn't fit. Not for Madeleine. Even with her cane, Madeleine Riordan was a woman always on the move, if not physically, at least mentally poised to jump. She wasn't one to sit silently hour after hour bullying a woman when she could have gotten the same effect with one swat of her tongue. Fatal disease may make some people less vindictive. If they're still out to get their neighbor, it doesn't change their M.O.

The passive-aggressive approach Delia described was in fact more suited to Delia. But there was something beneath Delia's comment. I didn't know whether it would reveal a layer of Madeleine or of Delia herself. Careful to conceal my excitement, I asked, "Delia, what would make you think Madeleine was that angry?"

Delia wrapped a lock of wiry red hair around her finger absently observing the process. "I've seen her, talking about her cancer. She was furious."

"Furious at?"

She leaned toward me. "Medicine. People's carelessness. The laws of the universe. See, the thing was that she'd been real responsible about taking care of herself, going to checkups, doing self-exams, getting mammograms. She had a mammogram one year. 'Everything looks fine,' they said. 'Come back in a year.' And when she went back—almost a year to the date—they found not only a tumor, but cancer that had spread all the hell over. Inoperable."

"Oh shit!" I swallowed, turning away from Delia. There was a draft from under the door; it chilled my ankles. I couldn't imagine what Madeleine must have felt—I didn't want to probe deep enough, personally enough into the possibility of death ambushing me to experience the dread, anger, the rock-bottom fear she must have had—but fury seemed a reasonable reaction to me. When I turned back to Delia, her skin was pale, her face taut, and she was unconsciously holding her shoulders high and tight —probably mirroring me. Our eyes met briefly and in that moment I could feel the balance between us shift from authority-and-subject to two women sharing a small stab of grief and a pile of fear. We both swallowed. I took a breath, gratefully refocused on the steps of the interview, and asked, "Did Madeleine blame her doctor?"

"Her doctor, the lab, the government. She said the country spends more research money looking for a cure for baldness than breast cancer." Delia settled back again, but the tension didn't leave her body. Her shoulders poked into the barrel cushion and her arms hit her thighs at an awkward angle. "Maybe meditation would have helped. I know people who've had tumors shrink. But Madeleine couldn't get beyond her anger."

If anything could blast apart Madeleine's façade of control, discovering she'd been ambushed by cancer should have triggered it. I could picture Madeleine laying into the woman who took the mammogram, the technicians who read it, and the doctor responsible for it all. I could imagine her biting off the heads of well-meaning friends. My only surprise was that she tolerated having a sort-of landlady like Delia who blamed her for not overcoming her illness. Everything is in your mind; therefore, everything is your fault. *Therefore, it won't happen to me.* "Tell me about her anger. Was it spurts of fury or a low-burning rage, the kind that's always there threatening to burst into flame but never really does? Was she still angry the day before she died?"

"Smoldering, that's exactly it," Delia said, clearly surprised. "She could have taken my head off any minute. Like my mother, always ready to tell me I was doing it wrong, or not doing it enough."

"So even when she wasn't saying anything, her presence carried with it unspoken condemnation?"

Delia jolted forward. It was the most animated I'd seen her. "Yeah. How'd you know? There was no chance of doing anything well enough; the only question was how much of a mess I'd make, how late I'd be with it, how . . ." She shrugged. "I just gave up."

I didn't tell her that I'd had a grandmother just like that. But I'd been luckier than Delia. I'd spent only my summers with my grandmother. Every June my parents would drop me off with dutiful instructions to be good. Grandma would shake her head and settle in to tighten up the slack they had allowed during the winter. Each summer was worse than the last; each winter I swore no one could make me go back again. I'll never know whether I would have held out the year I was eleven; before school was over, while I was still swearing, my grandmother had a stroke. I only saw her once more, in the nursing home, and then I was sure every one of her complaints, every fetid smell, every moan and howl down the hall, was my fault.

I knew how Delia felt, but if she expected sympathy, I was the wrong person to tell she'd defeated her bully by giving up.

I couldn't resist saying: "Maybe she *could* do things better." With Delia the possibility didn't seem out of reach.

"I'm sure *she* thought she could." Delia shrugged, pushed forward, and rested her tie-dyed forearms lower on her tie-dyed thighs. "We had it out eventually. The way I saw things, she corrected everything I did. But for every correction she made there were probably twenty she bit back. She was almost choking on things she didn't say. In her eyes, she should have been sainted for restraint."

I laughed, uncomfortably; Delia's method of handling the household tyrant had some advantages. "Was Madeleine like that—a dormant volcano that could blow any time?"

"Blow and smother you in lava without even noticing."

"All that suppressed passion," I murmured. "Contained, boiled down till the taste burns your tongue." I thought of Howard when he'd worked undercover, gone for weeks at a time, and of the nights he came back, and the days before those nights, days when no matter what I was doing I could almost feel the ridges of his chest, the hardness of his body against mine. And when he finally got back . . . But what did Madeleine do with her passion? Delia, of course, wouldn't know. Instead, I asked, "So, Delia, then what is it that brought Madeleine back to Canyonview?"

Delia didn't know that either. I rephrased the question twice, but if she had any notions she didn't put them into words. Earlier I would have attributed her lack of response to laziness; but Delia McElhenny was more than a woman so laid-back she'd flattened into nothing; she was a careful observer; she carried a grudge like a raw egg in a spoon race; and she'd been savvy enough to arrange to live in a very desirable Berkeley neighborhood and let other people support her. If something or someone threatened her life here, I suspected she wouldn't "just give up."

I left her with the usual warnings and walked back down the companionway between Madeleine's and Claire's rooms and stared into the almost total darkness, wondering about Madeleine. That contained passion of hers was, of course, her strength. No one who had been seared by comments, her prevolcanic sparks, was likely to wait around for the major eruption. But what was at the core of it?

I had the feeling that I was dealing not so much with a case of a murderer stalking in and killing her as one where her very being drew her murderer to her. And if I could find the core of that being, I'd find the killer.

I sighed. It'd be a damned sight easier to track down a murderer than to uncover the secrets of Madeleine Riordan's soul!

Turning back, I knocked softly on Claire's door. Heling opened it. The woman in the bed was asleep. I put my finger to my mouth; Heling walked back to her seat at the foot of the bed, half hidden behind a Chinese screen, and sat. I wondered if that was how Madeleine had spent her time in here, except that Madeleine would have been holding Coco. Tormenting Claire because of a thirty-year-old political difference? Hardly.

The room was about two thirds the size of Madeleine's. Whereas Madeleine's had the sense of tasteful efficiency, with its framed Sierra Club posters, small red carpet, and straight-backed chair, Claire's room reminded me of a guest room in the home of a relative you don't visit often. Doilies, ceramic figurines ever in danger of breaking, ruffled white curtains. The sheets were decorated with tiny flowers, and the blanket was baby yellow. The woman in the bed looked like the dictionary illustration of "maiden aunt."

Whatever compelled Madeleine to return to Canyonview, I just couldn't believe it was in this frivolous room.

Nodding to Heling, I walked back across the companionway. In contrast to Claire's doilies and dust ruffles, Madeleine's room seemed refreshingly stark and even her method of death sensible, convenient, no fluff— make use of what's available, slap it over her face.

Grayson was sitting in her Shaker chair, checklist on his lap. Grayson! Damn! I'd suspected he'd be the scene supervisor here; still, what rotten luck. Or was it just bad karma? I was almost sorry I'd exercised that last touch of spite leaving his Hostage Negotiation report listed as late. Almost.

I glanced at Madeleine's bed and smiled. Madeleine would have left that report listed late, too.

But Madeleine wouldn't have had to wonder every time a call was delayed or report late for the rest of this case if it was Grayson getting his own back.

Briefly, and with remarkable care on both sides, Grayson and I conferred. Neither of us mentioned the Hostage Negotiation report. "Pereira scanned the deceased's checkbook and address book. *Nada.* We can't contact Riordan's husband, Dr. Timms. Patrol went by the house, no one there. Neighbors don't know anything—no big fights, no hurried exits."

"Damn! What's with the guy? His wife's dying; he's not here and he's not home. Where is he?"

"We'll find him. Husbands of murder victims don't stay gone." Grayson shrugged off my frustration.

I took a breath. I'd be damned if I'd give him the satisfaction of hearing me snap at him. "What about the neighbors here?" The backup units should have finished their rounds by now.

"Zilch."

"Big surprise."

Grayson leaned back against the slats of his chair and took his time resting an ankle on the opposite knee. "So, Detective, you finished the room search? Seen everything you had to?" For the first time his voice was animated. He was leading me—somewhere.

"Yes. Why?"

"You're ready to sign off on it, so to speak?"

"Yes."

"You didn't check under the bed, then?" His moustache twitched as if batting back a smile.

I muttered, "No."

"Then you must have missed these." Grayson dangled a pair of binoculars.

I took them from him and silently moved to the window and let up the shade, partly to look out, and not in small part to have my back to him until I got over the worst of my humiliation. How could I have overlooked them? And to have Grayson of all people find them! By tomorrow morning this tale would be all over the station!

But there was nothing I could do about that now. I adjusted the binoculars and looked into the canyon. It was too dark to see down. Rectangles of light from houses across the canyon blurred through filmy fans of oak or eucalyptus leaves. I moved the binoculars slowly counterclockwise, till I was nearly facing the bay, till the lights in the distance were too far to be more than an abstract pattern in black and gray. Then I refocused on the window directly across the canyon.

Why had Madeleine come back here when she could have stayed home with her husband, the absent veterinarian? What made the lava boil? Or freeze? When I turned back to Grayson, I was smiling. "There is only one window visible across the canyon." Maybe the answer wouldn't be there, but what was there was a telescope pointing at Madeleine's window.

CHAPTER 11

□

Madeleine Riordan had left her home and husband to live in a single room among people who, with the probable exception of Michael Wennerhaver, she either didn't care about or actively disliked. The one significant thing she'd brought with her was her husband's binoculars.

I didn't picture her returning to Canyonview to watch birds.

With binoculars Madeleine Riordan might have been able to peer into the canyon, into the lair of our parking pest. Had she seen something there she was considering telling me about? Had she needed time to decide whether to take that unnatural step? She would have hesitated to call us, her old adversaries. If you spend years embroiled in citizens' complaints, you end up viewing the police as a passel of bullies who exist only to threaten and maim. And a crime has to be dire indeed before you'd pass them another club or bit of information. Harassing meter maids hardly fell into the dire category.

Again the thought jabbed me: did she just need someone to talk to? Could she have been so lonely she'd abandon her principles for the sake of an hour's visit? Or had she been stringing me along? Two days ago I would have accepted "stringing along" without question, just another antipolice maneuver in Madeleine Riordan's life. But the imminence of death reveals layers people didn't know they had, didn't *want* to know.

Or maybe the answer to my questions lay behind the telescope lens across the canyon.

The far-side canyon is Kensington, in Contra Costa County. The afflu-ent city is unincorporated, as its road pavement makes clear. (Of course, judging things on that basis, one would assume much of Berkeley was unclaimed by any governing body.) I called the dispatcher and left word with him to notify the Kensington police that I was heading over the line. Inspector Doyle would have been in touch about the hostage operation last night. The county line runs east-west through the canyon. When we went down there last night, we had no idea on which side of the line we'd find the action. And even after we had found the stash of tickets, we didn't know which jurisdiction they were actually in nor were we likely to, without a whole lot more trouble than any of us wanted to go to. But the meter pranks were our case, the meter prankster our perp; with its tiny police force, Kensington would be glad to merely assist.

I drove up to the Kensington shops and cut back to the rustic road that skirted the canyon. The Berkeley side of the canyon had streetlights, park-ing problems, and living room windows that faced onto the street. But here in Kensington, thick trees blocked out the sky. There were few streetlights, few blurs of light in street-side windows. I could have been in the moun-tains winding through roads made from pony express routes. Kensington homes perched like bobcats scanning the canyon for their prey.

It took me three stops to find someone home who admitted to knowing the location of a canyon wall cottage and the steps that led down to it—wooden supports holding back earthen platforms—that were wedged in so tight between two rim houses that I'd have taken them as stairs to a back stoop.

I made my way down between houses with roofs level to the street. The stairs weren't steep, but the supports had been worn down with time, and once I passed out of range of the light from the canyon-facing windows, I had to feel for the edge of each step. Maybe one false step wouldn't have flung me into the lair of skunk and parking perp, but it felt that way.

A single light shone off the roof of a walkway between halves of the cottage. Mostly it lit the walkway, but from what I could make out of the cottage it could have been a copy of Madeleine's. Was that what drew her binoculars here, and the telescope in the window of this house to Made-leine's cottage?

I stepped onto the companionway and knocked on the carved red door that led to the mirror image of Madeleine's room. When I got no response, I tried the door across the companionway. No answer there either. I gave them both another round, and stood looking across the dark canyon, aware of the smell of fresh dirt and bay leaves and eucalyptus. Only one square of light was visible on the far side, but to my unaided eyes it was nothing more than a yellow square in a black background. Over here, the outside lights illumined hydrangeas offering violet and pink balls at the end of drought-thinned stalks. And I could see the remains of a couple of rose bushes that had doubtless provided an aperitif for the deer.

The resident might well be in bed at this hour, but three knocks should get anyone up. I pounded on the door one last time.

"Okay, okay, hang on. I'll be there in a second." The male voice sounded like it came from inside a closet at the far end of the building. If he could hear this knock, he'd heard the others. Not a man much interested in knowing who had tramped down to his out-of-the-way and—I thought, as police officers do—unprotected door.

It was a full minute before the red door swung open, revealing a lanky fiftyish man with wavy gray hair caught in a ponytail. The jeans he was wearing had not only the stylish holes at the knees, but unstylish ones on both thighs and a sub-zipper patch that saved him from indecency. His faded ZOO RUN T-shirt hung loose over sleekly muscled shoulders and arms. There was a cadaverous look to his face that made me flash back uncomfortably to Madeleine Riordan and her bare skull, her too-prominent bones. But there was nothing unhealthy about his tanned face. He just looked like one of those people who had more compelling things to do than eat. I suspected Michael Wennerhaver would view his decrepit garb with horror. But in most of Berkeley, where well-dressed is viewed as ostentatious, this man would seem an exemplar of proper restraint.

"I don't give out money at the door," he announced.

Proper restraint, indeed. And not a great sense of time, unless this neighborhood drew peddlers at eleven at night. "I'm Detective Smith, Berkeley Police. I need to ask you a couple questions." I smiled, in what I always hope is a disarming way. "Okay if I come in?"

He shrugged. "If you don't mind the mess. I was in the darkroom," he added as if that had substituted for a housecleaning binge.

I followed him inside. Maybe he had turned his closet into a darkroom. It certainly looked like he'd turned out the closet's contents into the room. Letters and clothes covered a refectory table against the side wall, books were piled haphazardly on the floor amid a thick cushioning of dust balls. Shirts, sweaters, and jackets littered chairs; in a magnificent statement of slovenliness three jackets lay on the floor beneath the wispiest arrangement of clothes hooks I'd ever seen, like half a dozen or so eighteen-inch tapers in a spray coming out from the wall. They probably would have buckled under the jackets' weight, but nothing suggested they had ever been tested.

I could barely keep myself from smiling. In front of the dark picture window was not the telescope I had thought I'd seen, but a camera with a telephoto lens. He could have looked into Madeleine's window this evening. He could have captured her murderer on film.

But if he had, he hadn't rushed to notify the sheriff, and he hadn't chosen to mention it to me. I would need to slant in on this. With a show of massive self-control I kept my gaze moving from the camera to the kitchen wall and back to him. "I'll need your full name and address here."

"Why? What's going on?"

"We've had another incident on the canyon."

"Berkeley side, huh?"

"Right."

"Connected to the business last night?"

"We don't know." When he looked skeptical at that pat reply, I added, "Honestly. It's too soon to tell, but you can see that with two calls in the same area in two days we have to consider the possibility of a connection."

He nodded, either in agreement, or acknowledging my having swept him into the in-group of those expected to understand. For my purposes it didn't matter which. "Your name?"

"Victor Champion."

I almost laughed.

"Firstborn son. My parents weren't people to take chances. Unfortunately for them"—he grinned—"they didn't grasp the concept of overkill. I played every sport in school and nearly had a nervous breakdown from the academic pressure. And that was in the days before it was respectable for boys to break down, particularly sons of colonels. It says something that I've chosen to spend my time alone in a darkroom, supporting myself in a noncompetitive field." He shrugged with pride of rebellion he clearly assumed I would understand. And, in fact, I did.

"Photography is noncompetitive?"

"Quantitatively at least. That's the best we can do. Life is competitive."

"I guess that's something you learn growing up on military bases?"

"Right. And every time you move, the competition starts all over again. It's like having a new cat move into the neighborhood; suddenly all the territories have to be fought for all over again. I could have spent my whole childhood hissing and with bite marks in my tail." He waited to see if I caught the significance of the wound placement, then smiled. It was a lopsided smile mostly on the left half of his face. I wondered if that was the side he'd kept hidden from his military parents.

I was dying to ask about Madeleine, but witnesses tend either to offer nothing or to talk nervously until you announce your purpose. Then, comforted or at least focused, they feel like they have more control over the interchange. Once I asked about Riordan, chances were I'd never get him to reveal another thing about himself. "So, how'd the colonel take to that kind of pacifism?"

"Sent me to boarding school. Three, actually. Took him two to realize that military school wasn't the answer. The third was the kind of place where you can major in photography, bicycling, and the philosophy of Gandhi. Pretty radical for the time." He offered that lopsided grin. "I'm pretty much through work and ready for a glass of wine. I suppose I can't tempt you, even if this is out of your venue."

"Right. But you go ahead." We love it when witnesses loosen up, not that wariness seemed to be a problem with Champion. Either he had nothing to hide, or he'd spent hours in the darkroom and it was taking a long time for his mental eyes to adjust to the light of police presence.

Taking advantage of his trip to the kitchen, I glanced around the room again. The floor was bare wood—no carpet. The three chairs were of tan canvas, the type you buy at discount import stores and that forever rub your sitting bones no matter how thick your gluteal padding, and Champion's, I'd noticed, was not a bit excessive. Firm, but definitely not excessive. The walls were white and held no photographs. Either Champion was a very modest artist, or one who found new faults in his work every time he eyed it. Off to the left the hallway led to a kitchen and bathroom. "Is the other room the bedroom?" I asked when he came back.

"Is that a personal question?" he said with a look that made me think he had observed me in the same way I had him.

"A structural question."

"Too bad. Still, the answer is yes."

Now I could place him. Suspects try a variety of strategies with us. One is to pretend we've dropped in for a social visit, that whatever we're questioning can wait. The innocent don't bother with strategies. But through them, the guilty reveal more of themselves than they realize. I said, "And you support all this as a photographer?"

"You haven't seen my work."

"You haven't shown it to me. But still, I doubt Edward Weston could have handled the payment on this house." Land in Berkeley, and more so in Kensington, is like little plots of gold. The steeper the incline the more carats.

"I inherited it after my father died."

"The colonel and his wife lived here?" A studio in the hills overlooking the most liberal city in the country seemed an uncharacteristic whimsy for a colonel.

He laughed. "Hardly. The colonel would never have set foot in Berkeley. After he died, my mother drove up from Arizona once, but all the steps here were too much for her." He glanced around the room proprietorially.

"The colonel would be rolling in his flag-decked grave to know how I spent his money. It took the whole of it, but it's worth it. So how do I eat, you're asking? My mother died a year ago. I inherited what little she had. I make the occasional sale, and well, Nature has been good to me."

I expected him to glance down at his lean body. Nature had, indeed, been good to him. And clearly from the tone of his conversation I was not the first woman to have noticed it. Had Madeleine with her binoculars noticed it? Was that all her return to Canyonview was about, a last burst of lust?

A smile played at the left corner of Champion's mouth as if he could read my mind. He said, "I don't usually mention Nature's gift, but a police officer will have heard worse." He caught my eye momentarily, grinned, and said, "One of the things I've learned along the way is how to bolt houses to their foundations. After the Loma Prieta earthquake people have gotten a whole lot more serious about keeping their houses where they are. I could spend all day every day crawling around foundations. It's straight grunt work. But if I do one a month, I'm in good shape. And I don't have to go far for business."

"Well, I can see why you don't go around here boasting about this boon. You work in the canyon?"

"On the rim. There aren't many houses as far down in it as this one."

"Have you seen anyone down there?"

"In the canyon? Kids. But I work during school hours."

"No one else?"

"Who'd you have in mind?"

I hesitated momentarily, then decided to go on a "need to know only" basis. "We had a solo hostage situation there last night. The suspect disappeared. Maybe you've seen something that could help us find him." What we'd found down there he didn't need to know.

He stiffened.

"Mr. Champion—"

"Pi-on. Call me Pion."

Peon, indeed. I laughed. "Socked it to your parents, huh?"

"Final straw in the second military school."

"Well, Pion, I can guess how you see us, the police. But give my question some thought. If there's a guy hanging out down there, he can be building fires . . ." I didn't have to elaborate on the danger. The fire storm of 1991 was in a canyon on the other side of Berkeley. Fire swept down the canyon; temperatures rose to 2000 degrees (the temperature of crematoria); twenty-six people died.

Pion leaned back. The light hit half his angular face, showing me how it might look in photographic art. His cheeks hung off prominent bones, his mouth was wide, his lips thin, and his spatulate nose a bit too long as if he'd spent his half century stroking it in thought. His eyes moved from side to side under heavy half-closed lids. Come-to-bed eyes, Connie Pereira would have called them.

He shook his head. "Sorry. When I'm doing foundations, I'm making a racket. And I'll tell you you don't get much of a view when your nose is against the support posts. But I'll keep an eye out. If there were a fire here, I'd be the first to burn."

"Good enough."

He leaned forward. "Can I get you something? Coffee? Tea?"

I had enough background on him. He was relaxed, complacent, his guard down. This was the moment I'd been waiting for.

"No, thanks." I looked over at the telephoto lens. "But tell me about Madeleine Riordan."

"Who?"

"Madeleine Riordan, the woman your camera's focused on."

His whole body tensed. It was as if all those lanky bones had shrunk a size, and all those sleek muscles compacted. He leaned forward, poised on the edge of the chair. "She's got no reason to complain," he whined. "I've got a release for her. She said she'd sign it. I just haven't gotten over there for it. Now that I don't have a car, it takes more time to get places. I know she was uncomfortable about the photographs, but, shit, she could have called me. She didn't have to bring you guys in. Ridiculous. The whole thing's ridiculous."

Suddenly the room seemed icy, the walls too bright, the picture window startlingly dark. What kind of man was this—this man who I'd found attractive—who spent his time taking Peeping Tom photos of a dying woman? I could feel the muscles in my neck clutching. What kind of man took advantage of the only things she had left: her view of the canyon and the body disease was sucking dry? And brushed aside her objections with the ease of a rapist insisting "she wanted it." I had to swallow twice before I could trust my voice. "Show me the photos."

He didn't move.

"Now!"

He jumped up. "Okay, okay. They're in the darkroom. It's just that I've never shown them to anyone."

With effort I restrained comment and followed his long loose steps into the hallway to a room that must once have been a laundry area. It was five by eight, with brown chemical bottles on shelves, shallow pans by the sink, and streamers of negatives hanging from clothespins. Champion walked to the far end and extricated three 8-by-11 prints. "These are the best," he said in a voice that barely resembled the sure, easy tone he'd had before. This was the voice of the boy afraid of the consequences of not fighting for territory, afraid what territory he'd managed to steal for himself would be snatched away and he'd be standing on nothingness.

I stepped out into the hallway. He followed, shut the darkroom door, and walked back to the living room. With the sweep of an arm he cleared the refectory table. Letters and clothes thudded to the floor. Carefully he propped the photos on the table, then moved back.

I steeled myself, silently apologized to Madeleine for compounding Champion's invasion, then stepped up to them. The telephoto lens had made the pictures startlingly clear. One was a nighttime silhouette taken through the window. Madeleine must have been sitting on the foot of the bed; her legs must have been crossed, but I couldn't be sure. Her back was utterly straight, and the light formed a halo around her bare head. She looked both like a candle and like a Japanese monk. Strong, self-contained, a light in the darkness. Utterly sexless, just insight and integrity. The Madeleine Riordan her clients trusted with their futures. The lawyer everyone respected but few asked to lunch. This was a photo I'd expect Michael Wennerhaver to have in the honored spot above his desk. It captured Riordan in a depth I hadn't expected from Champion. I felt a flush of guilt, recalling my suspicions about him. Still, the man who came on to me was as real as the sensitive photographer.

The second photograph was a daylight shot. Madeleine was sitting in the same place, clearly cross-legged, and Coco had his paws on her shoulders. They were nearly nose to nose and Madeleine was smiling. Her smile was so intense I had the sense that everything else, including her illness, had dropped away. In the photo there was no dying woman, only one delighted with her pet. Only the delight. I stared at it, amazed that these two pictures had captured sides of her so disparate they might have been of different people. And I found myself strangely relieved to know that the first picture wasn't the whole, that she had had at least this one moment of joy over there in the room she was to die in. Of course, I realized almost immediately, there had to have been more. *I* barely knew her. It shocked me anew on how little I had made my judgment of her, not just now in this case, but in the image I'd had of her over the years.

The third photograph was from a different angle. A palm branch cut into the edge of the window. I hadn't noticed that palm. Madeleine was facing the other direction. She seemed to be looking at or beyond a partition or doorway; I couldn't tell just what—it was too hazy. Her head seemed like a skull, dead and yet vivified by outrage—an outrage as burning as the joy had been glowing, the calm inspiring. If I wondered whether Madeleine Riordan had accepted her dying easily, I had my answer.

I turned slowly to Pion. "Are there others?"

"Nothing worth printing."

But he would have made contact prints at least. "I'll have to see them."

He nodded and headed back to the darkroom.

I would ask him if he saw anything today in Madeleine's studio. But I knew what answer I'd get. He would tell me he hadn't. And I would believe him. I could imagine these portraits would have made Madeleine uncomfortable. She had probably never been adored like this. I couldn't stop looking at the pictures, looking from one to another, from the joyous to the outraged to the controlled. I found myself glancing faster and faster as if I could mentally flip them like animated drawings fast enough to create one picture of the essence of Madeleine Riordan.

When he brought the other prints I could see why he hadn't earlier. They were ordinary shots of an ordinary woman. I looked back at the three, wondering if Champion had captured the triumvirate of Madeleine Riordan or had recorded three of any number of her hidden sides.

Whichever, he'd shown an insight I couldn't believe of a stranger. I handed him back the rejected photos. "Now, tell me about Madeleine Riordan."

CHAPTER 12

☐

I pushed aside a windbreaker and sat on one of Victor Champion's canvas chairs. It was every bit as uncomfortable as I'd expected, as if its entire purpose of existence was to pinch the skin between it and my sitting bones. But when Champion settled, not on his sitting bones but lounging on the flat plate of his sacrum, it was clearer to me why he found these hard surfaces tolerable. He wasn't nearly so tall as Howard, but the long sprawl of leg was the same. Before he could respond to my question about Madeleine Riordan, I said, "I owe you an apology."

He looked up from under his come-to-bed eyelids, surprised. "Is this an official apology, Officer?"

"As official as you're going to get. Jumping to conclusions isn't just unfair to you, it's real bad police procedure. So, I'm sorry."

He hesitated so long before offering a slight nod that I wondered if he realized my apology had been partly a ploy. I may have misjudged him; a detective is judging all the time, reconsidering constantly, like a computer justifying the margins every time a new phrase is thrown in. Normally I would add "Champion as Peeping Tom" and wait to reform the picture of Champion around it. I wouldn't make a final judgment till the case was closed. I'd keep my professional distance. With the Riordan case, I had a hunch that if I kept to the rules and played from a safe distance, I wouldn't skim the surface.

Or, perhaps Champion hesitated because my suspicion had touched a sore spot. Perhaps these photos of his weren't quite so innocent as they seemed. Or maybe they were, but others he'd hidden weren't. "So, tell me how you know Madeleine?"

"I don't."

"Your work betrays you."

He smiled, not that lopsided grin but a soft expression that encompassed his whole face and wiped away the residue of resentment. "Well, I didn't know her when I took the first roll. But after I developed it, I decided I'd better go over and get her okay."

The truth? Perhaps. Or had Madeleine with her binoculars spotted him and called him over? "When was that?"

"The end of last week."

I sighed. "Pion, again your work betrays you. You've cut to the marrow with those portraits. You've seen her as her colleagues never have. You're a superb artist, but, dammit, you're not good enough to have intuited her on a day's acquaintance."

He laughed, sending a lock of gray hair over his wide forehead. "God, the blarney. I love it," he said, pulling himself up straighter in the chair. "Okay, you've found me out. But only by a month. It was the middle of last month. I saw her sitting out. In a wonderful pose. And I just decided on the spur of the moment to bike over. I wanted to photograph her close up but she refused. She said it would make her too self-conscious."

"You didn't think of that? The woman had just lost all her hair!"

"But she looked wonderful. I told her that."

The man was an idiot-savant.

"I told her she was beautiful, magnificent. And she is. The way she moved, even with the cane, it was like a stream over old worn rocks. She's changed since last month. Thinner, more contrast between bones and flesh. But she's even more beautiful. Her soul shows through now."

I hadn't told him she was dead. I felt a pang of guilt, but the way things were going I suspected he'd say something in the next minute to make me forget it. "But you did photograph her."

"She said it was okay if I did it from a distance, so she didn't know. And if she didn't want me to, she'd pull the shade."

Was that part of Madeleine: it's okay if you don't get close enough to touch me? "And did she? Pull the shade?"

"No. But she left a week after that. I was devastated. All those nothing prints you just saw, they were from that one week before she left. Most of the good ones I didn't get till she came back. I almost tracked down where she lived and went there."

"Almost?"

"No, this is the truth. Maybe I would have, but I got an emergency bolting job. By the time I finished, I decided to wait for Madeleine to come back."

Nothing Champion had told me suggested that level of patience. "You knew she'd be back?"

"Yes, but not so soon. She'd had some kind of awful treatment and gotten over the bad effects. I assumed she'd get a longer respite than just a couple weeks."

"Did she move to Canyonview again because she'd gotten worse?"

He shrugged. "I guess."

I looked at the three portraits again: her smiling at Coco; outraged; and at peace. Anew I felt amazed that in the nearly ten years I had known of Madeleine Riordan I had never seen anything to suggest this depth of feeling. The pungent smell of sandlewood incense blew past and was gone. Like the glimpses of her, I thought. The glimpses she had never shown us. Irrationally, I felt angry. Then I thought of Champion resenting Madeleine's going home; I had a little more sympathy for his self-focus. "When did you shoot these?"

He picked up the smiling picture. "That was the day before she left. It was the only decent one of that batch."

I looked at it again, trying to see beneath her skull to the emotions she hadn't shown us. Was she ecstatic at the prospect of going home? Did she think she had a second chance at life? Slowly I put the photo down and picked up the second. "And this one, where she looks so peaceful?"

"Friday, the day she came back."

"Ah, good." As much as the next person, I knew the emotional steps the dying take, from denial, through bargaining with the cosmos, to acceptance. I was glad she had made it to the end. "And how long before that was the other one taken?" I said, lifting the photograph with the palm frond and the look of outrage.

"That one was on Saturday night. About seven thirty."

"*After* the peaceful picture? It was the last one?"

"Yeah. Then she pulled the shades."

If she had followed the normal steps and reached the calm that made death acceptable, was that calm we all hoped would protect us from the terrors of death so shallow it could be destroyed by rage? And what could have been so compelling to have given rise to that rage? "What was she so angry about?"

"I don't know." He dropped into the chair again and looked down the length of that spatulate nose of his the way he might at a print that hadn't come up right in the developer. "Just why are you asking me all this? What's going on?"

I put up a hand. "Bear with me a minute. Let's look at what happened. Madeleine came back when?"

"Friday."

The hostage operation had been on Sunday, and this evening, when she died, Monday. "What made her come back?"

He didn't answer.

"Did she come to be with you?"

He shook his head. "I wasn't with her. She didn't even know when I was taking her pictures. And then she shut me out of that."

"But you know her so well," I insisted. "You must have an idea."

His eyes half closed. He wanted to come up with something, I could tell. But in the end he said, "What it comes down to is, she lost her nerve. She had it a long time. You can see it in those portraits, the nerve to live, to do things to the utmost. But I guess dying caught up with her." He shrugged. "I guess you really can't blame her."

But I could tell by the sag of his body, the little catch in his voice, the way the skin on his cheeks seemed to sink in, deflated, that he did blame her. He cared more about the woman in his portraits than I had imagined anyone caring for Madeleine Riordan. "Okay, why she came back might not be the issue. What happened after she got there?"

"You'll have to ask her."

"I'm asking you."

He slumped lower in the chair. "I don't know. Maybe nothing. It probably wasn't anything that would make sense to anyone else. Talk to *her*."

"I can't, not now," I said slowly. "She's dead."

His eyes opened wide and his face seemed to sink back as if the air had been let out of his head. Then he jumped up. "You've known this all along. You've sat here, not telling me she was dead, letting me talk about her, and all the time she was dead." He stalked across the room and yanked open the door. "You just get out of here."

I didn't move. "When you level with me. *Anything that would make sense to anyone else.* So it's something. And Victor," I said deliberately using the name his parents must have used, "you know what it was. Now you tell me."

"You lied to me before that."

"Victor, this is not a contest—the person with the most blame loses." Purposely I didn't look him in the eye. But I watched for some small movement—an easing of the jaw, a stretching of the hand—something to indicate he accepted the truce. No sign came. He was too much of a brat to be pushed; if I backed him into a corner, he'd just put his fingers in his ears and stick out his tongue. There was no way but to give him more information than I wanted—the inner-circle lure. I leaned forward. "I'm going to tell you something we're not going to make public. Can I count on you to keep it to yourself?"

His thin lips tensed, drawing that spatulate nose closer. He was sharper than Delia McElhenny. He knew I was playing him; he yearned to tell me just where I could put my information, but that would mean his doing without it, and from the look of him he wasn't quite ready to make that sacrifice.

To prod him I said, "I'm asking because I need your help."

He waited just long enough not to appear eager. "Okay. Really there's no one I'd tell anyway—unless I run into a skunk under one of the houses I'm working on."

"My assignment is to Homicide Detail. Madeleine didn't die of cancer. Madeleine was murdered."

He drew in breath sharply. He hadn't put two and two together, or at least it didn't add up to wondering why I was asking about Madeleine's death. It's not uncommon for people to be too startled by the arrival of the police to run a secondary line of thought; and we're pleased about that. He swallowed. "How did she die?"

"Asphyxia."

"Somebody strangled her!"

"No, not that violent. I'm afraid that's all I can say. It's already more than we'll make public. Now, you, what is it you haven't told me?"

He got up and paced across the room, snatching up a shirt and tossing it on his fragile-looking coatrack. He picked up the angry picture and stared at it. "Okay, Madeleine wouldn't have told me if she didn't want it known. And maybe it doesn't mean anything anyway."

I waited, hoping he wouldn't just fade away in the miasma of anythings, anywheres, and anyhows.

"Like I said, I'd never seen Madeleine look like this, like she had one last—I didn't know it was the last then—moment of fury. I'd watched her for days and never seen anything remotely like that. I was amazed. I waited till she got back to her room and called her."

"Where was she when the picture was taken?"

"Claire's room."

"She was looking at Claire?"

"Facing the bed."

"How long did you have to wait before she got to her own room."

"Forever," he said with a huge sigh. He looked again at the photo but I had the sense he wasn't seeing it anymore, but rather feeling the frustration of his wait Saturday night. "Actually it probably wasn't more than ten minutes. Maybe less. I just can't say."

"That's okay for now. So what happened when you called her?"

"Well, her light went on. She pulled the shade. If she hadn't . . . but she did. I just couldn't be left hanging. And after all if she was that angry, she probably needed someone to talk to."

I smiled. "She snapped at you for calling, huh?"

His thin lips twisted into a smile of their own. "Boor was her term."

"So what had made her so angry?"

He shrugged. "Like I said, I don't know. I can only tell you what she said, and it didn't answer questions for me. I could hardly make out what she was saying. Like her words were bubbling up through water. Or sludge. Or whatever image you want of despair. Anger almost smothered in despair. Like it was all she could do to get the words out."

I was holding my breath.

"She said, 'We can't have people choosing which moments of our lives are important enough to deserve respect.' "

I gasped. That was essentially the question she had asked me at the Coco Arnero hearing: "During which moments is his life important enough to deserve your respect?"

Was that why she had asked me to come back tonight? Was the reason she had been killed enmeshed in the Arnero hearing? Or was it now in me?

"Did she say anything else?"

"No. That's all. She hung up. I don't know another thing. Except that she's dead, and now I will never get the one picture that brings it all together."

I asked him to come down to the station in the morning and dictate a statement. Then I walked out and up those hundred earthen steps.

Was Victor Champion in love with Madeleine? In his fashion. But I couldn't imagine him killing her unless he were promised access to her embalmed body and could photograph it till it was shoved into the crematorium chute.

I might scoff, but from across the canyon with his telephoto lens he had managed to see more deeply into Madeleine than I had in years of work acquaintance. In his pictures he had captured a hint of what I'd hoped Madeleine would show me tonight.

I realized as I reached the Arlington that I was not just disappointed about that; I was annoyed.

And I was insulted. That surprised me. It wasn't as if I'd ever had a nonbusiness contact with Riordan. But investigating was my job, my profession. How could someone like Champion have seen more than I? And how could Madeleine Riordan have allowed him to see what she had hidden from everyone else? *Why* had she?

And perhaps most infuriating was the fact that I still didn't know why she had decided to move back to Canyonview and what there had caused that look of outrage in Champion's picture. Maybe she had told him, but if so it was in a code he couldn't decipher in his pictures, and he certainly couldn't pass on to me.

I checked in with Inspector Doyle just long enough to agree we'd get together in the morning.

When I got home Howard was already asleep. I took a long bath, then slid in beside his warm sleeping body. I didn't wake him, but just lay listening to the comforting sound of his breath and wondering what could be so compelling as to make me elect to spend the last months of my life without him.

CHAPTER 13

□

The big news of the morning was Doyle's vain attempt to contact Madeleine Riordan's husband, one Dr. Herbert Timms, D.V.M. According to his service Timms was at a conference in Carmel, three or so hours south of here. They didn't know where he was staying. And after three calls last night and two this morning the only thing Doyle was certain of was that Timms was not answering his phone here. With a smile of relief, he passed the number on to me. I headed back to my office to tackle some of the accumulated paperwork and the numerous necessary calls.

8:30—To Timms. No answer.

8:33—To his service. No new info there.

8:35—To coroner's office. Got Matthew Harrison who said Madeleine Riordan had been taken first for autopsy. He'd check with the pathologist on cause and time of death and get back to me.

8:40—To Raksen. No fascinating fibers, pertinent prints.

8:45—To Timms. No answer.

9:00—To Timms, still gone.

9:10—From Harrison. Madeleine had indeed been smothered. They'd found particles from the pillowcase in her nostrils. The time of death would not have been more than two hours before I found her. Not before seven P.M.

At nine fifteen the dispatcher called. "Smith, you got a fracas at Walnut and Vine, Walnut Square." The meter maid perp had escalated.

A crowd of about thirty clustered on the sidewalk, right outside the original Peet's Coffee & Tea, the coffee cups in hand. Dogs meandered; one guy was posting signs for a weekend benefit-protest march (a leftist variation on the walkathon—protesters gather pledges for their participation in the march—one dollar per mile or hour. If they're arrested peacefully, the pledge doubles). Behind him a mauve-turbaned street person demanded spare change. The sky was blue, the air still warm—a perfect day for Berkeleyans to enjoy theater al fresco. The crowd stared at a venerable beige Mercedes and beyond at Parking Enforcement Officer Celia Eckey.

Eckey was purple. Literally. Purple from her formerly gray hair to her previously merely tanned fingers. Purple coated the right side of her Parking Enforcement vehicle and a swatch of street. Eckey smiled, but I knew her well enough to realize that was only because she was talking to the reporter for KRON news. "Some variety of explosive matter." She pointed to a sagging black rubber container affixed to the one-o'clock-to-three-o'clock portion of a Mercedes sedan tire.

"And it blew up in your face when you tried to mark the tire?" the newscaster prompted. Behind him a covey of print reporters crowded in, notepads in hands.

"It's water soluble." Eckey was masterful at defusing a situation. She'd had plenty of practice. "If spit were champagne," she'd said one day, wiping her face, "I could open a vineyard."

"And here you have it," the newscaster said to his camera, "another entry in the Parking Pranks Parade. Brings to mind the clown with pie-in-the-face gags, doesn't it? Coming to you from—where else?—Berkeley, this is Gary Frellis."

Murakawa was standing behind the Mercedes tire guarding the most essential part of the scene till Raksen arrived. We hadn't gotten a fingerprint off the parking vehicle when the perp released the brake, nor from the stolen helmet when it was finally recovered. I didn't have much hope now, but at least Raksen might find something from the explosive bag.

"I don't suppose you think the Mercedes's owner is the perp, Eckey?"

"Nah. Too easy. Flaunt's just a regular."

"Flaunt?"

"Three FLT two something something. Damn, I don't usually get so pissed off I lose a plate. Three FLT two eight . . . Damn! Flaunt's a big one for letting his meter run out and hopping in his car just in time to pull out before we get to him. We know the vehicle's been sitting there illegal for an hour." She glared at me. "It's a game to him, Smith. Then he drives around the corner and sits reading his paper until we get through here and move on."

"Why don't you turn the corner and collar him?"

"I circle the block, yeah. But I never get the bastard. I come back; he's waiting. He lopes up and tosses another dime in the meter and gives me a big, fat grin. Tiress has nabbed him, but not me. Smith, the man's got more time than sense."

I nodded. Eckey spent her weekends at some kind of retreats that she claimed helped to keep her centered. She was the most diplomatic parking enforcement officer we had. But clearly Flaunt was responsible for a serious centrifugal relapse.

Eckey braced her right hand on her purple hip. "I ask you, what does the fool do that pays him enough to keep a Mercedes and gives him nothing more to do than spend his mornings sitting around watching for us? Whatever it is, it's some kind of job I want."

The reporters ambled back to their own vehicles—double-parked. The coffee crowd was dispersing into small discussion groups, doubtless to consider the fine points of the incident. Raksen pulled up behind the Mercedes and bent over the offending tire.

"Hey, what the hell . . . !" A tall, sandy-haired man in his late forties ran toward Raksen, waving both arms. The crowd turned toward him.

There are crowds and crowds. On Telegraph Avenue, with its mixture of students and street people, tourists and drug dealers, there's always the danger of violence. But north Berkeley boasts a more mellow citizenry. This crowd was older; they'd seen it all before. And from the look of them they'd particularly seen this guy before. They were watching him, but they were smiling.

I dug in the glove compartment and handed Eckey a package of towelettes. "In case you'd like to freshen up."

She ripped one open and started on her purple face. I'd thought she would climb into the car for her ablutions, but she was too intent on watching the scene.

I ambled over to it.

"Can't have my car here all day!" the tall one screamed. I glanced back at Eckey. She grinned and mouthed "Flaunt." "We won't be any longer than necessary," Murakawa told him.

Flaunt stepped toward Murakawa, who was nearly six feet. Flaunt towered over him.

"It's already longer than necessary. I've got an appointment on the other side of town in fifteen minutes." He looked down at Murakawa. "You guys put up so many traffic lights in this town you can't get across it in less than a quarter of an hour."

Eckey edged closer. She'd done a wipe and a promise on her face. Her skin was only slightly blue, the lines around her eyes bluer, and the creases beside her nose and mouth still purple. She looked like a caricature. I decided not to bring that to her attention.

Flaunt pulled keys from his pocket and waved them in Murakawa's face. "I've got to leave—right now."

Behind Flaunt, Eckey made "draw it out" motions to Murakawa.

Slowly Murakawa said, "Lower your keys and give me your reasoning, sir." Murakawa's dark brown hair flopped over his forehead. His wide-set eyes looked relaxed. But there was no compromise in his voice.

"I'm giving a workshop. I am the leader."

"The leader," Murakawa repeated straightfaced. Behind Flaunt, Eckey rolled her eyes.

"Take Responsibility for Your Life," he announced.

Eckey's eyes shot wide open. She let out a gurgle I took to be an unsuccessfully swallowed guffaw. But Flaunt was too busy staring at Murakawa to notice. The coffee drinkers eyed one another knowingly and started up the street. Clearly Flaunt did not hide his workshop under a barrel.

Behind me a tow truck rolled to a stop.

"What's that?" Flaunt demanded. "Hey, you're not going to tow away my car because one of your meter maids got sprayed by it. *I* had nothing to do with that."

Eckey stepped around him. "We're not saying you did, sir." She was eye to eye with his bottom shirt button.

"Then, lady, you can't tow it for that!"

She let a beat pass. "We're not. Not for that. But our records indicate you have five outstanding parking warrants."

"So?"

She tried to maintain cool composure, but the heat of victory won out and a smile crept back onto her face. "After five warrants"—she tilted her head up and looked Flaunt in the eye—"we tow."

Tow truck drivers have the dexterity of jewelers and the speed of thieves. Flaunt was still screaming as the Mercedes lurched away behind the truck. Thirty seconds later he jumped in a cab (I suspected Eckey of calling it but didn't ask). The last I saw of Flaunt he was leaning over the seat pointing at the Mercedes and shouting at the cab driver words I took to be "Follow that car!"

Raksen would do his number on the car, tire, and bag. I didn't hold out hope for that. In any case, he wouldn't be done for an hour or so.

We canvassed the crowd. No one admitted seeing the perp affix the explosive bag on Flaunt's tire. At that time Flaunt himself had been inside Peet's, boring a postal employee with recollections of his workshop.

No one in Berkeley was going to expose the parking perp. Everyone but Parking Enforcement loved him. The Robin Hood of the expired meter. Even I had mixed emotions. If the perp kept poking meter minders long enough, eventually he'd jab Elgin Tiress. That was one puncture I'd sure hate to miss. But the perp had staged the hostage negotiation fiasco and made fools of the entire team. I wasn't about to let him get away with that. And I couldn't shake the notion that the hostage setup in the canyon was connected to Madeleine Riordan's death.

I stopped back at the station, made another try at Herbert Timms, D.V.M., and got no answer. Dammit, where was the man? Then I grabbed lunch—a chocolate shower sundae at Ortmann's—and drove on to Canyonview to meet the woman Madeleine had spent her time tormenting.

This was one of those days when the fog never clears. Looking into the canyon, I could see where the common allusion to soup had arisen. The canyon looked like a huge tureen, and the fog in it, one of those chowders that had been thick and warm and wonderful the night before. Too good to have merely one bowl. Sufficiently heavy to weigh on you all night, viscous enough to have rolled as you did and when you lay on your side to pull your overstretched stomach down toward the bed. In the morning when you opened the fridge door looking for ice water to pour over the Alka-Seltzer, you would see that tureen holding a dirty beige congealed mass with wrinkled edges of mushroom and wizened celery slices. Or in the case of Cerrito Canyon, live oak branches.

At Canyonview I spotted Delia McElhenny through the front window of the main building. She was stalking across the room carrying a basket, and looking like one of the Furies. If this was her normal state, what caused the lethargy of last night? With Delia McElhenny I'd need a lot more data to make any final judgment. I kept moving around the side of the building to the rear cottage.

The light skimmed the surface of the canyon fog, reinforcing the image of congealed soup. Under my gaze the rubbery surface seemed to give way and the live oak branches shivered in the quickening wind. I could picture Madeleine Riordan sitting alone in her room, in the dark, staring down into the canyon. Seeing something someone assumed was safe from peering eyes. At the same time, across the canyon, Victor Champion would have been peering back at her.

I glanced at Claire's door. From what little I knew of her, I didn't picture her broaching the darkness, but perhaps one of those days while Madeleine sat next to her holding Coco just far enough away, Madeleine had talked about what she had seen. *If*, indeed, she had ever seen anything.

I knocked on Claire's door. It was a moment before a shrill voice said, "Come in."

I stepped inside. Again the feeling that struck me was of a guest room in the home of a distant relative, one of those aunts or older cousins who referred to me as Louisa's daughter and never mentioned what I did for a living, or, more damning yet, where I did it. It was a room too pink, too ruffly, with too many ceramic statues waiting to be broken.

Claire fitted in perfectly. It took me a moment to realize that of course she would. It was her room; she owned it, she'd have decorated it. The foot-high ceramic dancing lady with real lace ruffles had probably come from her bedroom at home.

The head of the bed was beside the door. Claire lay against the raised pillow. Her gray hair was pinned up in a roll in the back. There was a softness to her features—none stood out on her still delicately made-up face. Despite being alone she wore a pink brocade bed jacket, and I wasn't surprised to note its lace collar. Nor was I surprised to see the unfinished letter she'd put on the bedside table. Or the tape recorder softly playing Beethoven. What did startle me was the unlit cigarette next to it. In Berkeley adult smokers are rare as Republicans. The smell of old smoke mixed uncomfortably with powder and lilac perfume.

"I'm Detective Smith," I said.

"About Madeleine's passing," she said in a quivering voice. She offered me one of those inappropriate smiles that dot formal female conversation. *Pay no attention to me*, they say. As the smile faded I could make out the edges of something beneath it. But I couldn't make out what.

"Yes." A flowered stuffed chair sat behind a paisley print screen by the foot of the bed. This had to be the chair Madeleine had been sitting in when Champion caught her expression of outrage. I pulled it up next to the bed, and wondered with a shiver if Victor Champion was now snapping pictures of me. Like Madeleine, would I become his possession in his darkroom? I glanced down at the chair leg. The fabric above the left leg was brown with rubbed-in dirt. It was the only less-than-immaculate spot in the room. I could picture Madeleine sitting here, holding Coco against the chair, him rubbing impatiently. The edge of the screen, too, was marked. At least some of the time, she must have kept Coco behind it. And Madeleine, had she enjoyed her power? Had she really tormented Claire? While she held Coco behind the screen, had she dangled the threat of bringing him closer, close enough to lick a hand Claire couldn't get up to wash? Or had Madeleine, like most dog owners, just not been able to believe that anyone could *not* love her pet?

I decided to play the interview as if Claire and Madeleine had been friends. Sitting in the chair, I said to Claire, "Madeleine's death must be a terrible loss for you."

She looked directly at me. Her eyes were hazel and surrounded by so many lacy lines her skin looked in danger of tearing if she blinked. "I saw my parents die when I was young. And my brother twenty years ago, and then my sister five years ago. I nursed her for a year. I was retired then." She spoke with that whine some people get with age, as if all the softness of their voices have dried out. She breathed in with difficulty. Emphysema? Automatically I glanced at the cigarettes. "Death's faster than you think," she said speaking more strongly. "They're sitting in bed watching the morning quiz show one day and that night you hear the death rattle." She switched on the smile again, fencing me out of whatever was beneath it. If by this time there was anything down there.

"When did you last see Madeleine?" I asked, trying to keep my tone conversational.

Her gaze drifted down to the smudge on the chair and back up to me. She pulled the edges of her bed jacket together and stared at me, her eyes moving back and forth nervously. "Too close."

Was the event of Madeleine's death too close to talk about? Or did she mean me? I pulled the chair back, but her brow didn't relax, and her eyes kept moving. I could almost smell her fear mixed with the chalky sweet odor of her powder.

She glared at the smudge, and whispered, "He was too close."

"Coco?"

"His breath smelled." She wrinkled her nose, and lacy lines around her eyes deepened to furrows of fear. "He came right up to me. He touched me." Her shoulders pulled in together, her head down toward them so I could barely see her neck. Her voice was just audible as she whispered, "I couldn't keep him away."

"And Madeleine knew how you felt?"

She nodded tightly. "She sat right there where you are."

"And did she understand?" As soon as the words were out I heard the ridiculousness of the question. If Claire had looked like this, no one could fail to understand. Even Madeleine. If Claire had been a client of hers, Madeleine would have been outraged at this torment. What odd cut-off valve did Madeleine have in her mind? Madeleine had been unparalleled at defending the rights of street people, of protesters, of the defenseless; surely she should have been able to relate to Claire. Was Claire too bourgeois for her to care about? Or had she, the dog lover, simply seen Claire's reaction as misguided, and been sure that exposure to Coco's charms would loosen her up? "When you told Madeleine how you felt, did she keep him away?"

Without releasing her bed jacket she wrapped her arms tighter across her breasts, pulling the pink quilted fabric so taut I was sure it would rip. The words croaked from her throat. "She couldn't. He sniffed her out." Her watery eyes shifted to the doorway and back to me, and she laughed that little ladylike giggle.

Something scraped the window. Claire jolted, then laughed, a shrill nervous sound. I laughed, uneasily too, noting the palm frond as it took another swing. Had Madeleine steeled herself time after time as the frond scratched? I'd have to take another look at Champion's pictures.

The door blew open a few inches with the gust. I turned, noting the latch on the inside, a latch Claire couldn't walk to. And catching a glance of the cigarettes, it occurred to me that the unlockable door was a necessity. Delia, Michael, and even Madeleine had to have been able to make sure Claire hadn't dropped a butt to smolder on the bedding. Still, anybody could have walked in. From the street, making their way quietly around the main house. Or up from the canyon. If Madeleine had sat in my chair partially behind the screen long enough to fill Claire with this kind of fear of Coco, what had she seen? Had Madeleine noticed something in the canyon? Maybe something she mentioned to Claire, or even pointed out to Claire. As upset as Claire was, I figured I'd better start with the most obvious. "Did you see the hostage operation down in the canyon Sunday night?"

"Hostage?" She released her arms from their armoring position. "He wasn't a hostage. He was hiding out. We didn't want him there."

"Did you see him?" I asked, feeling the adrenaline rush you always get when a tack pays off.

"No, I didn't see him," she insisted, her voice firm now, angry. Her watery eyes looked more solid and she glared at me as if to say: any idiot should know that. It was a look I might have expected from Madeleine Riordan. "The students were out front screaming. They pulled at the chancellor's fence, trying to tear it down. Nice young ladies—they had been before—screaming like peasants! It was disgusting! Appalling! The parents were horrified. They never forgave us. *Us* as if we started it. They should have blamed *him.* But he escaped. Ran out of the country. Over the border to Canada. A draft dodger! Left the mess he made and skedaddled!"

It took me a minute to realize she was talking about the Minton Hall demonstration and the *he* was Cisco, the draft resister who escaped. I said, "I was asking about Sunday night, in the canyon, here. We had a police operation."

"Police? The police came. Or was it the sheriff? They herded all the girls back into their rooms—"

"Miss Wellington, that was twenty years ago. I'm asking you about day before yesterday."

Her eyes seemed to unfocus as she stared at me. A blotchy flush spread from around them over her cheeks. "Was I in the past?" she asked in a small, fearful voice.

"Yes."

"Weren't we talking about the past?"

"No," I said gently. "I was asking about this last weekend."

The blotches deepened. She clutched a wad of the pink flowered cover. "They say I do that, wander into the past. I remember those days. It's this time—now—that drifts." She reached toward her bedside table, clumsily pulling open the drawer. What she drew out was a cloth-covered book, the kind with empty pages. I thought she would hand it to me, but she kept it in her lap, pressing it between her hand and her solar plexis. "I write things down so I can remember. I date each entry. I have to remember, you understand that, don't you?"

I nodded.

"Only crazy people don't remember. They think I'm crazy here. I remember but they don't believe me."

"What do you remember?" I said softly.

"You. You're a policewoman. You've come to see Madeleine."

I took a long breath, willing the pressure around my eyes to ease, the tense lines around my eyes not to mirror hers. "And do you remember Madeleine sitting in here, with her dog?"

"That awful animal," she said with a shudder.

"Why did Madeleine bring the dog in here?"

The lines around her eyes eased. Her eyes blanked. I wondered if the kind of speculation I'd asked was beyond her ability now. "Because I couldn't ask her to remove it."

"Why not?"

She released the red-and-green book and adjusted the lace collar of her bed jacket. "Well, my dear, you seem a nicely brought up young lady. You know you can't be rude to a guest you've asked to come. It was up to me to maintain the proper standards of deportment. Good manners do work, dear. The last few times she didn't bring him."

I had no idea how long this flash of temporal lucidity would last, or in fact, how lucid it was. Was she speaking about this week or thirty years ago? I'd have to judge that later. "You asked Madeleine to come here. What did you talk about?"

She raised a finger. "Now I did tell you, my dear. You weren't listening, were you? They don't listen to me. They think I'm too old, too dizzy to bother with. They've all packed me away like a summer carpet."

I swallowed, unable to think of a reply. Her analogy was too accurate. I remembered my grandmother talking about taking up the summer carpets, getting them out of the way of the winter ones. Then I'd hated those dry, brittle, hemp rugs that signaled my visits to her. And when they were packed away—when I'd be going away back to my family—I'd been overjoyed. I had the same feeling with Claire. I desperately wanted to be done with her, and I'd been here only half an hour. How much more routinely would Delia or Michael dismiss her, particularly knowing that her memory was so ephemeral that she probably wouldn't remember being waved aside?

I swallowed again and made one last stab. "Did Madeleine talk about the meter maid's carts? Someone's been after them. Did she mention that?"

"The meter maids?" Claire laughed. "It's the best game in town. That's what Madeleine says. She has spyglasses. You ask her."

"I can't ask her," I said slowly, wishing I could avoid reminding her about Madeleine. Murder investigations don't allow that option. "She died yesterday."

Claire shrank back into her ball. She stared over my head. Every part of her was shaking, her hands, her head, her whole body. The tape recorder clicked off; the click resounded like a gunshot in the silence. "Ask Madeleine," Claire insisted, her voice barely audible. "You'll see. She laughs. You ask her."

I moved toward her, reaching a hand to comfort, but she pulled away, wrapping her arms tighter around her. "You ask her."

I pressed the call button. Then I reached for the cigarettes, lit one, and held it out to her. For a moment I was afraid she'd refuse something that had been between alien lips, but she didn't hesitate. I sat back tasting the acrid taste, and waiting until she stopped shaking. What had Madeleine Riordan felt sitting here? Had she seen her own future, when her disease destroyed her nerves and muscles and sapped her strength and she could no longer walk? When people dismissed her words? Had the sight of Claire been too frightening to allow it to be real to her?

If so, why would she have come in here—unless she forced herself, refusing to let herself take the easy way out? But I didn't know Madeleine well enough to draw that conclusion. No one I'd talked to had. I wished I could get hold of her husband.

When Claire stubbed out the cigarette, I realized something. Sitting here, watching her suffering, I, too, had blanked her out and concentrated on other things. I glanced at my watch, relieved that it was nearly time to meet Eckey. Eckey wouldn't care a whit about Claire, but I was willing to bet she'd be surprised at the picture of Madeleine Riordan sitting by her canyon window staring through spyglasses, possibly down at Eckey's parking perp.

CHAPTER 14

□

"She was watching that pain in the ass down in the canyon?" Eckey demanded. Eckey was still outlined in purple. But now that she was red with outrage the purple didn't stand out as much. "She had him in view and didn't report it!"

May have had him in view, I could have corrected. Wisely, I didn't.

Eckey paced heavy-footedly to the end of the tiny aisle between Howard's and my desks in our minuscule office. Eckey's movement required mincing steps which on anyone an inch bigger than she would have looked ridiculous. As it was, purple-marked Eckey could have passed for an enraged grape stomper. "Madeleine Riordan," she snorted. "Well, that says it all!"

"Had a few run-ins with her?" I asked when she'd made her way back from the small slatted window to the door. She turned and stood, her foot tapping, engine idling, waiting to burn rubber.

"Run-ins! You wouldn't believe the idiots she defended. I'll tell you, Smith, you get the cream of the crop in Homicide. And you"—she turned to Howard, who had just wandered in—"even in Vice and Substance Abuse you get a saner group than the fools we see any day of the week. At least your guys got enough sense to want to make a living. Ours—"

"Eckey," Howard said edging around her fast-idling form. "I deal with the scum of the scum. I have to bring these folk in. You, Eckey, deal with doctors and lawyers."

"Humph! Some doctors. Can't imagine these dudes making any sickness better. They're too busy saying 'Not my fault! Can't blame me!' "

Howard plopped into his chair and stretched his legs across the aisle. Howard is six feet six, most of that legs. In order to stretch them out in this office he's got to sit at a forty-five-degree angle that lands his feet beyond the edge of my desk—just where Eckey was standing. He started to stretch but thought better of it as Eckey glared down at him and continued to rant, "Give you an example. Guy's expired."

"You mean his meter," Howard put in.

Eckey was not amused. "On his Mazda. So I ticket him. He's got no complaint, right?"

"Well—"

"Wrong, Howard. He's got plenty of complaint. He comes racing out of the bakery screaming like a banshee. Don't I know it's Veterans Day?"

"And you said?" Howard was getting into the rhythm here. There were few things Howard liked better than a good sting story.

"I didn't *say* anything. I nodded. You got to be a psychiatrist in my job, Howard. There's a reason shrinks make eighty bucks an hour saying nothing more than 'Mmm.' If they kept their mouths shut all the way and just nodded, they'd probably make a hundred."

Howard nodded silently and put out an upturned hand.

Ignoring that, Eckey went on: " 'You can't ticket me on Veterans Day,' he screams. They only scream, Howard. Never talk, only scream. Like they think the city advertises for Parking Enforcement personnel in the hearing-impaired column."

Howard's mouth opened. I'd lived with him long enough to know he was about to suggest that the impairment the perp had in mind may not have been merely hearing. Wisely, he let his mouth close.

"So I give him the regulation spiel that if he has questions he can call the complaints number."

Now I nodded. If there was a law of karma, I hated to think what vile crimes the person who spent eight hours a day handling parking complaints had committed in a previous life.

Howard pushed his chair toward the windows, preparatory to drawing his feet in and swinging them under his desk. He was too gracious to comment that as sting stories go, Eckey's had been a bust. None matched his, but—

"That's not all!" Eckey insisted. "You might think so. Any sane person would guess that would be the end. God knows it should have been." She glared down at Howard. "But not in Parking Enforcement. No siree. No way. Half an hour later I'm driving along Shattuck Avenue and the Mazda comes racing up behind me, screeches to a stop, and the fool comes bansheeing out of his car. Leaves the Mazda right in the lane. 'Veterans Day!' he yells at the top of his lungs."

I put a finger to my lips before Howard could open his.

" 'Veterans Day is a holiday!' He looks down at me like a dragon. He's breathing fire. 'I called the city, just like you told me. Do you know what the fucking city said?' He's screaming and flapping his arms like a dodo bird." Banshees were mythical, but dodoes were extinct; things were getting worse. And Eckey was flapping her own arms, a decidedly injury-inviting operation in this office. "Cars are braking in the other lane to watch him. I mean this guy's got Shattuck Avenue stopped in both directions, Howard."

"So you nod?"

I got my finger back in front my mouth before he could refer back to the psychiatric techniques.

"I do the next best thing. I repeat his question: 'The city said?' "

" 'The goddamn fucking city didn't say anything,' he yells to the masses, 'because the goddamn fucking city is closed today. BECAUSE VETERANS DAY IS A HOLIDAY!' "

Howard had a serious lapse of control. He guffawed. In for a lamb, in for a sheep; I gave up and laughed, too. Eckey has a good sense of humor. I've seen it. But in her bailiwick some things are beyond levity.

"Do you know what kind of position that puts me in? You're laughing, sure. The city didn't set you up and leave you out to dry, and hang spinning in the wind," she snarled, mixing and mangling metaphors like a master chef. "It was all I could do to get out of there with my cart in one piece."

Now I nodded. "I assume the city heard from you."

"Yeah, they did when they got back from their day off. Heard from me, heard from him. And probably a hundred other irate parkers. But my point is, any sane person would realize that I am a single mother trying to feed my kids. I've got a high school education and I'm damned lucky to have a job with medical and dental and retirement. But I don't make the parking regulations." She stopped and took a long breath. "Now you would think a doctor would understand that, wouldn't you?"

Howard might have dug himself in deeper than he already had with his untimely laugh—they had their own stories about doctors in Vice and Substance Abuse. But before he had the chance I returned to my original question and said, "So, Eckey, I take it from this that you knew Madeleine Riordan."

"She's past tense?" Eckey didn't look sorry. She'd only have seen Riordan in the company of guys like the Veterans Day dragon.

"Died Monday. In a nursing home on Cerrito Canyon. The point is,

Eckey, she had binoculars and she might have been watching the guy who's been hassling all of you in Parking Enforcement."

"Like I said, it doesn't surprise me."

"Why so?"

"You sleep with donkeys, you're going to wake up braying."

I had the feeling she'd done some swift editing on that one. I said, "Could you be more specific, about Riordan?"

She leaned back against the wall and scrunched her purple-lined eyes in thought. "I never trusted the woman. Too cool. She came into the hearings like I wish my kid did with her algebra problems. Like there were no people involved, just rules. And the rules are, no matter what the screamers say, no matter what they throw at you—and I don't carry Wash 'n Dris for nothing—no matter, Parking Enforcement personnel must never respond to rudeness." She shook her head. "Woman had no heart."

I pictured Madeleine sitting in that figurine-filled room with Claire. Was she another figurine, sleek and cold to the touch, and hollow in the middle? "Coldness doesn't suggest she'd have been watching the perp."

"She was cold, but every now and then she'd catch the hearing commissioner's eye and she'd almost laugh. And those times, Smith, were— Let me give you an example. She represented my Veterans Day asshole."

That surprised me. Madeleine Riordan had represented the oppressed, the chronic poor so used to being shoved aside they didn't think to complain, the yellers of "Wolf!" who this time really had seen bared teeth, the guys on the Avenue too disoriented to fight for fair treatment. Coco Arnero. Pretty much I envisioned immaculate Madeleine Riordan representing anyone she'd be uncomfortable having in her own home. The Veterans Day guy sounded too upscale for her. "What was his complaint about *you*?"

"Well you might ask. You'd think it'd be me bitching about the city. Or him bitching about the city. And he'd have done that if she'd let him. But she was too smart. She kept his lips buttoned. That was the only good thing. Drove him crazy not to be able to say anything. I looked over at her once and I'll swear to you, Smith, I think she enjoyed that as much as I did. It almost made me think better of her."

"Almost?"

"Almost, until she started on me. First the woman made me out to be an idiot too lazy to read the municipal holiday schedule. Then, with barely a pause for the transition, she paints me as so cowardly that I sent the fool off on a wild-goose chase so I wouldn't have to come up with an explanation of how a holiday cannot be a holiday. *She* understood my position, she told the commissioner. But it wasn't her position to decide whether the city had created this circus because one hand simply didn't know what the other was doing, or from barefaced greed, because they were making such a killing on their meters they didn't want to miss a day. Well, I'll tell you, Smith, that set off the whole room. Everyone in town's got an opinion on parking meters."

"Right." Everyone on the force has heard those opinions. On most issues in Berkeley there are as many views as there are speakers, and as many people to tell you the rest of them don't know what they're talking about. But come to parking and the citizenry speaks with a single mind, a mind glad to explain that years ago the city fathers decided to combat traffic. "Keep the car out of the city!" the starry-eyed patriarchs proclaimed. "Teach the masses to take the bus! Make it more costly to drive, much more costly to park. Cut pollution, save the air!" Parking meters grew like oaks. Nickels, dimes, and quarters fell like acorns. And soon the city fathers were squirreling those coins away as if they'd seen glaciers on the horizon. Did mass transit improve? Not noticeably. But the city coffers were another issue, and by now, the single mind insisted, the city was making a fortune off its drivers!

Eckey braced her hands on her hips. "So, Smith, she's got the whole room united. She's kept the fool so quiet that he's become a pawn to represent them. All this with a matter-of-fact presentation and the garnish of sarcasm. It was a performance like you'd see at Berkeley Rep. And when she told the commissioner that after her client had endured the lunacy of the city the least he could expect was not to get the runaround from Parking Enforcement, the audience actually applauded." She threw up her hands. "So, I ask you, what chance did I have?"

"Snowball's," Howard grumbled. The type of situation Eckey faced would have driven him crazy. Even the thought made him want to smash walls. He pushed himself up, motioned her to his chair, and strode out. Eckey eyed his chair but remained standing.

"So what are you saying, Eckey? I mean, how do you connect Madeleine Riordan with the buggy basher?"

She shrugged. "Just nothing I'd put past that woman."

"Could you be a little more specific?" I hadn't said, "That's it?!" but perhaps I could have controlled my sarcasm. If I had, maybe Eckey wouldn't have left in a huff, with a parting comment that mimicked my own offending tone. "Well, Smith, you're certainly the right person to be investigating Madeleine Riordan. Won't be a stretch for you to think like her."

I sat back, stung at first. It took me a while to realize that however Eckey may have intended her comment, I wasn't entirely insulted. And her observation opened an avenue that could lead behind the closed gates of Madeleine Riordan's being.

I let my eyes close and tried to feel what it would be like to have been

Madeleine. With some people that's easy, they're so like me. With others, like Pereira, it's as if her body is divided into ten front-to-back sectors and I could slip as comfortably into half of them as I could into her clothes. The other half are too small, the wrong colors, or styles that look good on her but make me feel pretentious.

With Madeleine Riordan there were probably only one or two sectors I felt at ease in. But I could tell from how my body felt when I used that tone of sarcasm that there was a match there. Some similarity of view, of feeling, something too deep to draw right out.

I laughed. If this is the way I was conducting a homicide investigation, maybe I'd been in Berkeley too long.

I called Raksen for an update, but it was too soon for the compulsive lab tech to part with any drop of undistilled information.

Dr. Timms, Madeleine's husband, was still not home. Was it time to consider an APB on him? Not yet, but if he didn't show by tomorrow, it would be another story. In the meantime, I left instructions for Pereira to find out who Timms had spent time with at his conference in Carmel and interview them. Murakawa I'd have canvass Timms's neighbors at home. In a murder the spouse is always a prime suspect, and the absent Dr. Herbert Timms was making himself more suspect by the hour.

I finished my reports on the scene, but I couldn't shake the idea of seeing things as Madeleine had. She hadn't orchestrated her death; few carry power that far. But I had the feeling of her still holding the strings to the investigation, posthumously manipulating the suspects and me. If I could just see things through her eyes . . . I could never let on to anyone what I was doing. Woman's intuition? Or should I square my shoulders, adopt a manly voice, and call it playing a hunch?

I shivered. Either way I was going to have to do the one thing I wanted to avoid—get inside Madeleine Riordan's skin and feel what she felt as she lay dying above the canyon.

CHAPTER 15

□

It was a desperation move, this business of getting into Madeleine Riordan's skin. I didn't really believe I would learn anything. I didn't think you could slip into another person's being. In the Bay Area there are plenty of classes in that type of thing. We've got a whole catalog of counterculture classes and services, from channeling for beauty (inner and outer) to crystal healing to an astro-hypnosis dating network. A directory comes out monthly. One month Howard and I had gone to a workshop in which we sat cross-legged knee to knee and matched our rhythm of breathing. I'd felt a certain closeness during the exercise, but it had been hard to say whether that came from the breathing, or the incense and candlelight, or, more likely, the seductive pressure of his knees against mine. The next class, we'd decided, would be massage.

What would happen now, I was sure, was that I would sit in the dark in Madeleine's room until Delia or Michael came in and said, "What, are you still here?" and then I'd snap myself together, make some official-sounding comment, and slink away.

Nothing would come of it. In any case I didn't want to do it. The idea of sliding into the hidden sectors of Madeleine's being made me so uncomfortable I could barely stand the thought. For that reason I couldn't let myself *not* try.

I grabbed the last doughnut (a chocolate-coated vanilla creme) from the box at reception, deposited a dollar, and headed for my car. Whatever Madeleine Riordan might have been, she hadn't mentioned hungry. It was

Howard's night to bring home food. Chances were that meant pizza. A couple pieces should survive till I rolled in. One of the joys of living with another cop was he never expected me home for dinner or to call when I wasn't.

The wind scraped leaves across the sidewalk. Usually at this time of night it pushes fog in from the ocean, backs it into canyons, and shoves it up against the hills. But maybe even the weather gods tire of gray. Tonight they were sweeping out the Bay Area, blowing hard enough to scoot the fog up over the hills to die above Concord, Pleasant Hill, Dublin. The night sky was navy blue instead of its normal dark smudgy gray, and so clear it seemed to be made of crystal. I drove up the Arlington, an alligator's back of a road, narrow and curved with cars parked across the gutters and onto the sidewalk and still leaving barely enough room to twist past at the 40 mph everyone goes. To my left, way below, the yellow lights of Richmond and El Cerrito glistened like gold breastplates. I had to drag my eyes back to the road, yanking the wheel sharply into a bumpy abrupt curve. With the radio off the car seemed like a being of its own, its big engine breathing like a long-distance runner, the constancy of it tickling my ears and coating the walls and windows and creating a capsule around me that sealed me off from the rest of life.

I passed Victor Champion pedaling his bike slowly up the steep street before I recognized him. And if he'd had any reaction to seeing a Berkeley Police car, it hadn't been to move closer to the curb.

I turned down San Antonio, letting myself pause momentarily to stare down across the bay at the string of lights drooping from the towers of the Golden Gate Bridge. All those golden lights down there, it looked like the New Year's Eve party of the century. Like I could walk anywhere and be welcomed in. Up here the streetlights behind papery tan leaves created a world of rice paper broken only by drooping dark fronds of short palm trees. Warm creamy rectangles hinted at the life within the houses along the canyon, protected behind curtains I'd never broach. A raccoon skittered across the street, between the houses, doubtless down into the canyon to join the deer and skunks and field mice.

I pulled up in front of Canyonview and rang the bell.

The speaker crackled a moment before Delia asked, "Who is it?" She didn't add "intruding at this hour, creating more work for me," but her tone carried the message.

"Detective Smith. I'll be in Madeleine's room for a while. Don't bother to come to the door." I realized I was as pleased to avoid her as she was me. I needed to keep the capsule feeling.

I made my way around the house and onto the companionway and stood listening to the voice of the canyon, the beat of the cicadas, the unexplained rustling from below. The last person I wanted to see was Claire, but I couldn't head into Madeleine's room and leave her helpless next door wondering what was going on in there. I knocked and in a moment Michael opened the door. He had that same protective look he'd had when I first came to question Madeleine. "Claire's just ready to go to sleep. Can you wait till morning?"

Behind him the head of Claire's bed had been cranked down so it was only a bit higher than the foot. She looked at me from those watery hazel eyes, and I had the impression that she was about to apologize for Michael's abruptness but decided against it. Michael, after all, wasn't her student. His poor manners didn't reflect on her.

"I just wanted to let you know I'd be in Madeleine's room for a while. So you didn't hear noises and wonder."

Michael's face flushed, he nodded a bit too vigorously, and murmured, "Thanks for letting Claire know."

I walked across the companionway. Madeleine's door was unlocked. I pushed it in slowly, expecting the room to be cold. It wasn't. The sick, I reminded myself, don't have the circulation for cold. In all the commotion no one must have thought to adjust the thermostat. The air felt steamy, and as soon as I closed the door, I had that uncomfortable feeling of too many clothes but not having layered so any could be removed.

Madeleine's things were still here. The binoculars were on the bedside table. I picked them up and turned off the light, then moved to the window and sat back against the bed. No, that wasn't good enough. In Champion's pictures Madeleine had been sitting cross-legged. I lifted myself up onto the bed and crossed my legs. My skin was clammy and I could feel the muscles of my shoulders, my back, my stomach tightening, pulling back, hiding from that exposure, all happening exquisitely slowly so I got the full slap of each step. And then I saw her again, in my mind, as I had when I'd first walked in here Sunday night: gaunt, icy pale, her hair gone, her face tiny in the ashen expanse of her scalp. And that so-out-of-place *Far Side* nightshirt that hung on her bony shoulders. I could feel the shock I had hidden staring at Coco and the gray rod he'd been carrying. My chest was shaking now with that swirling cold emptiness like the kind you get from breathing in too much smoke.

My hand tightened on the binoculars. With relief I put them to my eyes. I was here to get a sense of what Madeleine had experienced. I didn't need to relive what *I* had felt.

The canyon was dark, darker than night for city eyes. No streetlights or flash of headlights to outline forms long enough to set them in memory. I stared down and after a minute I could make out shades of dark, but nothing more. Had there been a light down there, though, it would have

But Madeleine hadn't been "most people" before she was dying. Most people don't spend weeks interviewing witnesses for a case like the Arnero complaint, stitching together an event at three o'clock Tuesday afternoon with a sighting of Arnero Wednesday morning, with a memory of him when he'd been an anthropology graduate at Cal. Ninety-nine of a hundred people would call the case a waste of time, and the remaining one wouldn't believe he could make the case.

I could see Madeleine determined to find out what went on in the canyon. But Madeleine was not known for patience. They say you learn it when you're forced to. There were a lot of things different about Madeleine Sunday. But patience was not one of them. She wouldn't just watch and wait. Not when her time was short.

But what would she have done? Would she have dispatched Delia into the depths? I almost laughed. The picture of laid-back Delia in her tie-dye lumbering down the hillside was too ludicrous. No, Michael, her protégé, would have been her choice. Whether or not he wanted to go, he'd have been obligated. Or Coco; maybe she'd have sent him with a note.

No! She couldn't be sure what was in the canyon. She'd never take that kind of chance with the one creature she loved. And Michael, she'd invested a lot in him. Would she ask him to go down there unawares? He who was very allergic to poison oak?

I hoisted myself farther back on the bed and sat against the headboard as Madeleine had done, my legs extended. The mattress was softer at this end, like sand. I could feel it pushing against me as it had her. Imprisoning.

I remembered Coco lying next to her, her hand clutching his fur, him burrowing in against her leg. She'd needed that contact. I hadn't put it into thought at the time, but it had been clear that if it had been physically possible she would have wrapped the dog around her till he cocooned her from . . . from death?

No, it wouldn't have been death, not for someone like Madeleine Riordan.

When I'd avoided coming here I had expected to sit on her bed and be filled with the black fear of death closing in. But I wasn't. What I felt was worse, an icy, unmovable sense of loneliness that filled my entire body. If I'd been Madeleine I'd have burrowed into the bed, clung to the dog, and grabbed onto whatever I could with the diversion in the canyon to keep that loneliness from freezing me before I died.

The ebb of my breath resounded against the walls. Outside the night wind battered live oak leaves, scraping sharp points of one against the shiny surface of the next, the wounds unnoted.

I slid off Madeleine's bed and spent a minute straightening out the covers, as I would if I were a guest, just visiting, not living here. And then I stood out like the moon. Even the flicker of a cigarette lighter or the flame of a candle. And if I had seen that, the canyon was varied enough that I'd be able to place the spot and look at it in the light of day. So what? If Madeleine had seen something she certainly was in no shape to clamber down the canyon side. What would she have done if she'd seen a candle flame? That one was easy. No one would hesitate dealing with fire in a canyon after the Oakland hills fire. If Madeleine had spotted a flame she'd have had the fire department here in a minute.

But what if she'd seen a flashlight beam? Would she have sat here in the dark like I was, staring down, collecting pieces of the puzzle as she had done when questioning clients, making a reasonable case? Would it have been a game to her, taking what she was given, waiting for nightfall to see what new clues came her way, trying to figure out what was going on down there? According to Claire, Madeleine called the parking enforcement bashings the best game in town. Did she realize activity in the canyon might be part of that? If so, it didn't take a detective to know whom she'd be rooting for. Would she have sat here night after night watching for a clue to his next move? The uphill wall of her room was windowless; no one would have known her light was out. The perp in the canyon depositing his cache of traffic tickets like a squirrel in autumn, would he have been an outlet for her? A connection of sorts as she sat in this isolated room waiting to die?

The cold poured through my body. Slowly I lowered the binoculars. I ached to turn the light on, but I forced myself to stay put, not to escape the fear that she couldn't.

It must have been minutes sitting motionless before sensations congealed into thoughts. I'd known when I decided to come here that there was something I couldn't face and yet couldn't allow myself not to face. I'd seen the surface of Madeleine's life. But, as she had said, you can't know in half an hour the depths that it's taken another months to reach. Depths of fear, despair, sorrow? Depths.

I dive at the pool. Maybe ten feet. Fifteen max. The first five feet are fine, but get beneath that and the pressure squeezes my eardrums. Usually I come up, not because it hurts but because I'm afraid it will pop my ears. Because I'm afraid. I hadn't wanted to get too deep into Madeleine's consciousness. I was afraid it would pop something and whatever that something is, I'd never get it back the way it had been.

For Madeleine anything in the canyon would have been an escape. But if what was going on down there was merely the perp and his parking tickets, as diversions went that would have had a short run. After seeing that scenario a few nights most people would either have called in patrol, or shut their blinds and turned on the TV.

took the first sure step I had in this case. I felt certain—*police certain* (i.e., not too certain to double-check)—that Madeleine would not have sent Michael or Coco down into the canyon. She would call the man she had always chosen to handle her investigations: Herman Ott.

But getting Ott to admit that would be a lot harder than my coming to this room.

I opened the door and nearly smacked into Michael.

"I wanted to catch you before you left," Michael whispered.

"Were you waiting here?" It unnerved me that I hadn't heard him outside the door.

He pulled the door shut and motioned toward the main house. It wasn't until we'd taken a few steps that he said, "I just needed to make sure you understood how fragile Claire is. Madeleine's death's been tough for her. She won't show it. Some of these old ones, particularly the ones who've lived alone, they're real good at keeping things to themselves. The way they act, you don't think they feel anything at all. But they do; it's just that the feeling is buried so deep you have to dig it out." The moon shone down on his glossy hair and muscled shoulders. He looked sleek, and agile, and young: all the qualities Claire no longer had. I wondered what she felt like seeing him each day. As if responding to my unasked question, he said, "Claire's state changes day to day. Good days and bad days, like a lot of the old folks. She's given to fantasies. Maybe they're what get her through the bad ones." He stared at me, waiting for a nod of understanding.

I got his point, but police training is too ingrained for me to allow myself to be swept along. Refocusing his view, I said, "Fantasies concerning Madeleine?"

"Sometimes she carries on like Madeleine's her best friend, her protector, and then the next day she'll mix her up with one of the characters from her afternoon soap operas, and she'll think Madeleine is saving her from one of the soap opera crises." He shook his head. "Sad. And"—he swallowed —"well, it was real hard on Madeleine." He swallowed again and seemed to be waiting for me to acknowledge Madeleine's plight. Or was it Claire's? Or his? When I nodded, he said, "Living a long time isn't free. They pay for those extra years, don't you think?"

I decided to ignore that unpleasant possibility. We were at the front stoop now. Hoping to take him by surprise, I said, "Michael, what was Madeleine looking at in the canyon?"

"When?"

"When she was using the binoculars."

He turned away. "I don't know," he mumbled unconvincingly.

"But you've got an idea, don't you?"

"Well . . ."

"What do you *think* she was looking at?"

"Well, there are houses on the other side, partway down in the canyon. Guys leave their shades up. They figure no one's going to be staring in their windows but the deer."

"What was Madeleine looking at in those houses?" I insisted.

"I don' . . . I don't know," he stammered. "I didn't ask. It was her business. If she was staring into guys' bedrooms, it was none of my business. She had few enough pleasures. It wasn't like her husband ever stayed with her, you know."

There were plenty of questions about Herbert Timms. But for the moment I pushed them aside. "Did she ever ask you to go down into the canyon?"

"No. Why would . . . oh, you mean to check out the guy you guys were after. Ah, you figure she was watching him, huh?" he smiled, clearly relieved. "Yeah, I could see Madeleine handling a case like that, a guy half the police force came after. Oh, yeah," he said with a bit more glee than I found appealing.

"But she didn't take you into her confidence about it." I waited to see if the jibe worked. It didn't. Michael Wennerhaver barely missed a beat before muttering, "No."

I would have given a lot to know what went through his mind in that missed beat. But all I could conclude now was that in the arena of self-control he was indeed Madeleine Riordan's protégé.

I walked on around the house looking up at the office window in time to catch sight of Delia McElhenny slouched in a chair staring at my car. I quickened my pace; even police cars get ripped off. But the car was intact. When I glanced back at the house, Delia was gone.

I could have gone back to the station to dictate reports of the day's interviews while they were still fresh. They might be fresh; I certainly wasn't. I longed for my bathtub, water to the rim, almond-scented bath oil. Soaking would be wonderful. But guilt would dilute the pleasure. We pay for more than extra years. And besides, I was hungry.

I decided on a compromise. Food for the stomach; food for the search. Pizza and Ott.

CHAPTER 16

□

It was the easiest entry I'd ever made into the Ott Detective Agency.

It's not everyone who can arrange to have the best pizza in town delivered in tandem with their own arrival. But we at the Department provide a good and steady business for a number of pizzerias. At midnight —just about the time when franchise managers are asking themselves why they waste money staying open late—a second dinner begins sounding pretty good to the guys on Evening Watch. Ott's office is on the third floor of a building that's been a walk-up since the elevator broke sometime in the sixties. In the past I have knocked on his opaque glass door, pizza in hand, and convinced him to open up. More recently I've knocked but he hasn't opened. I was damned if he'd win tonight.

Herman Ott, a man who has survived as a private detective since before the demise of that elevator, could not afford to be a fool. A knock and a boy's voice calling out: "Pizza!" did not encourage him to open his door; it made him suspicious.

"I didn't order pizza," Ott called.

I could tell he was right behind the glass, sniffing the aroma of oregano, garlic, anchovies. Ott adores anchovies.

"It's from Jill Smith," the boy called. I'd given him a script. I know Ott so well by now that I could almost have had the boy read the answers without my hearing Ott's questions. But for safety's sake the boy was to check with me before he spoke. Now Ott would be thinking: *Smith? She doesn't owe me anything. Maybe it's not from Smith. Or if it is there's a catch.* Which, of course, there was. *Take it away,* he'd almost say. Almost, but not quite. For Ott, passing up a free meal was like a canary turning up his beak at a tray of suet.

The delivery boy eyed me. I nodded.

"It's got double cheese."

Ott's idea of pizza was suet on dough. If he'd had his way each slice would hold so much cheese that only a weight lifter could get it to his mouth. Herman Ott with barbells was a picture few could have imagined. Even on the warmest days Ott's arms were usually covered by the long sleeves of a yellow, brown, or beige shirt. I had seen them bare once—it had been 100 degrees out that day and closer to 120 degrees in his office with its windows that opened on the air shaft. That day his ensemble had included Bermuda shorts with gold, rust, and chocolate stripes; his V-necked ecru T-shirt exposed an appalling amount of his blond-tufted chest and bony arms with the loosest skin I'd ever seen on an adult male.

I nodded again to the delivery boy.

"Double anchovies," he called.

I could swear I heard breathing behind the door. Ott couldn't resist anchovies. I'd seen him going after them, swooping down into that sea of yellow cheese like a giant canary of prey. I pointed to the paper.

"And pineapple." The boy wrinkled his nose. I didn't blame him.

There was still one more line on his paper. I didn't expect Ott to turn down anchovies and pineapple, but I knew him well enough to wait for the final round before he capitulated. I gave the nod.

The boy looked at the paper, then at me. He shook his head in disbelief. "Say it," I mouthed.

He shrugged. "And sunflower seeds."

The door opened. The boy walked in and plopped two boxes on Ott's desk. He was still shaking his head. "Hey, man, I don't know what you even call this mess."

Ott looked down at the two boxes as if expecting a pizza and a bomb. The latter suspicion was not entirely unreasonable, considering Ott's clientele. Most of his clients were more familiar with *The Anarchists' Cookbook* than *Betty Crocker.*

As Ott was lifting the lid of the second box, I strode in. "You wouldn't expect me to eat that concoction of yours, would you?"

He turned to glare at me, his deep-set hazel eyes narrowing, his round cheeks flushing an unattractive shade of orange. Hands bracing his plump hips, he looked poised to flap his wings and squawk. "Smith! I should have known you'd engineer a trick like this."

Coming from him, I took that as a compliment. But I couldn't let on.

With Ott, if you lose your reputation, you don't get a second chance. Despite his marginal clientele and his hand-to-mouth existence, Ott had standards as rigid as Madeleine Riordan's. I extricated a five from my pocket and handed it to the delivery boy. He hesitated, perhaps expecting Ott to protest a woman paying the tip, but Herman Ott is no chauvinist, particularly when it comes to money.

I lowered myself onto one of the wooden client chairs. The slats cut into my back. I'd been dropping into Ott's office for more than half a decade—virtually never invited—and not once in that time had I come across a chair any but the most desperate of persons would sit in. "Do you furnish from Discomfort Is Us?"

"No one invited you, Smith." The one padded chair stood behind his desk, a caramel job with rips in the plastic the length of the back. He eyed it but didn't sit.

"No one but me would bring you your favorite pizza. Being seen ordering that is like buying the *National Enquirer*. Now the Diner's Club will never give me a card!"

I opened the lid of the double cheese, double anchovy, pineapple, and seed. Straight cholesterol. Raising the lid on the second, smaller pie, I reached for a piece of pepperoni, anchovy, and onion.

Before he could restrain it, a tiny gasp escaped from Ott's mouth. Surely *he* couldn't be offended by *my* choice. How could a man whose clothier of choice was Goodwill, who refurnished from the nearest curbs on the city's annual trash-pickup day, view my taste as unacceptable? But he was still standing over the pizza boxes, his beak sniffing in disapproval. He looked from it to me, to my hand poised to extricate a slice of pepperoni. Finally, he said, "Just a minute," walked to the trash can, and pulled out the day's *Examiner*. As he lifted the boxes and spread the paper over his desk, I had to restrain a laugh. I'd forgotten how finicky Ott was about his office. The adjoining room, in which he slept, was a slovenly nest of discarded clothes, blankets, books, newspapers, and magazines, but in his office the queen could have perched without fear of soiling the royal tail feathers. Once again I reminded myself that Herman Ott had a very distinct set of rules; they were just different enough from the norm that most of us didn't recognize them as rules.

Printed tablecloth in place, Ott pulled out a piece of the anchovy, pineapple, and seed. The double cheese put up a good fight. But Ott, a seasoned eater, yanked it loose, slurping up the stalactites of cheese in his waiting maw.

A lesser woman would have lost her appetite, but police training prepares you for desperate situations. I chomped down on the pepperoni.

Ott finished two pieces before he said, "She killed herself."

I stopped, pizza in midair. It wasn't that I was surprised Ott knew I was investigating Madeleine Riordan's death. No one in town was arrested or died without his knowledge. In the realm of information Ott was a black hole, inexorably sucking every fact, observation, or theory into that mental space from which neither light nor matter ever reemerged. What amazed me was that without begging, cajoling, or promise of money, Ott gave information to an officer of the peace. It was a first. It was also a second: Ott was wrong. But I wasn't about to say that—yet. "How do you know?"

"I've known Madeleine for years."

"How well?"

"I've done some work for her. I've referred clients to her. She was a woman of unbending principles."

I could see the bond of respect between them. And I recalled Madeleine's cane, and the two long flights of stairs up to this office. "You made Madeleine Riordan come here?"

Ott laughed humorlessly (as he did most things). "Smith, I didn't *make* Madeleine Riordan do anything. She insisted."

I leaned back in my chair, jabbed my ribs against the slats, and sat forward. "Okay, I can picture that. She'd never have let anyone think that cane slowed her down." I picked up a piece of pizza, folded it, and tapped a finger against the crust. "How'd you meet her?"

"An antiwar protest, like half the people I know." But he said it too flatly; he was asking to be convinced he should elaborate.

"In marches?"

"Yeah, that's what we did." He reached for another piece of pizza.

Someone who knew him less well wouldn't have noticed the slight relaxation in the arch of his eyebrows (eyebrows that were so light that most people wouldn't have noticed *them*), but I had seen it often enough when I missed the mark he wanted to avoid, when he was settling back to watch me wander off on a wild-goose chase. "Ott, she wouldn't have been a marcher. The woman walked with a cane."

"Not always." He moved the pizza to his mouth and began his vacuum imitation. The double-cheese, double-anchovy mix was rising from the middle of the folded piece, Vesuvius-like. A less skilled eater could have been asphyxiated. But while Ott persevered in a manner that would have impressed Henry VIII, I could tell he wasn't enjoying it.

"You've known her since before she needed a cane?" I prompted. I wanted to ask what she was like then, before Nature had made every step a decision. "Why did she need that cane? What happened?"

"Auto accident."

"When?"

"Toward the end of the protest days." He wasn't eating anymore. His forefinger was rubbing along the edge of the box, courting a paper cut, but he didn't seem to notice. His gaze wasn't on me, but on some image that floated invisibly a foot in front of him. He looked like I'd felt when I first saw Champion's photos of Madeleine. Except that for him the compelling image was in his own mind. Or memory. I wished I could see what he saw.

"Ott," I said softly, "she didn't kill herself."

"She told me she didn't plan to linger on machines."

I shook my head, amazed he hadn't learned she'd been smothered, impressed by how well we'd kept that fact quiet.

"You didn't know her like I did," he went on. "Life was an orderly picture for her. Her job was to keep it that way. The kind of satisfaction that you get from a good dive in the pool she got from making you write your reports on time."

I nodded slowly. It shouldn't have surprised me that Ott knew about my newfound passion for diving. It just made me uncomfortable, as if the man were standing on his toes, stretching his plump body up so he could peer in over the edge of my eyelids.

"And when that order went, it was like a future of nothing but belly flops." Ott looked down at his hand. His finger was bleeding.

"The cane, Ott. What happened?"

Ott sucked the blood off his finger. Then he picked up a napkin and began tearing a strip for a tourniquet. His pallid face was more bloodless than usual, his neck drawn into cords. He tore each strip slowly, and when the napkin had been divided into eight interchangeable rectangles, he began wrapping them around the paper cut. Brain surgeries have taken less time. Brain surgery patients have looked less pained. Knowing the source of his discomfort, I held my tongue. But it wasn't easy. Finally he said, "Okay, Smith, I'll tell you about Madeleine. This is pretty much third hand because by the time I saw her again I didn't see any point in bringing it up."

I nodded, amazed. Ott hadn't even asked for anything in return.

"You think of her as an orderly, unflinching monitor, right?"

"Right."

"But before the accident, she bicycled all over. She didn't own a car. She wasn't one of these people who's at every demonstration. Even then she chose her causes, but when she was committed, she gave one hundred percent. A real firebrand. There was no stopping her. If she had to get a flyer to the printers, she pedaled that bicycle so fast you couldn't see her feet. When she rounded corners you'd think she was going to scrape her ear on the pavement. She'd cut in and out between cars so fast they didn't even brake, and she'd grin and slap the fender."

The Madeleine Riordan I'd known never made a move without weighing all the angles. "Was it the accident that changed her?"

"Of course," he said with disdain.

"Tell me about it."

"She shattered her pelvis." Ott paused so long I thought that was all he was going to give me. When he finally went on, his voice had risen half an octave and there were long gaps between sentences. "It was in the country. . . . The cops who found her didn't know enough not to lift her. . . . Maybe they got her to a doctor as fast as they could, maybe not. . . . Probably didn't make much difference. . . . Doctor was in a small town; he patched her up. . . . By the time she got to a hospital—" He shrugged, but his face held none of the anger I would have expected. I had the feeling I was listening to a ghost of the man. In all the years I'd known Herman Ott, I'd never heard him sound so drained.

There was more to this than a colleague who'd gotten inadequate medical care. I had the feeling he'd keep talking, if I could just come up with the right questions. But if I once erred, the spell would be broken. He'd finish his pizza and toss me out. "How did Madeleine come to have the accident if she didn't even own a car?"

"It wasn't her car. The Movement got it. If it had been her car, she would have made sure it was in better shape."

"What was she doing with it?"

Ott pushed the pizza box away. "One of her jobs in the Movement was to find drivers to take draft resisters over the border into Canada. It was a long, tedious, routine drive. All the driver needed to be was reliable, bright enough to find an unguarded border, and able to keep his mouth shut afterward. That was the normal run."

"But this one wasn't normal?" I prompted.

"Some weren't. In an emergency she'd take it herself."

"And the accident run?"

"Guy with a fifty-thousand-dollar price on his head."

I almost whistled—$50,000 is a lot of crime. I took a guess. "Someone connected with the bombing of the Oakland Induction Center?"

"No. Nothing violent. Madeleine didn't deal with violence. She insisted that's what we were against. The guy was the conduit to all the resisters the government hadn't found yet. He knew all the safe houses. You can imagine how much the FBI wanted him."

"And how bad it would have been for him, and the whole antiwar movement if they got him."

"Right. Madeleine . . . Madeleine must have thought that, too."

What had he edited out? "Madeleine . . . ?"

He shook his head. "She checked out the car and told them it was too old, too unreliable; they'd have to find another before she'd put one of her drivers in it. They'd have to get a good car and decent maps. They couldn't, or maybe just didn't; you know how things were in those days. In the end she decided the guy couldn't wait, so she drove him herself." He sighed so deeply I wondered if he had been involved in that disastrous decision or with that car.

"So they headed north?" I prompted.

"Yeah. And the word got out. After she crossed into Washington state, she called back to Berkeley. They told her to watch for cops. She was almost to the border when she spotted a car behind her. The draft resister was driving her car. She was in the passenger seat. What she told people was that the car was old, the door latch wasn't reliable. They were driving a winding country road. He took a curve too fast and she fell out."

"And shattered her pelvis?"

"Pelvis, leg, and arm. Hit her skull hard enough to knock her out."

I shut my eyes to block out the picture. Then I said, "And what really happened?"

Ott glared at me. "You know her well enough to guess."

I sat a minute thinking of Champion's pictures. Even in the shot of joy there was a focus in her smile. And in her outrage, she didn't look as if she were about to explode; she looked like she'd get someone. "How close was she to the border?"

Ott nodded approvingly. "Eight miles."

"She wouldn't let one of her drivers go in that car, but she went herself because it was vital to get the passenger over the border. She wouldn't have put him next to a car door he might slide out of. So, then," I said slowly, "Madeleine didn't slide out that door, either. The door didn't suddenly unlatch." My stomach lurched as I realized the corollary. "My God, then she must have waited for the right curve and opened the door." I could see her hand tightening on the door handle, bracing to pull it up, knowing as a wary person would that in another breath she could be dead, or maimed. "And did the man get away, Ott?"

"Of course. She knew the cops would have to stop to take care of her. The FBI was crazy to get him, but the cops, well, Smith, you guys have your faults, but you're not going to leave a woman to die by the side of the road." Before I could comment, he said, "The doctors told her she'd never walk again. It was a year before she could get around with the cane. And after that, Smith, she'd used up all her leeway."

"Ott, who was the passenger?"

"Code name Cisco. He kept his identity hidden."

"But you knew it," I said, feeling on firm ground.

"He didn't tell anyone."

"Ott," I said, exasperated, "that doesn't mean you didn't find out. Who was he? And is he back in town now?"

Ott shrugged. "He's dead. Been dead twenty years." It went against Ott's code to reveal an identity to the police, even an identity that had been dead twenty years. Before I could press him, he said, "He was hit by a bus in Vancouver. Wasn't looking where he was going. Just like him. He could concentrate on something that concerned him and do a first-rate job, but for the rest of life he was like . . ." Ott stared at me. A movement flickered on his face, as close to a smile as his thin lips were trained to handle. "For everything else, he was as flaky as Coco Arnero."

I swallowed, futilely willing my skin not to flush. Whenever I recalled the Arnero incident I'd assured myself that it was too insignificant for anyone else to remember. I hated to have anyone remember it, but particularly Ott. "Did Madeleine find Coco flaky?"

He couldn't resist a little smile of victory. "Smith, you of all people should know about Arnero. Lived wherever there was a free couch, always found a short-term job when he needed it, broke minor laws, missed appointments, but God, the man had panache. You had to love him, even when he drove you nuts."

"Did Madeleine feel that way?"

"She did." Ott pulled loose another piece of pizza. The cheese had cooled and congealed; it reminded me of turkey fat the day after Thanksgiving. "She had to work like hell to keep him in line every time she represented him. He'd weird out. But once Madeleine committed herself, his weird spells didn't bother her; like she didn't even see them, except when they affected the case. The thing was, Smith, she liked planning the hearing strategy; the bigger the challenge the better, if she believed in the client. But she also got a kick out of playing the game. It was like riding her bike between cars. She loved leaning over the brink." Ott stared over at me, his eyebrows raised in amazement. "She was something like you, Smith, an adrenaline junkie."

Coming from Ott, that was a compliment. And by Ottian standards he was forced to give it, no matter how it pained him. He was right. I love the chase—all or nothing—only this moment exists. And hostage negotiation, when lives hang on every word. Then it doesn't matter that I live in a room filled with unpacked boxes, that my car is falling apart. My life can be a shambles, but adrenaline makes it okay. It's an addiction—I can't imagine giving it up. And to be forced to, like Madeleine, was . . . "How did she survive, Ott?"

Ott was still staring at me, as if he saw a whiff of her escaping through my pores. "She focused."

I nodded. "She brought it all to her cases?"

"One helluva lawyer."

"But it wouldn't have been the same."

"Dammit, it couldn't be! She was just more adult than you." He looked away in disgust, the whiff dissolved in the mire of my ordinariness.

But he'd answered too quickly. I'd seen him do that often enough, throw the switch, send me angrily onto the siding. "No, Ott, I don't believe planning cases for even the most deserving of clients—"

"You don't understand, Smith—"

"No, Ott, I do. It wasn't the client, it was the cause, right?"

I held his gaze till he admitted, "Yeah, okay."

"Even so, planning courtroom strategy is not cutting between cars. It's not just the difference between intellectual challenge and the physical. The difference is that with the court cases she was always inside the law, always safe. You don't get the rush from that. You've got to do what we do, go where laws don't count, where you could get shot. Or you break the law."

Ott didn't disagree. His face remained utterly still.

"So what law did she break, Ott?" I said, my breath quickening.

"Her car was parked in red zones."

"Ott!" He wasn't lying, but he sure wasn't admitting to the truth.

"She had an old Triumph, a TR-3, I think." Ott was probably the only private detective in the continental United States who had to look up makes of cars in a book. "She loved it. She bought it after her accident and had it modified so she could drive. It was a dumb indulgence; there were times she could barely get in and out. 'Sports cars don't have cane racks,' that's what she said. But she couldn't bring herself to give it up."

"Was it a statement of freedom?"

Ott looked away and nodded. It was a moment before he said, "The car wasn't in good shape. Rust. Couple of different colors of paint. One of a kind. And, Smith, it was in red zones—different ones—Friday and Saturday."

"This Friday and Saturday, the days before she died?"

"Right."

"Surely she was in no shape to drive then."

"Of course not. I didn't say she drove."

"Then who did?"

But that question Ott was not about to answer. He sat in his lemon plaid shirt, his scruffy ecru vest, pressed back in his chair like a sick canary huddling at the back of his cage. Madeleine was an old friend, or as close to a friend as Ott had. "Ott, here's an easy question for you. Would Madeleine have let her dog run freely down into the canyon?"

The corners of Ott's mouth twitched, as if trying to laugh. "Madeleine was a no-nonsense woman, except when it came to that dog. She had her blind spots—"

"Like she loved him too much to take the chance of judging him? Or finding something wrong?"

Ott nodded and hurried on, "She never let him go where he might get wet, or step on a burr, or . . . The dog lived better than a lot of her clients."

In fact, I thought, he lived a good deal better than Herman Ott. I pulled my jacket tighter around me. I was about to admit I'd gotten as much out of Ott as I could, when I realized that he had not shifted into his normal end-of-visit etiquette: telling me to get out. There was something more he was willing to let me extract, not because he wanted me to know, but in response to something he owed his own code, or Madeleine. "Ott, just what was your debt to Madeleine?"

"No debt."

I stood up. "Can we skip the semantic games? You owed her something. Or maybe you promised her something. Ah, yes," I said watching the tiny signs of acknowledgment on his face. "Okay, you promised her something you couldn't deliver. I'm right, aren't I?"

"Yeah, well, it's too late," he said in a voice so low I had to lean in to hear. "It's been too late for years."

"It's not too late to help find her killer."

"Killer?" He started forward out of the chair then sank back, clearly deflated by the realization that he, Herman Ott of the Ott Detective Agency, had not even considered the possibility of murder.

Before he could regroup, I made an offer that even I found appalling. Detective to detective, we'd both understand it; but between two people who cared about a woman who had died, it stank. "Tell me what you promised her and I'll tell you how she died."

Ott didn't lift his head. "After the accident, Madeleine was in the hospital up in Washington state for nearly a year. Down here her mother had a stroke. She ended up in a nursing home, a place in Contra Costa County where they were so busy not letting patients go to the bathroom alone that they didn't bother to check that they took their medication. Just left the pills on the trays for the ones with brain damage to stick in their pockets or toss under the bed. The old woman's condition was fragile. When Madeleine called, she couldn't let on that she was injured; she had to wait for her own pain medication to wear off enough so she could call, and then she had to make excuses about why she wasn't visiting. But as she started getting better she realized her mother was sounding worse. She was worried. So she called me." He stopped speaking but he didn't move.

I waited.

He lifted the top sheet of newsprint and began tearing at it. "I was working on a case, my first big one. I needed the money. Hell, it was more than that, I needed to prove I could break the case." His right hand jerked; the paper tore free. "By the time I got to the nursing home, Madeleine's mother was dead."

"I'm sorry," I muttered, careful not to look at him.

"Madeleine never blamed me. She said her mother died because no one noticed."

Because no one noticed.

Her words from the Coco Arnero hearing seemed to come out of my mouth by their own volition: "Or, during which moments is his life important enough to merit your attention?" It kept coming back to that.

CHAPTER 17

□

I wished I could have gotten Ott to tell me what law Madeleine had really broken. Parking in red zones, or letting someone else park your car in red zones, is hardly a memorable crime in Ott's book. Clearly Ott wanted to lead me along the path to the unnamed driver. But was that path a shortcut to the killer or a just a torturous loop to nothing?

I was so stunned by his long-nurtured guilt and by his uncharacteristic decision to tell me about it that I left without the rest of my pepperoni-and-onion pizza.

Now, as I walked from Howard's nearly empty fridge into the living room, I regretted that oversight. It was small recompense to think Ott would have a better than normal breakfast off it.

"I'm comforting myself with that," I told Howard now, "and with remembering how cold and congealed it was."

"Noble of you, and tasteful," he said, settling back on the sofa in his living room. "I would have saved you some of my pizza—I could have, I'm a lot bigger than Jason." Jason was second to Howard on the tenants' list, and second to none in food consumption. So far the only item I'd found to be safe in the kitchen was chicken hearts, if raw. Anything else he took to his room to consume in silence. Jason was a student of one of our numerous local gurus, one who focused on Spiritual Consumption. He chewed each bite thirty times, noted the variety of tastes and textures and internal reactions thereto, and recorded all in his spiritual journal. I was willing to bet that was one diary that wouldn't be a hot property for publication. "At least it's kept him out of the living room," I said curling my feet under me on the sofa. I leaned back against the worn fabric in the corner. The whole sofa reminded me of the edge of Claire's chair where Coco had rubbed. "I just don't know where I am with this case."

Howard nodded, opened a beer, and stretched his legs, intertwining his feet with mine. The room smelled of sandlewood and garlic, suggesting that Jason had carried his incense to the kitchen and had a go at spiritual munching there before retiring to the holy table in his room.

I told Howard about Madeleine's accident. "I can picture her before that, Howard, whipping around corners on her bicycle, cutting in and out, gauging her chances in quarter inches. And I can see her as I knew her, walking with the cane. It was always like she really didn't need that cane, like she'd grabbed it walking out the door, just in case."

"She would have liked to hear that. It's a real testimony to how well she planned."

"How so?" I asked. Vice and Substance Abuse deals with a more righteously indignant clientele than other details, so Howard had faced Madeleine Riordan in more hearings than most. Still, I was taken aback by the familiar way he spoke of her. I couldn't recall his ever mentioning her before.

Howard felt around the floor for his beer can, leaned back against the sofa end, and rested the can on one knee. He seemed to have forgotten to drink. "A couple of times we were in hearings that dragged on till midnight. Five to twelve Madeleine's doing her thing like she's the head lion in the cage. Quarter after, we're leaving and she's wincing with every step. And hurrying off so no one sees. After that I kept an eye on her."

"What did you see?"

"She always parked near the door, or the ramp, or the elevator. She saved her strength. She"—he ran a finger slowly down the wet side of the aluminum can—"planned everything. All the stuff we just do, she had to plan."

"So she could look like she was just doing it," I said, finishing his thought. "Never a chance to ride free." I wiggled my foot in tighter between his. No one would have called Howard and Madeleine soul mates, but the lines of similarity they did have were etched very deep. Suddenly I felt intrusive, as if his knowledge was privileged and I was asking him to break faith exposing it to an outsider, even me. "Howard, she spent a year convalescing. Do you think she changed so much that the woman who cut between cars was entirely gone? I know she liked mapping strategy, being the architect of the sting, but would planning her legal cases have been enough?"

"Not for me, it wouldn't. But no one's ever accused me of being too mature."

I laughed. I couldn't imagine Howard as an adult; his recklessness, his spur-of-the-moment decisions, his uncontrolled glee in victory were his charm. If he lost those, I didn't know if there'd be enough left of Howard to still be Howard. Maybe the Madeleine Riordan who emerged from the hospital was only vague kin to the one who'd entered. I sighed. "Lots of college quarterbacks wake up twenty years later in BarcaLoungers happily drinking beer and second-guessing NFL plays. They accept the facts of life. Maybe Madeleine did, too." But even as I spoke my words sounded false.

Howard just shook his head.

"But, Howard, the fact is Madeleine did decide to come back to Canyonview. Either to get away from something or to get *to* something. Either to put distance between herself and Herbert Timms or because something drew her back to the canyon. And the only things going were Victor Champion standing in his window taking pictures, and there was our perp moving around down in the canyon." I pushed myself up and braced a leg on the arm of the sofa. "Dammit, I can't find Timms. I don't know whether Madeleine was on the sidelines there in Canyonview cheering on our parking perp. But the woman had spyglasses; she had to be using them for something. Lend me your binoculars."

"Why?"

"Because tomorrow I'm dressing in red top to bottom and heading down into the canyon. I'll put Pereira in Madeleine's room with the binoculars and we'll find out just what Madeleine could see."

"Jill," Howard began then stopped. He wanted to object—his mouth was still taut with the gulped-back words, his fingers were poised around the ball of admonitions. Even his legs were tensed, ready to leap up and insist on his point. He was dying to tell me to be careful, but he knew better. I grinned, walked over, and kissed those tense lips. I could tell it didn't give him the same satisfaction as that warm pleasure of holding forth to a lover "for his/her own good," but it seemed to come in a creditable second. In our time together Howard and I had come to relish talking about cases; we'd also learned the pleasures of stopping talking.

But later, before he went to sleep, Howard propped himself up on an elbow and demanded, "How're you going to handle Doyle when you present this plan to him tomorrow morning?"

I grinned. "The way any sensible officer does. Tell him afterward, when I've got the booty."

Howard chuckled. "And if there's no booty down there in the gully of skunk and poison oak?"

"Then I'll take the time-honored bureaucratic route. I'll bury the whole operation in the middle of some report he doesn't have time to read."

Having come to that managerial decision, I slept fitfully till the alarm went off at six, zombied up and headed to the pool to stretch those muscles I'd devoted the last six hours to tensing.

When I got to the station, the entrance was thick with the press, and the jail was thick with night visitors. Three In Custody reports awaited me and it took me every second before Detectives' Morning Meeting to round up the paper on them for the D.A.'s liaison.

As soon as the meeting ended—before Doyle finished with "Eggs" and had time to contemplate me—I co-opted Pereira, because I could count on her to keep mum if this operation failed, and headed for Canyonview.

I pulled into the space where I'd been last night, behind an old orange Triumph—Madeleine Riordan's beloved old Triumph Herman Ott had described. The temptation to go over it was strong, but it was wiser to put it off. As long as I ignored it, it still *seemed* to be a secret.

Pereira and I moved on around the house. Claire's door was closed. I could hear low voices in her room. I didn't knock, but moved quietly across the companionway. Coco was sitting on the sunny steps. Beside him, her long red wiry curls fluttering in the breeze, was Delia.

Life doesn't offer many opportunities for sneak attack; they shouldn't be squandered. I went with a hunch. As she turned I said, "Madeleine didn't know you were driving her Triumph."

Another woman might have gasped. Delia's jaw jutted forward. "I had to pick up some things for her, didn't I?"

Pereira moved around behind her. I said, "Driving a person's car without her permission is a felony."

"It's not like she's going to press charges, is it?"

"She doesn't have to."

"Look, she owed me that. She ruined my life."

I crossed my arms and stared down at her, restraining the urge to look pointedly around the grounds in this very desirable neighborhood in which she was sitting idle in the sun at midday.

"Well, if it hadn't been for the Minton Hall demonstrations, my whole life would have been different. I'd have a good job and some guy to support me . . . and . . ."

"And?"

"And I wouldn't be working my tail off watching over the dying." She jumped up with an uncharacteristic burst of energy and stomped up the steps.

I was tempted to stop her—I don't like to let witnesses decide when an interview is over—but I couldn't be bothered keeping her here just for principle.

Pereira shook her head. "Blame Madeleine, blame the meter maids?"

I nodded. Delia certainly had not ruled herself out of those adolescent pranks. She had ample time to cruise around town looking for piles of fresh manure or Dumpsters in which to deposit a stolen Cushman cart. And who knew the canyon better than Delia who'd grown up here? But could she have killed Madeleine? That wasn't so easy a call. Maybe I'd find a connection in the canyon.

This operation wasn't exactly by the book. But if you want to follow the rules till the game is over and you die, you opt for a career as a clerk, not a cop. You become a cop to be the one who enforces the rules—on others. And you demand answers, speed on the freeways, and step over the barricades that say "No Admittance."

"You look like you escaped from a science fiction movie," Pereira whispered. The restraint Howard had shown last night had ended with the dawn. This morning he had clucked around the room loading me up with enough equipment to head a survivalist organization. I carried one of the pokers with which work-furlough guys spear litter in the park and a backpack to haul my expected loot. And I had on hiking boots for traction, jeans, jacket, turtleneck, gloves, and sunscreen so thick that my face cracked when I talked. The last I'd wash off as soon as I got back to the station and hope to protect myself from the most persistent danger of the canyon—poison oak.

The companionway steps ended at a horizontal dirt path. Pereira and I followed it to my left under Madeleine's window and almost to the property line. There, camouflaged between two bushes, was a steep, narrow trail down into what looked like a trapdoor of leaves.

"Stay here," I whispered to Pereira.

I poked the spear into the ground and started down the steep incline, batting branches out of the way. The spear caught exposed roots; hanging on, I slid and nearly wrenched my shoulder pulling the implement loose. The bright sun flickered through the thick thatch of leaves, making the shadows darker and the underbrush fuzzy. My heels ground into the hard earth as I half walked, half slid down the path, and even when the trail leveled, I couldn't hear anything above the crunch of my boots and the rustling in the underbrush. There were rats and snakes, salamanders and slugs down here, but I was sure they'd find me more appalling than I them. If the parking perp were other than Delia, he could be sitting within three yards of me and I wouldn't know. Like the newts and slugs, he'd be keeping very still.

After the heavy fog of the previous days the canyon resembled a well-used coffee filter with wet grounds clinging to both sides. The musty smell of damp leaves and dirt mixed with the fresh scent of eucalyptus. The gurgle of water startled me; I was almost in the creek when I heard it. Fording the creek might have been a nightmare some other year, but drought has its benefits.

"I'm just crossing the stream," I said softly into the hand-held mike. I'd given Pereira a quick verbal sketch of the canyon floor. If she had to come to bail me out at least she'd have some idea where to come.

"Right," Pereira answered.

On the far side I moved onto a foot-wide path, a veritable freeway of the canyon, and turned right, heading back toward the Arlington from which I had entered two days ago. Above me, birds fluttered, or maybe it was deer swishing their tails as they decimated rosebushes higher up on the canyon wall.

The path twisted, following the creek, and rose till it reached an easy ridge, from which I could see the remains of the old quarry office where the perp had been headquartered, twenty feet ahead. The cement floor was the size of a one-car garage set between the canyon wall and the path. The surface looked more like rubble than floor, so deep were the cracks from decades of earthquakes. If an earthquake came now, I thought, I would become a permanent part of the California landscape.

The canyon floor was so narrow, the walls so steep that while one side of the cement slab was three feet higher than the path, the other cut into the hillside. The overhang where we'd found the collection of parking tickets had been created by an old aluminum door, probably from a shed, propped on twenty-four-inch cement blocks. The earth had been meandering down on top of it for decades.

"I'm at the quarry office."

"Can you see anything?"

I extricated binoculars from the backpack and looked up through the leaves, rotating the lenses till I could make out the branches beyond the oak tree overhead. "Only more trees. But I'm still on the ground by the quarry office. The perp would have been on the flooring." Ignoring the steps on the far side that I'd used Sunday night, I hoisted myself onto the cement and took another look.

"Can you spot me, Connie?"

"Nope. Walk around a little."

The rustling stopped. No leaf moved. The air was heavy and stale, as if it had sunk down here millennia ago when the canyon was formed. In the silence, the stream sounded like the Mississippi. I peered up through the leaves trying to make out Madeleine's window, to see Pereira looking back. But all I could see was more leaves.

I began to pace back and forth across the platform, moving like a lawn mower. "You see anything, Connie?"

"No . . . No . . . No . . . Wait, a spot of red. Maybe your shoulder."

I stooped. "How about now?"

"No."

"Damn, I've been over the whole floor."

"Maybe she saw something on the path?"

"Or swinging through the trees," I said in disgust. I could have the whole Department down here dressed in fox-hunt red, and if Pereira weren't looking at exactly the right spot, she'd miss the lot of them. "Try it from Madeleine's window. Call me when you're in place and I'll do the dance all over again. I'm going to give this platform one more search through while you're moving."

"Right."

If there was anything here we'd missed, it had to be under the metal overhang. And we'd gone at that thoroughly enough to come up with 187 parking tickets. Considering the likely outcome of this expedition, I was just relieved I hadn't used any more manpower on it. I eased myself across the floor, lay in front of the overhang, and peered into the dark. Nothing obvious. I pulled the flashlight out of my pack and shone the light. No more tickets—thank God!—no paper of any kind, not even a paper bag with discarded food. But there was a couple of inches of gray, plastic-looking gray, wedged in the back corner. With the point of the poker I scraped along the top. I expected the dirt to be years hard, but it gave way surprisingly easily, revealing six inches of thin tubing.

It took five minutes of scraping and then jabbing to free the cylinder. It looked like just another long gray dowel, until I spotted the leather loop that goes around the meter maid's wrist on one end and the hole for the chalk at the other. A parking enforcement wand!

I sat up, staring at it. Coco had been carrying a gray dowel Monday night! His stick hadn't had the telltale leather loop. I'd been too far away to notice a chalk hole that would have told me it was a parking enforcement wand. But it had to be. And it had to be somewhere up around Madeleine's room.

I called Pereira. "Madeleine Riordan's dog stayed close by. We didn't find the dowel in her room. Check the grounds nearby."

"Patrol hound at your service, Smith."

In four minutes Pereira said, "Got it! Dog might be a great retriever, but he's not much of a concealer."

"Are you sure it's a parking enforcement wand?"

"Oh, yeah. Chalk hole, ends of the leather strap—looks like the dog chewed off the rest. And if you want to go for a dental check, there are teeth marks all over it."

"Great!" Neither one of us said it over the airwaves, but I knew Pereira was thinking the same thing I was: Madeleine Riordan never let Coco roam down in the canyon, yet the dog had a parking wand! So Madeleine had been connected with the parking pranks!

And she wasn't merely watching the maneuvers of the parking perp, rooting for him as she might for Jerry Rice. She wasn't a fan in the stands. She was on the sidelines, near enough to accept the ball after he'd crossed the goal line.

I sat rubbing my gloved hand along the length of the wand, thinking of Madeleine sitting outside her room on that lower path. If she'd been near the bushes, she could have sat, unseen from Claire's window. And the perp could have sat right next to her at the top of the vertical path, hidden by the bushes from Michael or Delia or anyone who wandered down the companionway stairs. He could have sat there and regaled her with the thrills of his escapades. A transfusion of adrenaline?

But adrenaline doesn't transfuse. Only a diluted form trickles to the observer. But maybe she took what she could get. The thought should have comforted me; it didn't, at all.

I pushed myself up, realizing that Madeleine Riordan hadn't been as resourceless as I had pictured her.

I undid my backpack, unzipped the top, and stuck the wand in it. It protruded. I shifted it to the side. The end caught on the backpack seam. Grabbing it with my glove, I pulled. The glove pulled half off my hand and the pack slipped. I grabbed for it, missed, and ended up batting it in the air. The pack flew forward and landed hard on the step.

The light burned my eyes. The bang was deafening. Dirt and rocks spewed everywhere. The explosion blew me off my feet.

CHAPTER 18

For a moment after the explosion there was silence, as if every creature in the underbrush was standing taut, too shocked to move, every leaf and branch paralyzed, and even the air holding its breath. Then leaves shook free of their branches, twigs snapped, paws and hooves ran frantically across rocks, and claws raced up the bark of the live oaks. The roar of the blast echoed off the canyon walls, batting back and forth like a barrage of Ping-Pong balls.

The force of it threw me on my butt. Pellets of cement and rock and hard wood flew like buckshot. I rolled over and covered my neck; the rubble hit my arms, my ribs, the back of my head. I pulled my revolver free, rolled to the side of the platform by the stream, and slipped over the edge, squatting near the protection of the raised cement. The dirt-filled air clogged my nostrils with the smell of spent explosive and dry earth. My scraped hands throbbed. Through the swirling dirt, I eyed the shiny-leafed live oak trees, the dry brown underbrush, the little stream. The perp could be anywhere, with a stash of rifles, grenades, bombs. . . . The low cement ledge gave me almost no protection. Both hands on the revolver, I moved back against the canyon wall next to the metal overhang—seemingly un-jarred by the explosion—and crouched.

It was the most dangerous kind of wait. Nothing moved abnormally; the sounds grew dimmer. No one was out there—probably. Just one perp who'd booby-trapped this place and left—probably. One perp with one Flash and Sound device aimed at disorienting rather than maiming. One stun canister. I was just wasting time here. I could be . . . but I stayed put. Those 120 hours of training with the Hostage Negotiation Team had at least taught me that.

How far had the noise carried? Were the residents of Canyonview panicked? Had they heard it at all? Pereira would have, through the walkie-talkie. She'd be on the horn, calling for the bomb squad. In a quarter of an hour the place would be swarming with Exposive Ordnance Technicians. It'd be a show that'd make last Sunday night look like a lounge opener.

I forced myself to scan the hillside, to look twice at moving branches, still sure I was reacting to nothing more lethal than deer or squirrels. I kept looking, all the time knowing I wasn't seeing beneath the obvious. If the bomber were perched on the oak branch over my head, I wouldn't spot him. "Observe, dammit," I muttered to myself, shifting my gaze more slowly. Fifteen minutes. I'd make myself stay that long. The bomber wouldn't have that kind of self-control. He'd be out of here long before, if he wasn't already gone.

I thought of Pereira, my closest friend on the force. I'd put her in an awful spot. She be trying her walkie-talkie and getting no answer. She'd have no way to know I wasn't dead or maimed. She'd ache to get down here, but there was no way she could leave her post; she had to be there to direct the EOTs, and to protect the civilians from the battalions of bombers she couldn't be sure weren't down here.

That meant she'd call for a lot more than just the EOTs. Half our force would be coming down the canyon side. *All* of Kensington's small department would be involved.

My legs began to shake. I scanned around me, then figured *screw it* and sat. My gloves were in shreds; I glanced at my palms. Dirt was embedded in the scrapes. I was probably going to die of tetanus. I'd end my days muttering incoherently and foaming at the mouth—or was that rabies?

Another minute passed before an awful possibility crossed my mind. Could the explosion *not* be the work of the parking perp? Could this perp be merely a canyon loony? Could this be an entirely unrelated case? Had Berkeley become so specialized that we had a loony for every need? Then I remembered the tickets and the meter maid's marking stick. No, there was only one perp; the quarry office was our parking perp's lair.

It was close to the ten-minute mark when I heard branches shaking and shoes sliding down a path. I leaned forward into a crouch and braced the revolver.

"Anybody down here?" The voice was Michael Wennerhaver's.

How had he gotten past Pereira? Or was he already down here? I pushed back under the overhang and waited silently. I wanted to see him before I decided friend or foe.

As he came into view the sun was glinting off his short dark hair. His jeans were smudged with dirt, his striped shirt bedecked with leaves and twigs that would have shaken loose from the trees. But his hands were free and there was no place he could have been hiding a gun. I eased forward.

"Officer Smith! Are you okay?" His pale flat cheeks were red and shiny with sweat. He couldn't have faked the fear and excitement in his eyes.

"Yeah."

"I thought it was kids down here. I didn't know what was going on. It's so frightening for our residents when something like this happens, something down here. They need to know what it is."

I nodded. Was he protesting too much? I wished I could see to the canyon rim, to note whether windows along both sides were open revealing curious faces. Michael had made it down here awfully fast. Most people wouldn't even have known I was coming down here. But Michael could have seen me. And if he'd set the explosion, he'd have been listening for it to go off. Most people wouldn't have known the location of the explosion, they'd just have heard the bang and seen the smoke. But Michael had come right here. I hadn't considered him for the parking perp. But he fit the psychological mold—a loner, one who feels life has overburdened him. He had no history of parking tickets, but still . . .

"Weren't you worried about leaving your residents, Michael?"

"Of course. But they'd tell me to come down here and find out for them, like my aunts were always doing at home. They'll want to know. And anyway, Delia's there. She'll reassure the residents in the main house."

"And Claire?"

The creases around his mouth deepened. The sun hit his face like a spotlight, and the contrast with the deep shade made his pale skin look translucent. "Claire won't notice. She's—well—had a bad night. You know how she is—here now, and then back twenty years ago. I was hoping that would protect her, that Madeleine's death would mean no more than if she remembered a friend who'd died back then." He closed his eyes and breathed in slowly, as if the air were still thick with dirt and it wasn't easy to draw it in. "But I was wrong. It must have been an awful shock for her. Death is too close for these old people. Something like that, a friend dying in the next room, it's like the Grim Reaper peering over their doorsills."

"How bad shape is she in?" I asked. Michael had propped a foot on what remained of the edge of the office floor. He might have been standing in the street at the top of the canyon resting a foot on the curb, instead of next to a bombing site, however minor. This was, it struck me, a remarkably odd conversation.

"Last night Claire was frantic. Delia couldn't calm her. I sat up with her till dawn. Now she's asleep. The questioning and all: it's been too much for her."

Behind him I could hear someone coming through the underbrush. "Michael, get over here, and get down."

"What do you—"

"Now. Move!" I pushed him under the overhang next to me, backed against the canyon wall, and braced my revolver.

I was barely there when I spotted Victor Champion, hurrying toward the platform, camera in hand. He glanced at the platform, his mouth drooping in disappointment, before he spotted me. "I heard a bang, an explosion. Was it around here?"

"Right here," I said.

He glanced around again, his expectation clearly unfulfilled. Beside me Michael scooted free of the overhang, stood, and began brushing off his jeans. Champion, in his well-holed denims, looked at him as if he thought Michael was a maniac.

I wondered what Champion would have given for a bit of artistic carnage.

Before either of them could speak again, I stood up and said, "We need to get out of here now."

I'd have to question both of them and hope one might have seen someone coming down here, or might be that person. Chances were the greatest danger now was of their talking to each other and muddying their memories. Odds of the two of them being in this together were slim. I moved between them and started our procession along the path. My legs worked awkwardly as if the explosion and my fall had knocked my joints out of kilter. When we came to the path up to Madeleine's, I hesitated momentarily. Across the canyon came the rustling of leaves, and in a minute I spotted one of the Kensington officers. I called to him, took him aside for a quick briefing, and passed Champion on to him.

Champion, none too pleased about the prospect of dealing with yet another law enforcement agency, began hedging: "It was just a muffled bang," he said, ignoring the Kensington officer. "I was in the darkroom. The negatives weren't ready yet. I couldn't open the door for another two minutes. So, I didn't see anything."

"Sometimes you see more than you realize. Particularly if you're an artist."

He wasn't entirely mollified, but flattery exists for a reason. He started to protest, then shrugged and gave me a mock salute.

The colonel's son—who had inherited from the colonel. "Champion," I said, "we're going to need to see any weapons you have, ones you bought, and any that were your father's."

The Kensington officer nodded.

Michael and I started up the path, grabbing onto branches, feet slipping on the damp grass. Michael was having little more success with the ascent than I. He was stiff-jointed and climbed as if he'd never seen a tree as a boy, as if those aunts had kept him too busy gathering gossip. He was halfway up when I heard a siren shriek and die.

"Michael. Get behind me," I yelled. In seconds EOTs would be racing down the hill, grabbing the first "perp" they spotted.

Michael stopped. Yanking myself up by a shrub branch, I edged around him. It was only then that I realized we were almost at the path. I could make out a figure at the top. Not one of the EOTs, but Inspector Doyle, hands on hips.

Damn.

I motioned to Michael to wait by the companionway. To Doyle, I said, "The steps to the platform where our perp kept his parking tickets was booby-trapped. He had one of the meter maid wands down there." Putting the best face on the situation, I added, "I tossed my pack on it and set it off. Lots of dirt, spray of cement: Flash and Sound device."

Doyle's eyes narrowed. He glared at me and muttered something I couldn't make out.

From the street new sirens whined. Brakes squealed.

"Place'll be crawling with press," Doyle grumbled. "They'll be here before the EOTs roll. We'll have patrol contact everyone on the rim, again. We scoured the canyon Monday morning. This device has been planted since then." He glanced around the rim of the canyon. I could almost see him figuring how many men, how many hours it was going to eat up, how long he and I were going to have to fend off the press.

Slowly, he focused on me as if he'd never seen me, or any other representative of my species, before. "Mother of God, Smith, you look like the missing link. That's all we'll need on the front pages. Not only can't we get a clue to the parking perp, but we can't even stay clean."

"In future I'll only take on nuclear blasts!" I said in full sarcasm. I hadn't realized how wired and stressed and downright angry I was.

He started to retort but caught the words before they came out. Then he looked me over again. "You okay? You're not hurt, are you?" he asked in a tone I suspected he used with his daughters.

"I'm fine, just a little stiff."

"I'll have a uniform take you to Emergency."

Pereira strode across the path. "Inspect—"

I laughed. "Inspector, I climbed out of the canyon; I can drive to the Emergency Room."

"Inspector!" Pereira stepped partway between us. "We found Madeleine Riordan's husband."

Doyle turned his glare on Pereira.

"I've been after the man for days," I said. "Where is he?"

"In town. In his office. Seeing spaniels like any other day."

"Holy Mother, Pereira! What kind of man is he?" Doyle demanded.

"His staff *must* have told him to call us," I added. "So he ignores ten or twelve messages from the police?" I tried to run my thoughts fast-forward. Where had Madeleine Riordan's husband been? Why hadn't he come back before? Why hadn't he even driven her to Canyonview? Was he too disinterested to care, or had Madeleine left without his knowing? Had she escaped? Because of him? Herbert Timms had ignored me for days; now he would pay attention and he'd give me answers! I could feel the muscles of my back and legs tightening, ready to go after him.

Still, it galled me to leave the investigation here. When the EOTs gave their first report, I wanted to hear every word. And wanted to question Michael who'd made it into the canyon so fast; ditto, Champion, and Delia, who hadn't shown her face yet. What was with her? No one is so laid-back they can't be bothered to step out their door when a bomb goes off in their backyard. I had to decide quickly. There'd be plenty of patrol here to do the preliminary interviews. I could finish with Timms and get back here to do the final. "Inspector, I need to get to Timms before any more time elapses."

"Smith, I'll tell you what you need to be doing. You need to be going to the Emergency Room. Now go on."

"I'll stop by the hospital later. After I finish with Timms—"

He grabbed my shoulder. "You get yourself to Emergency now. When they finish with you, then you worry about these meter maid incidents. You pull every report on every one of them. We've got to find this guy before he blows up the entire city."

My fingers were squeezing together as if Herbert Timms were about to slip out between them. "Inspector, we don't know this explosion is connected to the meter pranks."

Doyle breathed slowly, angrily. "If it's not, fine; you can write up a report supporting that theory. But, Smith, if this is the work of our perp, we've got ourselves a guy who's gone over the edge. He's setting traps for no apparent reason."

I started to speak but he stopped me. Giving my shoulder a pat, he let go. "You could have been killed down there. You or one of the neighborhood kids if they'd gotten there first."

I sighed. No amount of complaint was going to sway him. Medical treatment after an incident like this was regulation; I didn't have any choice. Being an officer injured on duty allows you to cut to the front of the line in Emergency. But that "advantage" is less of a boon when it just means you get back to the station sooner to start pulling reports. And Herbert Timms goes on seeing spaniels.

I could have asked who would be assigned to Timms, but that meant admitting his decision was final. Grudgingly, I nodded and left.

But I couldn't bring myself to trot right up to my car. I stopped in the main house. At least I'd find out what Delia was up to.

Delia was nowhere in sight. I checked the dining room and the kitchen. I stood at the bottom of the stairs and called her name. I walked up the carpeted steps to the second floor and glanced in each of the rooms. One resident was asleep, the other was sitting by the window as if he had a front row seat. But no Delia. Defeatedly I walked back downstairs and was almost to the front door when Pereira burst in.

She was panting. "I was afraid you'd be gone. We just got word from Santa Cruz County."

"Yes?"

"The sheriff contacted the guy running the Seaside Veterinary Conference. Would you like to guess what the topic of that conference was?" She smiled.

"No."

"Veterinary dentistry. Brushing for Bruno, flossing for Fido, periodontics for puss. Dr. Timms was a lecturer. Root canals for Rex."

"Connie!"

"Right," she said, swallowing a grin. "Seems our Dr. Timms is a big name in the world of canine canines. But, Smith, that's not the really interesting part."

My leg and back muscles throbbed. "What?"

"Dr. Herbert Timms's presentation was Sunday morning at nine. He checked out of his motel beforehand. And at ten he left the conference for good."

I whistled. Sunday night was the hostage operation. Sometime Monday Madeleine Riordan had been killed. It was now three days later. Where had Timms been between ten A.M. Sunday and whenever he got to his office this morning? It was a long time for a man to be gone when his wife was dying.

I picked up the office phone and dialed Dr. Timms's, D.V.M. office, a number I knew nearly by heart now.

"This is Detective Smith, Berkeley Police. I need to speak to Dr. Timms."

"I'm sorry, the doctor is in surgery."

"So he is in the office."

"Yes, but he's very backed up. We had to reschedule all his patients. He's got patients till eight this evening."

I took a breath, repressing the urge to snap: *The man's wife has been murdered!* Instead, I said, "This is a police matter. Tell Dr. Timms I will be at his office in an hour, and I expect him to be available."

"But he's got patients—"

"An hour!"

CHAPTER 19

□

I stopped by Emergency, cut in front of a woman on crutches, a man holding his side and moaning, and two teenagers so green I didn't want to think what disease they might have, or be spreading. Ten minutes later I was out and on my way home for the world's quickest shower and change of clothes—black turtleneck, green wool slacks, and a blazer—and made it to the veterinary office right on time.

Dr. Herbert Timms's office was in a dark, wood-shingled Victorian on Telegraph Avenue, but not in the four blocks nearest campus, which most people think of as "the Avenue" with its sidewalk table displays of tie-dyed long johns and red feather earrings. There, there was no place to park when bringing a chihuahua for a checkup. Parking is an important consideration to a veterinarian and his two-footed clientele. And, I suspected, the folk who considered splinting the teeth of their Shar-Peis were not likely to park their Mercedeses blocks away.

I thought of Snowball—my brother Mike gave the Great Pyrenees his name, which quickly was shortened to Ballsy, a distressingly apt name. His vet's office was a cheery place with pictures of all of his patients and their people, and a huge family tree chart of the dog world from the beginnings of *canus familiaris.* Happy hounds stood next to eager sporting breeds, smug miniatures, and serious working dogs. And each time I saw Ballsy's vet, I made him explain again how the Russian tracker, ancestor of the golden retriever, could possibly have become extinct. Spotted owls become extinct, not big furry red dogs.

But there were no cute snapshots or genealogical maps on the walls of Herbert Timms, D.V.M. The tiny waiting room looked like a Victorian front parlor with linoleum floor slanted down to a drain in the middle. The only decoration was a time flowchart of the progress of dental decay, each stage accompanied by dire prognosis of misfortunes of the nonbrushing dog. The smell of vinegar battled with wet fur. And my entrance had raised a communal howl worthy of a *National Geographic* special. It suited my mood—cold, damp (hair), stiff (from the explosion tossing), and grumpy (from Doyle, the lack of progress on both cases, and from Dr. Tour-California-While-Your-Wife-Dies Timms).

I made my way past three cringing cock-a-poos and a very smug-looking shepherd to the counter. Behind it sat a woman with file cards in one hand and the phone in the other. "I'm afraid, Mrs. Templer," she said above the chorus of barks, "that shedding is not Duke's only problem. The main issue in his contact with humans and other canines, is that he is simply inadequately socialized." She glanced up at me and quickly returned her gaze to the cards.

I plopped my shield in front of her. Then I pointed to the door.

She shook her head.

In a voice that would carry through the waiting room, I said, "I'm here to see Dr. Timms on police business." Behind came three distinct *shhh*'s. I chose to believe they were aimed at the dogs.

"Mrs. Templer, I'm going to have to put you on hold." The woman pushed two buttons and said in a soft but no-nonsense voice, "Doctor, I think you should see the police officer now."

His voice rumbled incomprehensibly in the receiver.

"Doctor, I'd see her now." She clicked off.

I expected her to tell me he'd be with me in a minute, but she merely switched back to Mrs. Templer and her socially stunted dog.

I strode to the surgery door and stood tapping my foot. Ballsy's vet used to have a doghouse roof painted over his office door with DOCTOR where ROVER might have been. Timms's was just a door.

A plain wooden door, nothing to ease the passage in, that suited the kind of man who cared so little about his wife of two years that he went off for the weekend when she was dying. He didn't even bother to drive her to the nursing home. I tapped my foot more sharply, vainly trying to keep an open mind about him and what caused her to leave him and go back to a place where she was lonely and vulnerable enough to be murdered.

I hadn't really formed so much a mental picture as an image of Herbert Timms. But when the door opened, I knew the man who emerged didn't fit it. He was tall, tan, with a long, exceedingly narrow face, bagged brown eyes, and silky chestnut hair that hung flyaway from his narrow bald pate—a Saluki in medical garb. His attenuated fingers looked as if they could reach all the way down any hound's throat.

Madeleine Riordan had waited a long time to marry. The man before me wouldn't have been my first guess for one to sweep her off her feet.

"I'm already backed up," he said, ushering me in through his plain wood door. Salukis were temple dogs, seated next to the pharaoh, hounds to be revered, not told to sit and stay. Madeleine Riordan was not a woman who revered.

The dogs in the waiting room were still barking. From the back of the surgery came low whines, presumably from patients coming off anesthesia. Timms led me into a small white room. A large rectangular metal tray jutted out from the wall—the examining table, I recalled, on which a dog spends his time futilely trying to control his splaying legs. Timms stood on one side like a clerk behind a low counter. The only chair was beside him. It was a room suitable to concluding an interview rapidly. Whether from habit or the urge to avoid eye contact, he looked down at the tray. "I've just gotten back. I'm running behind." His hands were steady, his voice matter-of-fact, as if he were asking me to condense the description of Fido's symptoms.

I remembered Madeleine Riordan propped up in the bed, her hand digging into Coco's fur, and that wrenching aura of loneliness that had chilled me for hours. "Dr. Timms, the cock-a-poos can wait. Your wife is dead. Where were you all weekend?"

He cringed—minutely—as if reeling from a jab in the ego. I couldn't imagine him having a normal-size reaction to anything. "I had to give a paper. Madeleine and I lived with the prospect of her death for over a year; I couldn't stay home every moment. I have a responsibility to my science."

No wonder Madeleine had been willing to come back to Canyonview. Michael, Delia, Claire, and even Champion with his camera had their faults, but any one of them was better than this hard kernel of self-absorption. I took a moment to steady my voice before saying, "Your wife was murdered. I will stand here as long as it takes to find out your exact movements from the end of your lecture till now. Is that clear?"

Still staring at the tray, he said, "Officer, I don't like your attitude."

"You wouldn't be getting this attitude if you'd bothered to call us anytime in the last three days."

"I didn't know—"

"Your wife's death was in the papers."

"I didn't see the local papers. I was too far away."

"Please! We left messages with your service. Surely you are not so irresponsible that you don't check in with your service." Sarcasm was spilling off my tongue; I knew it, but I couldn't make myself control it.

"They didn't tell me."

"That's not what they told us." I was guessing.

"I didn't know it was important."

"Not important? A message from Homicide!" I leaned forward over the tray. "Look, Dr. Timms, when there is a murder, the best suspect is the spouse. When the spouse has an alibi and is cooperating, we're still suspicious. In your case I'm on the verge of putting you in the cage and taking you down to the station."

"I am cooperating. I'm holding up my surgery schedule to cooperate. Look, I will write out what I did hour by hour after I left Carmel if you want, but it's not going to make any difference. I drove around. I ate; I can't remember where. I walked on the beach. I can't give you a precise enough description of my time to be of any use. That's why I didn't call you."

"You didn't comply because it didn't benefit you. And now you're acting like that excuses you." He started to speak but I held up a hand. How had Madeleine Riordan put up with him? "We'll deal with that later. But I have to tell you, Dr. Timms, you seem remarkably unconcerned about your wife's murder."

"I'm not," he said, his mouth barely moving.

"Okay, then let's start with why your wife left her own home to return to Canyonview."

"She needed supervision."

I raised my eyebrows. Timms must have caught the meaning, for he said, "Not supervision like control. She just had to be someplace where there was always someone around. She went there because she didn't want to be a bother."

"A bother to you?"

He nodded: the silky chestnut strands flapped gracefully in response. "So she wouldn't interfere with my practice."

I breathed in slowly. The smell of antiseptic filled my nostrils, and I had the sense of it drying out the lining of my nose. I could picture Timms and Madeleine together, so restrained, talking about her death as if it were an appointment that necessitated some rearranging of their social schedules. "Was that an agreement you two had?"

"I'm out of town a lot, lecturing. This is an exciting time in veterinary dentistry; there are ground-breaking procedures in odontology, particularly exciting in endodontics—vital pulpotomy. It's wonderful to be—"

"Couldn't she have hired someone to care for her at home if you were out of town?"

It took him a moment to gear down from the heights of endodontic enchantment. "She didn't want me to worry. And there would have been all the hassle of hiring someone, dealing with them."

I didn't bother pursuing that. Trying to keep my voice neutral, I said, "Her decision to go back to Canyonview, was that something you discussed and decided on together?"

"We discussed it. She decided."

"And you concurred?"

He ran a long lean finger along the edge of the tray, watching its progress. I had the feeling he was using the time to search for an answer he prepared. "It was the sensible decision. Why should she have spent her last days home alone, with just hired help, when she could be with other people in her own condition?"

Like all the dogs coming off the anesthesia in the cages down the hall. I just caught myself before I shook my head in disgust. "You haven't been married long. How did you meet?"

"Professionally."

"You were in court?"

"Oh, no! Coco had been hit by a car. He was in terrible shape, had a—"

"I don't need the details," I said quickly.

Again his finger traversed the tray. "Well, it was touch and go whether Coco would pull through. It required extremely tricky surgery to save him, and virtual around-the-clock care. Madeleine got a month's leave from work. She sat with him in here—I don't usually allow that, but Coco was in such bad shape I felt it was the right decision. And after Coco went home and she couldn't transport him properly"—he hesitated—"I initiated home visits. And, things progressed from there."

I hadn't realized how flat his voice had been when speaking of his wife until I heard the normal highs and lows as he described Coco's condition. Clearly both he and Madeleine had responded much more warmly to the dog than to each other. I knew people who'd stayed together for the children. But this was the first couple who'd married for the dog. It seemed so ludicrous, a situation with which sharp-witted Madeleine Riordan would have had a field day. And yet it made me think better of her. It was a mistake that made her seem more human. "Tell me about her. What was she like?"

He looked blankly at me.

"What did she enjoy doing?"

"Oh. She was meticulous about her work. A lot of times I'd come home from evening hours and she'd be sitting up at her computer, or on the phone with someone connected with her cases."

"Who?"

"I don't know. She never talked about them."

Not if she got that type of response, I guessed. "Did she ever mention the name Herman Ott?"

"No."

"Delia McElhenny? Claire Wellington? Michael Wennerhaver?"

"No."

I closed the pad. I wasn't going to need notes to remember this interview. "What do you inherit from your wife?"

"That's rather a personal—"

"I can contact her lawyer; that will just delay me. Or you can assist the investigation of your wife's murder and tell me now."

Again he ran his finger along the edge of the tray, watching its progress. Not once had he come near making eye contact. I wondered if that level of personal recognition was within his range. "The bequest," he said slowly, "isn't to me, it's to the clinic here. And being married doesn't matter. She told me about the bequest after I saved Coco. She was so impressed with that and with my inroads in endodontics she wanted to make it possible for me to teach others—"

"But she was willing to have you wait to do that teaching till after her death?"

He looked up and nodded slowly. "She had to live."

"But you will benefit from her death."

"I suppose. But my point is, she made the will before we married. Before we thought about marrying. There was nothing personal in it."

All the fury I'd been holding back erupted. "Of course, there was nothing personal. Your wife was dying and you didn't even bother to drive directly home from your conference, much less stay home to spend the weekend with her!" My voice echoed off the metal tray. I was too close to this case; I was losing it entirely. "No wonder she left you to go and die somewhere where she at least had her dog for company!"

His chestnut hair was quivering. Then I realized his whole body was shaking. He stared hard at the tray, peering down as if into a crystal ball. "I couldn't stop her." His voice was so low I had to lean forward to hear. "You think I wasn't much of a husband. I wasn't. I didn't know what to do, not with her. I tried, really, I tried, but I couldn't reach her. Even when she got the diagnosis, knew she was going to die, and I lay next to her in bed, holding her against me, I knew it didn't do anything except make clear to both of us how ultimately alone we were." For the first time he looked at me, his eyes big, brown, wet. "I didn't have to go to this conference. I wasn't on the schedule. Hardly anyone came to my lecture. But I couldn't stay here, not when I knew she was dying and she'd chosen to move back with people she laughed at instead of having to stay with me." He wiped at his face with his fist, but he was too late. A tear hit the metal tray. Instead of spreading out and evaporating, it rolled to the side, and then down the trough that his finger had traversed, becoming smaller and smaller till it ceased to exist.

I'd let my own assumptions blind me; I'd speared into his grief for no excusable reason. I felt awful. For the second time in this case I felt compelled to say: "I'm sorry."

He wiped his eyes again and looked up, a wavering smile on his thin lips. "I thought being a cop meant never having to say you're sorry."

"We should be so perfect." That wasn't the slant he'd meant, I knew that, but my answer seemed to satisfy him. Again I was aware of the low, frightened, lonely whines from the dogs in the cages. I could imagine Madeleine and Timms, edging around each other, he too awkward, too wary to pierce the hard wall covering her emotions, and she? Was being in control so vital to her that she was too stiff and guarded to feel the warmth of any touch? Was she like the dogs in the cages, desperately wanting to be comforted, but unlike them, not knowing how to even moan?

Or was I still pasting the face I'd drawn over hers? If there was one thing I should have learned from this investigation, it was that no one really knew Madeleine Riordan, least of all me. I shut my eyes and swallowed hard against the utter emptiness of the face I'd drawn. I hoped I was wrong, but this time I doubted I was. "I'm going to have to ask you about Madeleine's decision to go back to Canyonview. What happened prior to that?"

Timms wadded up the tissue and tossed it in the waste can. "Claire, from Canyonview. She called the house. Right before Madeleine left."

"Claire called the day Madeleine left?"

"No, I wasn't home then. When she told me she was going, I stalked out and called the conference director to get him to squeeze me in. So her call from the Wellington woman would have had to be the day before."

"What did Claire Wellington say?"

"I don't know. I didn't usually answer Madeleine's phone, but I was walking by and she was across the room, so I picked it up."

"Did you hear her conversation?"

"No, I wouldn't have intruded."

"But you argued about the call?"

He shook his head. "No. I couldn't. When she told me she was leaving, I felt like I'd been sucked down the drain. I just walked out."

"You didn't try to tell her how you felt?"

His long fingers squeezed against the metal tray. "With Madeleine it wouldn't have mattered, not if there was something she had to do. Doing the right thing, that always came first. People were forever second." He glared up at me, daring me to disagree.

But I wouldn't have. I wondered if Madeleine had had any inkling how devastating that dismissive way of life was. Had the possibility that Timms would be hurt even entered the equation? I doubted it. I was willing to bet she wouldn't have hurt him intentionally; she'd simply have assumed he understood the importance of whatever need she was responding to. Checking against Michael's statement, I asked, "Did you drive her back to Canyonview?"

He squeezed his eyes shut and it was a moment before he got out the word: "No."

"Why not?" I said softly.

"She didn't need me." His shoulders hunched forward and his narrow face drew into the hollow they made. He looked like a Saluki cowering in the corner. But his voice was angry, like he'd been slapped. "She had some guy come drive her in her car. Some sleazy guy in a stained yellow sweater. The kind of guy she wouldn't have let near the sofa."

All the tension of the day exploded; I had to bite my lip hard to keep from guffawing. It would have been unprofessional, and there was no way I could explain it well enough for Herbert Timms to understand. But the picture of Herman Ott filtered through his respectable, upper-middle-class mind was just about more than I could handle. I asked for a description, just to be sure. And as he gave me his picture of Ott, my amusement faded. Ott could have told me about that drive. He hadn't. That didn't surprise me. I tucked that bit of information away; later I'd see what it could lever out of Ott.

I questioned Timms about calls from friends, or business associates, or anyone, but for all he knew of his wife's social world he might have spent the last year locked in his veterinary clinic. I had the sense that he loved her much as he might his dog: he could hold him close and scratch behind his ears, but he wouldn't ask him for a recount of the day's events. I asked about motives. He had no idea why she was killed. "Dr. Timms, you lived with her for two years. What did she do with her time besides work?"

"Well, she watched football. She was a big 49ers fan. She knew every play, and she could call them before the quarterback did."

"She guessed what they were going to run on every down?" I demanded. Sportscasters who've boned up all week can't do that.

"Well, no, sometimes the coaches made the wrong calls."

Now I did laugh. That sounded like the Madeleine Riordan I'd known.

Timms stared at me. Slowly, he smiled. "She was a very intelligent woman. Not being in charge drove her crazy. You wouldn't believe what she put up with from her clients; she didn't care, as long as she called the shots. Even after all these years, it infuriated her to have to lean on a cane."

I recalled Coco Arnero threatening her, and her still keeping him on as a client. So she could plan his next hearing? "She didn't choose to just watch the football games, she was sort of a backseat coach?"

"She even bid on the KQED–TV auction last year when the prize was a day with the quarterback coach."

Neither one of us commented on how such a day might have altered the 49ers' season.

I might have misjudged Herbert Timms before, but I was clear on Madeleine Riordan now. I thought of the long gray tube Coco had been carrying and its double down on the platform in the canyon. Madeleine Riordan was connected to the parking perp, all right. And unless that relationship was entirely out of character for her, she wasn't merely an amused observer to his escapades.

The Madeleine Timms described was the woman like Howard; she would never have been content to sit and listen to someone else's sting.

I could picture her sitting outside on the path at Canyonview, next to the bushes that concealed the parking perp. She had been on the sidelines, all right, and not as a favored fan; she'd have acted as coach. She would have been no more able than Howard to resist the urge to plan the incidents.

Madeleine didn't condone violence. Even during the antiwar demonstrations she'd refused to drive bomb-makers. I thought back to Eckey and the purple dye. For a woman who wanted to make Parking Enforcement look ridiculous, that sting was perfect. No danger, just ridicule. Even the most patient of Parking Enforcement personnel would be outraged. Eckey was. And the meter minders citizens hated, the Elgin Tiresses who stood in wait for meters to click onto EXPIRED, who puffed up like bantams when citizens accused them of quotas, they'd be the laughingstocks of the city. I was willing to bet if Madeleine had a regret, it was that her last play was wasted on Eckey.

It sounded like a crass reason to leave a husband. But it wasn't just a game, it was one last clutch at life.

□

CHAPTER 20

It was one thing to be sure Madeleine Riordan had orchestrated the parking enforcement capers, quite another to prove it. Her husband, Herbert Timms, denied it: "My wife was a lawyer; her life's work was upholding the law." But after he had uttered those uninspired words, a tiny smile pricked at the corners of his mouth. And that little fleck of impish pleasure showed me what Madeleine had seen in him. Alas, I also believed he was being truthful—not that Madeleine hadn't been the culprit, but that he didn't know she was. She wouldn't have told him.

I couldn't imagine being involved in a caper I enjoyed as much as Madeleine must have this one, and not telling Howard—not planning it together sitting cross-legged on the king-size bed, our knees nearly touching, an open box of pizza within reach, both of us interrupting with *What abouts* and *Why don't wes* one on top of another, our voices getting louder, hands clapping with glee, until we found the perfect plan, flung our arms around each other, and in all probability kicked the pizza box off onto the floor. That, more than the actual event, would have been the fun of the capers: the planning, the closeness.

But Madeleine had been a solitary woman. For her the strategy, the execution, the panache of the caper would have been reward enough. And since the success of the caper would have reminded her of the fact she never questioned—that she was more clever than anyone else involved— there would be hardly anyone worth sharing the success with. Still, the temptation to savor—to gloat—must have been overwhelming.

But if Madeleine had confided in anyone—who? Someone clever, ingenious, and who relished a victory over the forces of law and bureaucracy as much as she did. She'd choose a friend of long enough standing to assure trust. I was willing to bet that person was Herman Ott. Ott could have told me that, too. Ott had his standards. But so did I. I added this latest debit to his balance sheet. He was running well in the red, but I wasn't ready to cash in yet.

I could picture Madeleine sitting in her room at Canyon view creating the later—the clever—parking capers. She was a lawyer, a systematic, organized woman. A list maker. A woman who wrote down pros and cons before coming to a decision. She was from the world of legal pads.

There had to be written plans for the capers.

But Pereira had searched her room and found nothing.

I started the car. That did not mean there were no plans. We simply hadn't looked in the right place.

I would have given a lot to head right back to Canyonview, but Inspector Doyle could still be there. If so, I might convince him there was an overriding reason why I wasn't back at the station per his orders poring over the files on the parking perp—that I was hot on the trail of the one item that would tie the parking pranks to Madeleine's murder. *If* he was willing to listen at all.

I had two options. Number one: Take the chance of a furious Doyle co-opting my search, making off with the booty, and dispatching me back to files. Number two: Stop on Solano Avenue at Noah's for a lox schmear on a sesame bagel and walk down to Peet's for coffee, and give Doyle time to finish up at Canyonview.

I ate.

It was just after one P.M. when I walked down to the companionway. Murakawa was sitting next to the door of Claire's room.

"How is she?" I asked.

Pushing his lanky body up, he said, "Nothing's changed. She hasn't come out of the sedation. It's been a long time since last night, too long for a woman in her condition to be out without her doctor checking on her. I told Delia to notify him."

Delia must have been delighted to discover this new layer of medical authority. "And did she?"

"Got the answering service. I told her that wasn't good enough, that they'd have to call the emergency number."

"Didn't Delia know that?"

Murakawa nodded. "Yeah, she said they were tracking him down."

"So no one's been in there this morning, or in Madeleine's room."

"Right," Murakawa said a bit too quickly, as if I'd questioned his competence.

Lowering my voice, I said, "I think I'm on to something. Down at the end of the path." I made my way down the dirt and board steps and along the path. The bushes at the end seemed thinner now in the midday sunlight. I checked the path near them, not expecting chair leg or runner marks to have survived some number of days' wear plus the scrapings of any number of feet. But there was one round hole that could have come from a chair leg being pressed into uneven ground to level it. Bending closer, I could see another. It took me only a minute to separate the branches of the jade plant and, using a handkerchief to shield it, extricate an 8-by-11 metal box, one of those flat, fire-resistant boxes in which people keep their papers. It was locked. I carried it back to the companionway, and before he could ask about it, said to Murakawa, "Locked. But I have the feeling it will open itself in my office. Let me know when you've seen the doctor. Stay here till you do. We need a clear handle on Claire's condition."

"You want me to call you when the doctor gets here?"

"No, you ask him. Get his opinion of how lucid she was last week, yesterday, and what's going on now. You speak his language; he'll give you clear information." I walked across the companionway. "Oh, and when you see Delia and Michael, find out exactly the last time they took Madeleine down to sit by the jade plant."

I hurried around the house to the patrol car and made it back to the station in record time. Howard was at his desk when I walked into our tiny office. It was midday-bright outside, but in here it could have been a bear cave in January. The overhead light was on, as it was every day. And Howard, facing his desk, had his chair a foot out into the aisle to allow room for his legs. He looked like a parent at back-to-school night. He also took up half the aisle.

"You're bringing a gift?" he said swiveling around to face me and the metal box.

"Actually, yes. You'll enjoy this." I put the box in the middle of my desk. "Unless I am way off base, this was Madeleine Riordan's."

Howard looked at the flimsy home-safe box in disgust. "I'd have credited Madeleine with better judgment. I hope she didn't put anything she wanted to keep to herself in there."

"My guess is she didn't have much choice. She was most concerned about weather—the box was outside—and she had to use whatever she already had at home. Thus, this."

"What's Madeleine's contraband?"

"Papers."

He looked more closely at the silvery box. "Locked, huh?"

"Right. And the fact that she felt compelled to lock it, and to hide it outside, makes a good case that even in a posh place like Canyonview a patient can't count on anything in her room going unnoticed, or untouched." I cringed at the thought of orderly, controlled Madeleine Riordan living with the knowledge that nothing was private. It was degrading for a woman nearly half a century old to have to hide her papers like a teenager locking her diary.

Howard was already fingering a ring of keys. I reached out a hand. Howard grinned.

Still careful to preserve any fingerprints, I inserted the first key. It worked. Opening the box, I lifted out a crumpled and restraightened sheet of yellow paper and glanced at the drawing of a car wheel with what appeared to be a flaccid wart at the two o'clock position. "Eckey will be interested to see the ingredients in her purple makeup," I said, handing the sheet to Howard.

The yellow paper was just what I'd expected, and it confirmed my hunch that Madeleine had been the parking enforcement pranks planner. We would check the writing against hers, of course, but there was no question in my mind. I reopened the box. The second sheet was unrumpled, wedged into the bottom of the box the way papers get if undisturbed. I realized I was holding my breath. This was the paper that interested me. The first sheet—plans for a caper already done—had been handled, wadded, and straightened, but this one looked untouched. Leaving it as it was in the box, I read it, and ended up laughing.

"What?" Howard insisted.

"Tiress better watch out."

Howard was veritably rubbing his hands together. I could see why he was the one cop who had really liked Madeleine Riordan. And more to the point, I could see what he'd liked about her. I found myself almost relieved that the two of them hadn't known each other better. The stings they could have come up with together! "So she was out to get old Tight Ass? What'd she have in mind for him?"

I wished Madeleine could have been here to see Howard's reaction. Even by her stringent standards, praise from Howard would have been a trophy worth keeping. I pulled my chair free of the desk, slid it toward the window, and sat. "You know, Howard, the more I find out about this woman, the sorrier I am I didn't know her. This caper she's worked up here is a masterwork. First of all she sets the scene at Haste and Bowditch, at the top of Peoples' Park, by the spot under the trees where the regulars hang out."

"The regulars, who view Tight Ass like the city's contribution to street farce."

"Then she has her minion block the slots on four parking meters on Haste—three together and the fourth three spaces down. Look here, Howard, the woman is so thorough she's even listed that the slot blocks need to be three eighths of an inch in from the outside surface of the meter."

Howard nodded approvingly, his curly red hair flapping in response to the enthusiastic assent. "So the blocks won't be visible to the people who parked in those spaces."

"Three meters so it will give her minion at least four minutes to do his dirty work."

"And the park regulars will keep Tiress focused on his tickets or on them."

"And while old Elgin is writing away?" I quizzed, shielding the sheet, and waiting for Howard's inspiration, as if this were the Super Bowl of Sting.

Howard leaned back. "Well, she's already chained the Cushman to a phone pole, stolen the marker sticks, sprayed purple paint . . ." He began pulling at his already long, prominent chin. "Tire theft? Dangerous, but . . . In four minutes New York thieves could take apart the whole Cushman. Of course, not silently."

"Nope. Nothing so destructive. In every one of the capers she had a light tone. In this one, her minion paints the Cushman seat with glue." I pointed to the bottom of the sheet. "Here's the recipe for the glue."

Howard clapped his hands together. "Stick Fast! I haven't seen that stuff since I was a kid! I always knew Madeleine had potential, but I never suspected. She had such a good act. God himself wouldn't have figured her for this." He shook his head. "I am so sorry she's dead." His shoulders slumped forward, and the hands that had clapped together pressed into his thighs. "You know, I never even visited her after I heard she was sick." He stared down at them. "I don't do well in hospitals and places like that." Places people go to die, he meant, but he didn't say that. "It's real hard for me; I get there and I can't think of anything to say, and I feel like an ass talking about myself, but I don't want to ask her how she is, or hear her answer, or, God forbid, have to respond to it. I feel like a heel talking about the future, and a jerk if I just stand there saying nothing . . . It's all I can do to send a card." He swallowed. "I didn't even do that. But if I'd known all this about her, I would have. For all the difference that makes now."

I rolled my chair closer and covered his hand with mine, weaving my fingers in between his. "Howard, Madeleine had something she loved doing right till the end—the adrenaline of the caper. You of all people understand that. Maybe that was more important than another visitor." She'd made it clear it was more desirable than her husband.

Howard nodded, a bit too quickly to have given my thought real consideration. He'd swallowed the comfort whole. Looking back at Madeleine's instructions, he said, "Ah. So Tiress writes his three tickets, then he climbs back into the Cushman, plops his broad ass on the seat, and settles just long enough to become affixed." The grin returned to his face. "Then he comes to the fourth meter, starts to get out, but his pants stay on the seat!"

I could see first the confusion, then the outrage on Elgin Tiress's perpetually enraged face. I could hear the rough sound of the rip. "And the beauty of it is, he's still close enough to give the park regulars a clear view of his drawers."

"Right, and, Jill, you know what a grapevine they've got on the Avenue. Old Elgin would never write another ticket anywhere near Telegraph without street people, students, craftsmen, and half the shoppers pointing and laughing. They wouldn't be calling him Tight Ass anymore. Bare Ass! Madeleine Riordan, I salute you. It's not just a sting, it's a sting in perpetuity!"

Again, I felt a pang of sadness for what she had missed. And for the way she had walled in her life, and all she had kept out.

As if reading my mind, Howard said, "She was a hard woman to know, but if you could get through that crust of hers, there was a nugget of something great." He shrugged. "Or at least that'd be my guess."

My phone rang. "Oh, damn, Howard. I forgot about Doyle." I grinned at Madeleine's plans. "At least this'll cool his pique." The phone rang again. "Homicide Detail, Smith."

"Smith." It was the dispatcher. "Haste and Telegraph. Another parking enforcement assault."

I held up a finger to Howard and laughed. To the dispatcher I said, "Don't you mean Haste and Bowditch?"

"Nope, Telegraph. Peoples' Park Annex. And don't be laughing when you get there, Smith. Eckey's not laughing."

CHAPTER 21

□

Peoples' Park is the most famous two-point-six acres in Berkeley. Since 1968 when the University of California prepared to build a high-rise dormitory there, protests and riots have kept the park in the public eye. The three quarters of a block between Telegraph and Bowditch was home to flower children in the sixties and seventies, the homeless in the eighties, and homeless and drug dealers in the nineties. Through it all the university regents have never forsaken their quest to build *something* on this only clear spot of land around Telegraph.

When the latest riots let up, the park sported a volleyball court. The park dwellers had evictions. Some of them moved across the street to what was dubbed Peoples' Park Annex, a tent city on the razed rubble of a transient hotel at the corner of Telegraph Avenue. Compared to the Annex, Peoples' Park had been like Grosse Pointe, with the discipline of West Point. Annex tents sagged in stagnant water, and the occupants juggled fights, drugs, and the complaints of the absentee owner. By the time they were evicted from the Annex, too, they had few supporters left. The lot returned to rubble. All that was left to remind people of the interlude was a tall black spike fence.

As I neared the scene, I noted the Cushman protruding from that fence.

I'd been to enough parking enforcement capers to expect to look for a meter minder gritting teeth and scrubbing face, feet, or any part between, to see reporters taking notes, television cameras whirring, and a crowd of

Berkeleyans laughing their heads off. Here, on Telegraph, I would have expected a circus. Instead, the thirty or so civilians were almost outnumbered by sworn officers, Parking Enforcement personnel, and guys from Advanced Life Support. The onlookers stood nearly silent staring down at a spot ten feet beyond the Cushman.

I pushed through them. The A.L.S. medics were kneeling next to a blue-uniformed body. I moved closer, though I already knew the body would be Eckey's. She lay still, eyes closed. Bruises marked her forehead and circled her eyes. I glanced at her arms: her sleeves were ripped, her skin cut and bleeding. Her hands were too bloody to tell whether the bruises came from an accident or were defensive wounds. A faint residue of purple was still visible in the creases beside her mouth, giving her skin a bluish tinge. She lay on the broken cement; water had collected in the cracks beside her head and tendrils of brown hair hung into the mud. I wanted to pull them free, dry them off, make Eckey not look like a corpse in the gutter. I swallowed hard and looked down to see if her ribs were moving. They were. She was still breathing.

I rested a hand on the shoulder of the nearest medic, a guy whose white turban suggested he was either a Sikh or a follower of one of our Hindu gurus. "What's the prognosis?"

Before he could speak, Eckey opened her eyes and muttered, "Shitty."

"Shh!" the medic snapped. Clearly it was not his first suggestion along this line. "Either you lie still, shut your eyes, like I told you, or I empty this whole syringe into your vein and you don't need to think about what you're going to say till a week from Wednesday."

I laughed, mostly from relief, and gave the medic's shoulder a pat. "Having Eckey as a patient is going to burn off any bad karma you've got from your last three lives."

He shook his turbaned head.

I'd been so focused on Eckey it was like all my other senses had shut down. Now suddenly, I smelled the musty mixture of blood and dirt that surrounded Eckey. On Telegraph Avenue brakes squealed and the staccato beat of rap music indicated a drive-by gawker had rolled down the window for a better look. Behind me one of the patrol officers asked for a name and address, voices speculated on "Crash?" "Brakes?" and "One ticket too many?" A whiff of strong coffee floated past. There is no disaster too great for Berkeleyans to observe with a *latte*.

I moved around to the other side of Eckey, standing where she could see me. Her neck was immobilized in a foam collar.

"What're you staring at, Smith?" she growled.

"You."

"Whadaya mean, me?"

The door clicked shut. I caught the medic's arm. "She's going to be all right, isn't she?"

"Yeah, no thanks to you." He rounded the truck's corner and ran for the driver's seat.

"Bat outa hell," I heard someone say behind me. I turned to see Leonard standing next to a guy with matted brown hair, a Peruvian army blanket, and thong sandals. The guy was one of the park regulars. "She coulda killed someone flying down the street like that. This is a city of laws, man. What's the point of having laws, if you cops don't follow them? Tell me that, man?"

Patrol had divided the civilians into three groups and had thinned the herd by half. I checked with them, but no one they'd interviewed yet had seen more than the Cushman crashing into the fence.

The Cushman was still affixed there, but now feet protruded from its underside. I recognized the short, bejeaned legs. "Misco," I called. I didn't expect him to roll out. He didn't.

"Yeah, who's that?"

"Smith. Can you tell what happened?"

"Oh, yeah. Nothing fancy. Brake line's been cut. Just sliced through like any high school kid could do," he said in disgust.

Misco could, and too often did, recapitulate tales of crunched doors, broken grilles, bent fenders from careless left-hand turns, ignored red lights, and full-circle turns in intersections (the Bay Area's improvement on the old U-turn). Traffic Investigation's work was regular and routine. So when Misco got something as exotic as sabotage, it made his day. From a saboteur he expected quality work, and he was downright offended when he didn't get it.

"How long would it take to cut the lines, Misco?"

"Good pair of clippers? Ten seconds."

"Suppose you weren't real familiar with the innards of the Cushman?"

Misco stared blankly. To him unfamiliarity under the hood was a concept as foreign as was elbow grease to Delia McElhenny. "Minute or two, I suppose. But, Smith, brake lines are brake lines. Any idiot can cut 'em."

"Thanks, Misco. Get me your report as soon as you can."

"No problem. Won't be more'n half a page."

Raksen was prowling between the crowd and the Cushman, head down.

"Anything of note?" I asked.

"No skid marks. The dispersion of glass fragments suggests the vehicle was moving at a good clip."

I gazed more closely at the hood. It was serrated and pressed half a foot in between the metal fence posts. The windshield was totally gone, and

A smile crept back onto my face. "You, Eckey, you look different"

"Different how?"

"I've never seen you with your mouth shut."

"Can you save the banter till after the Emergency Room," the med said, clearly disgusted.

"Just two questions."

"Okay, but we're ready to move her."

"No way!" Eckey snapped. "You don't touch me till I say so. Now, what do you need, Smith?"

I squatted down next to her. "What happened?"

"Brakes failed."

"Do they go often?"

"Never like that. I've had to pump up brakes before. But we're not traveling the freeways in these carts, you know; we've got plenty of time to pull over. I never heard of anyone injured 'cause of brakes. I—"

"Keep your head down!" The medic pressed his hand on her forehead. Her head hadn't been quite off the ground, but Eckey's intention had been clear. And from the look of his tight jaw and pressed lips, he wasn't burning off karma, he was adding more.

To one of the patrol officers, I said, "Get Raksen here. I want the entire cart gone over, plus the scene. And Misco, from Traffic Investigation. The Cushman doesn't move till he's eyeballed it. He and Raksen can fight for firsts."

"They're on their way, Smith."

Leonard, the beat officer, was making his way around the edges of the crowd. Three patrol officers were taking names and addresses, beginning the tedious task of interviewing everyone who'd seen anything. But Leonard would get more just ambling around picking up a word here, an observation there. He'd know which of the park regulars had been in residence today, who else's presence was noteworthy, whose absence a red flag.

The medics slid a support under Eckey, lifted her onto the gurney, and started rolling it toward the ambulance. I moved along behind her head. "My other question, Eckey. This route today, this wasn't your regular assignment, was it?"

"How'd you know?" she demanded as the medic pressed her head back into the gurney.

"Tiress's?"

"Yeah. Goddamned lucky bastard. I'll tell you, Smith, much as that pain in the ass screeches around stirring up messes for the rest of us, if this had happened to him, I wouldn't be crying."

"I'm sure, Eckey," I said as the medics started to close the doors, "that you'll let him know that."

the steering wheel had been jerked off its column. My shoulders drew in tight, and I could feel the flush of anger in my face. Eckey could have been killed.

To the nearest patrol officer, I said, "Take charge here. I'll be back." I headed across Haste, walking uphill past the old stage in the park, the free box where a jumble of coats and sweaters lay for the taking. The university had installed its volleyball court, but the aura of Peoples' Park had merely settled around it. Groups of three or four guys sprawled on the lawn; singles stood nervously next to their grocery carts that held their worldly goods. One leaned on the cart, his ancient raincoat hanging open to reveal a T-shirt advertising *Les Misérables*.

Howard stood next to a parking meter seventy-five feet from the far corner; his lantern jaw was tense. There was no hint of the merriment that normally brightened his eyes. "Exactly like Madeleine planned, Jill. This meter here and the three farther up have their slots blocked." He shook his head. "I just can't believe Madeleine would orchestrate something like this."

"I can't either. And, Howard," I said with sudden conviction, "I don't think she did."

He tilted his head questioningly.

I lowered my voice. "We'd be a lot better off if this were her plan. Then it would just be a matter that you and I let ourselves be fooled. But Madeleine didn't come up with Eckey's crash. She planned exactly what we saw on her paper. Then she died. And whoever's been doing the capers doesn't have her sense of farce or of decency."

"Yeah, this was no caper. We're talking felony assault."

I nodded. "At this rate, sooner or later someone's going to be killed."

"Eckey?"

"No, this wasn't planned for Eckey. Telegraph was supposed to be Tiress's route today."

"And the goddamned lazy perp can't even take the time to drive around and see who's in the Cushman."

"We're dealing with more anger than skill," I said.

"Even so, you'd think any perp working on a sting like this would take the time to drive around town and find out where Tiress is. Tight Ass wouldn't be hard to find; it's not like he keeps a low profile."

"Right. It's odd that Madeleine would have put up with such sloppiness."

Howard nodded slowly in agreement, but he offered no explanation.

I glanced toward the onlookers still moseying across Haste Street for a closer look. "Next time our perp could run a Cushman *over* Eckey, or Tiress, or some two-year-old in the road." I turned and stalked across Telegraph Avenue.

Herman Ott had a big red debit with me. It was time he paid up.

CHAPTER 22

□

The aroma from the pizza shop next to Ott's building didn't make me hungry, it made me mad—at how little I'd gotten for that revolting pizza I'd taken Ott the other night. And I'd left the twerp half of my decent pepperoni and onion for breakfast!

I raced in past the defunct elevator and took that long double staircase two steps at a time. I was panting when I got to the third floor, rounded the corner, and headed down the south hallway so fast that I had to jump over a toddler and his collection of orange plastic gizmos. I skidded to a stop by Ott's door and banged on the glass.

No answer. Of course, no answer.

"Ott, open up! I mean it. I don't care who hears this, you understand. You get this door unlocked—"

The door flew open. Never had Ott opened up before the third threat. I was still panting; I didn't bother to hide it. I strode in, took one look at the tidy piles of papers on his desk and with a sweep of an arm, brushed the lot onto the floor.

"Jesus, Smith, what the—" He jumped to the floor like a canary off his perch and flapped around after the papers.

"You lied to me, Ott!"

"I . . . don't . . . lie."

"The hell you don't. There's lying in words and lying in silence. Silence is the coward's way."

He scooped up the last sheet and held it protectively against his chartreuse acrylic turtleneck. "You barge in here making up rules, then you carry on like I should follow them. Well, Smith, I'm not a cop; I don't play by your rules."

I plopped myself on his desk. He always hated that. "You make a big thing about your ethics. The last of the old-time Berkeley idealists. The holdout from the sixties who hasn't been co-opted by the system. Sure!" He started to speak but I kept going. "Madeleine Riordan was your friend, the woman you owed a debt to. Someone pushed a pillow on her face; she gasped for air. Picture that, Ott. What a helpless, terrifying death for a woman who was brave enough to throw herself out of a car for the Cause." Ott stood up, clutching his cache of papers with both hands. I should have stopped there, but I was too angry. "Even her mother didn't die like that, Ott." I didn't have to add that Ott had done nothing to make things easier for her mother; that he hadn't gotten around to checking up on her when Madeleine asked. "Her mother's death was a prize compared to her own."

Ott said nothing. He shifted the papers into a pile and tapped the edges on his desk. His silence infuriated me more than anything he could have said.

I looked directly into his small pale eyes. "You drove her there, to Canyonview. Why?"

"Her husband's car was in the shop."

That took me aback. Timms had talked about walking out when he realized Madeleine was leaving. It hadn't occurred to me he'd meant it literally. But it made no difference here. "Why did she ask you?"

Ott shifted onto one foot. It was an odd habit he had, dangling the second foot a couple inches off the ground like a bird on wet grass. I'd only seen it three or four times, but it always meant he was balancing almost equally distasteful options.

The spicy aroma of peanut and pepper sauce sifted in under the door to mix with the vague scent of coffee too long in the cup. I pulled my jacket tighter around me. The sweat I'd worked up running up here was icy now. If this building had been in New York, the heat would have shut off at ten P.M. In this one it had ceased in 1952.

Ott put the second foot down, opened his desk drawer, plopped the papers in, and sank back in his ripped tan chair. His pale cheeks were sunken, his thin, limp yellow hair almost invisible against the chair; his whole body slumped like a chicken ready for the pot. It was as close to defeat as I'd ever seen Ott. "I'll save you the steps, Smith," he said with none of his normal verve. "Madeleine asked me to drive her back to Canyonview because we were old friends. But I don't know why she decided on the move. I didn't ask." He looked up at me, his pale face revealing nothing. "And that's the real reason she chose me. She knew I wouldn't ask."

I stared at him, amazed. Herman Ott was far and away the nosiest man on Telegraph Avenue, if not the entire city of Berkeley. Or maybe the world. "The only reason you wouldn't ask is because you already knew."

"No."

"No—what?"

"She knew I wouldn't ask, Smith, because I suspected that it had something to do with the memory of her mother in that nursing home and I didn't want to bring up that any more than she did."

Madeleine's mother's poor care was hardly Ott's fault, but nothing would truly convince him of that. After twenty-five years it still haunted him, as he clearly assumed it haunted Madeleine. We all see life through our tinted glasses. Ott was being totally honest, painfully so. But, by my calculations, the tint in his glasses was off-color; he was wrong. A nicer person would have told him that—a nicer person without a killer to find. Instead, I went with his theory. "Madeleine's mother died in a nursing home because of poor care. No one got poor care at Canyonview. And the only older woman there was Claire, whom Madeleine didn't even like."

Ott shrugged. "Maybe Madeleine was the mother this time. I don't know, Smith. I didn't ask. And I didn't try to find out."

I gave a slight nod. His commitment to Madeleine meant that if she didn't want him to know, he would make sure the hidden knowledge didn't find him.

"But mother-daughter things go two ways," he added.

"You mean Delia? You think Madeleine had some sort of maternal feeling about *Delia*?" The concept of protective feelings about the whiny eternal adolescent was more than I could imagine.

"Like I said, I don't know." It was as helpless as I'd ever seen him. He looked as if a pot was full of boiling water and he'd just agreed to be dropped in.

I almost took pity on him, but I caught myself before I threw away my advantage totally. "Ott, Madeleine's mother had nothing to do with her decision to go back."

His pale eyes widened. He looked at me hopefully, desperately, as if he'd spotted my hand on the burner knob under the pot.

I dangled the possibility of turning off the flame. "You'll be totally honest with me? Nothing held back?"

He leaned forward tentatively, wondering: was it possible he could really climb back out of the pot? Another time I would have delighted in my potential victory. Now I held my breath.

Finally he said, "On this issue alone."

"On Madeleine and anything concerning her death, *including* the meter maid pranks."

"What?"

I slammed my hand on his desk. "Either you're completely honest, or you get nothing from me. And you can go to your grave wondering if driving Madeleine to Canyonview set her up to be killed—if you cared more for your ethics than for your friend."

Ott jolted back as if I'd taken his head and shoved it down back into the hot water. I was too angry to be concerned. Eckey could have been killed. But Ott didn't care about Eckey, and my being pissed off would only amuse him. I took a breath to calm myself and focused on what would get to him: "Madeleine masterminded the meter maid pranks. Now someone is using her notes, perverting her plans, making her elegant pranks into violent and banal assaults."

Very slowly he nodded. "Mockeries," he muttered. "Okay. Your game, Smith. But, listen, you tell a single soul about this . . ."

"No problem. As far as the world is concerned, anything that comes up here is just the result of my own brilliant hunches." I settled in his client chair. "The reason Madeleine went back to Canyonview was to control the meter maid pranks, nothing to do with memories of her mother—unless I'm way off base."

Ott leaned forward resting his chartreuse-clad arms on the desk. He wanted to believe me, but he couldn't quite bring himself to. That made me distinctly uneasy; he's rarely wrong. "Who was Madeleine's operative in the meter maid pranks?"

"Don't know. I'll save you time, Smith. She never admitted she was behind the pranks. We talked after each one. I applauded their panache. She never demurred. We understood, but nothing was ever spoken. So I don't know another thing."

We understood, but nothing was ever spoken: how utterly Madeleine. "Well, we know she had someone carrying out her plans. Did she go back to Canyonview because the prankster was already in the canyon when she got there the first time and she wanted to be nearer to him? Or did she go back to get away from him?"

Color returned to Ott's face. "You think the guy who pulled off these pranks was Herbert Timms?" He was not just startled, he was offended. He looked remarkably like Michael Wennerhaver when I'd suggested Madeleine might have confided in Claire things that she hadn't told him, her protégé.

"I can't picture Timms snatching parking enforcement wands," I said. "But a week ago there were a lot of things I now know about Madeleine Riordan that I could no way have imagined. I'm not closing any doors. She had the plans for the capers with her at Canyonview."

Ott straightened up. "Maybe Timms found out what she was doing. I wouldn't put it past the little wimp to threaten her. She could have gone back to the canyon to protect her helper—"

"And to save the scheme."

"He came after her for the plans. She told him he could sputter all he wanted. The wimp grabbed the pillow . . ."

I nodded. Smothering was the act of a very repressed, very angry person. I couldn't picture Herbert Timms as the meter maid prankster, but I could see him murdering his wife. "That would explain why Madeleine chose to go spend so much time with Claire when she got back to Canyonview. Claire was a woman she could barely tolerate, but so what? She was a barrier to Timms so Madeleine didn't have him coming in and bothering her about the caper plans, wheedling, threatening, whatever. Claire is the kind of repressed, frightened woman who'd been trained to accept the status quo, like the timid aunt you tolerate but don't visit a minute longer than you have to. Still, for Madeleine, sitting with her would have been better than being alone and having to deal with Timms."

Ott nodded slowly, and with a fair amount of skepticism.

"Okay, so that's just a theory, but it still leaves the question of who helped in the parking pranks."

He started to protest, then seemed to recall his agreement. It might have been to guide me into a convenient byway, but Ott said, "I'm going to save you a lot of time, Smith. Madeleine would never have used Timms in the parking pranks. She wouldn't have exposed him to the possibility of arrest, particularly when she knew she wouldn't be around to save him."

"You could make that case for Michael Wennerhaver. She wouldn't have made such an investment in his career, backing him for the scholarship and all, just to let him get arrested."

Ott, of course, knew about Michael. He'd know about Champion and the photographs, Claire and Delia and Minton Hall. He probably knew I hadn't unpacked my boxes at Howard's and if there would be any empty seats at Berkeley Rep tonight. He nodded. "Madeleine would never have put her own amusement above what was right."

"Her own or anyone else's. But, Ott, why would she particularly care about Timms being arrested? Because of his work?"

Ott glared, like I was the village idiot. "Smith, he has custody of Coco. She would never have died and left the possibility of Coco's keeper being jailed."

"And of Coco being without care. Of course not." Herbert Timms already felt cast aside; I hoped he never came upon this line of thought. I leaned back against the sharp slats of the chair. Timms could have driven to Berkeley and back to his conference in Carmel in seven hours and three hundred or so miles. If he'd been the parking perp, he'd have had to drive back to stick the purple powder on Flaunt's tire. If he killed Madeleine, he'd have had to make it in the night before. Ott had said Timms's car was in the shop Thursday. The shop would have an odometer reading. It'd be easy to check how many miles had been recorded since. Rolling back the odometer in new cars with all their electronic gear is not the simple thing it was twenty years ago. I didn't cross Timms off entirely, but I let him slide down the list below Michael, and Delia, Champion, and even the extreme long shot, Claire Wellington. For an angry person holding a pillow over the face of a weak and startled victim is not so hard to do. It could be managed from a wheelchair.

My pager went off. I pressed the reset button. "Ott, the last meter maid incident happened right across the street . . ." My normal words would have been, "I can't believe you don't know any more about it." In light of our agreement, I said, "What else can you tell me about it?"

He swallowed, clearly regretting the breadth of his indebtedness. "Look, Smith, none of the Avenue regulars is involved. And I'll tell you one more thing, since I'm being so totally honest. You remember that picture of Madeleine on the locker room wall down in your police department? The picture used for a dart board?"

I nodded, hardly surprised Ott had heard about it.

"Madeleine knew. Just in case you're tempted to delude yourself. Madeleine knew exactly what you guys thought of her."

I gulped. "She talked about it?"

"Oh, yeah. She laughed about one bureaucracy screwing another. She said if she were burglarized, her insurance company had better be prepared to pay off for everything she owned."

Normally the idea of besting the cops moved Ott as close to laughter as he came. But there was no glee in his expression now. I wondered if he understood how violated and enraged Madeleine must have felt—any woman would have felt—knowing her likeness was posted for ridicule on a men's locker room wall. I didn't want to ask.

My pager went off again. With relief I said, "Can I use your phone?"

He shrugged and walked into the hall.

When I got the dispatcher, I gave him my badge number. "Five twenty-seven."

"Smith, you got another Cushman incident. Bancroft and Bolivar Drive."

It took me a minute to recall where Bolivar Drive was. "By the lake at Aquatic Park."

"Not *by* the lake at Aquatic Park, Smith. *In* the lake at Aquatic Park."

CHAPTER 23

☐

I squealed the car to a stop by the wooden fence of a deserted chemical plant. A fire truck, three patrol cars, two Cushmans, and two unmarkeds sat at all angles by the edge of Aquatic Lake, a narrow strip of water between the freeway and industrial west Berkeley. The sirens had stopped but flashers streaked the gray dusk and echoed blue . . . yellow . . . red . . . yellow on the water. Staccato bursts of radios cut the air. Beyond Aquatic Lake, lights on the freeway blinked through the manzanita and junipers. Farther west the last stripes of sun seared the rippling water of the bay and the red glowing ball was settling into a bank of fog behind the red towers of the Golden Gate Bridge.

The Pacific wind iced my ears and snapped my jacket against my ribs. It unfurled Howard's loose red curls. Live oaks and junipers cringed away from the wind. Macadam paths snaked around man-made knolls and empty poles that once held PAR COURSE signs that had been trashed and not replaced. The signs that had been maintained warned: LOCK YOUR CAR and DON'T LEAVE VALUABLES IN YOUR CAR. Even early Sunday mornings, when bicyclists and dog walkers felt safe, the most common sight here was big American cars with lone men waiting behind the wheels.

If Nefarious Activity were looking for a place to picnic, Aquatic Park would be it.

Over the radio the dispatcher's voice came from three cars: "Four three nine call in. Repeat, Officer Four Three Nine call in."

Pulling my jacket tighter around me, I hurried past the patrol cars and across the few yards of lawn. The grass ended abruptly: no beach, just land chopped off and lake begun. And four yards into the lake the orange reflector triangle on the rear bumper of the Cushman protruded, inches above the wind-tossed water. I checked for the Cushman's driver, but there was no body lying on the lawn, no medics bending over. Instinctively I looked back at the sunken vehicle. Surely, the driver wouldn't still be in there. But, of course, he wouldn't, not with no one out there working on it. I grabbed the nearest patrol officer. "What's the story, Heling? The prognosis? Who was driving?"

"Elgin Tiress."

"Ah," I said, relieved. If the perp was after the most offensive guy in Parking Enforcement, he'd gotten him. The game would be over. He had won. Once again Parking Enforcement would worry about nothing worse than post-ticket tantrums. For us it would be worse though. With no new incidents we'd just be wandering down colder and colder trails. It said something about Tiress, or me, that I had contemplated all the logistic effects of his accident before wondering about him. "How is he?"

"Concussion. Arm and a leg that looked pretty bad. Ambulance was two blocks away when they took the call. They've probably got him in Emergency by now. His head went through the windshield."

Scrunching my shoulders up around my ears, I looked at the icy water slapping against the Cushman. "Tiress must have had that Cushman floored."

She nodded. "Tiress didn't say much. He was pretty out of it. But he did say 'stuck.' Said he started from Sixth Street and once he pressed the gas pedal down it never left the floor."

Automatically I looked east toward Sixth Street, six blocks away. In all that time why hadn't he gotten the cart stopped? Had he panicked? There was a certain justice in that picture. And if I, a fellow law enforcement officer, thought so, I could imagine the pleasure the parking perp would have taken in the image of Tiress's pallid triangular face flushed in fear. Tiress would have been started down a gentle grade, picked up speed, barreling through stop signs, shooting along the sleepy south Berkeley industrial streets and across the deep-rutted Santa Fe tracks, and down the suddenly steep grade to the lake. By then he'd had been moving fast enough to fling the Cushman four yards in.

"He was lucky he wasn't killed," I said.

"You could have said that before he stepped into the Cushman today," Heling put in. "You got all these new businesses down here, all these cars. Around here, Smith, a man'd rather discover a parking spot than a new gene splice. There are scientists running tests that have to be checked at three minutes after the hour or the experiment goes bust. You've got cut-throat computer companies with guys scared shitless of being late. You've got vehicles parked in front of anything that's not breathing. Tiress loved it. You know what they called him down here, Smith?"

"Besides Tight Ass?"

"The Hyena—and not because they'd discovered a sense of humor."

"No one ever accused Tiress of humor, Heling."

Heling adjusted her breath and continued undaunted. "Down here Tiress didn't have to bother waiting for meters to run out. Down here, it's just picking off the weak and dying." Heling paused and waited till she caught my eye. "And you know, Smith, that's Tight Ass's specialty."

Like many of us, Heling had considered herself Tiress's specialty at one point. She'd been late so often she started leaving her car in a loading zone while she checked in. In the two weeks she tried that maneuver, it cost her a hundred sixty dollars.

It was then that the beauty of this caper struck me. The perp hadn't had to count on Tiress panicking. He'd only made use of what there was in abundance here: parked cars. Or more to the point, not a free yard of curb space. Usually the lack of parking here infuriated only drivers. But today, it spelled disaster for Tiress, barreling along trying to spot a dozen yards of bare curb to scrape his wheels against, finding instead only the cars he so loved to ticket. I only wished I could have seen it. I also wished I'd gotten here a whole lot sooner. Tiress's frantic flight was one scene the parking perp wouldn't have missed. But by now our perp would be home sipping Chablis and chuckling over his memories.

Still, if he watched Tiress's cart go into the lake, he might have left a footprint or some other lead to his identity. Someone might have seen his car idling too long, or trailing behind Tiress. "Heling, cordon off the street beyond the Santa Fe tracks to the east and beyond that wooden building to the north."

She groaned, turned up her uniform collar, and trudged toward one of the other patrol officers.

From beyond that wooden building a vehicle that looked like the issue of an affair between a tow truck and a whooping crane moved awkwardly toward the lake, then veered to the shoreline. Feet planted on shore, it stuck its metal beak yards over the water and within feet of the fallen Cushman. In any other part of town we'd have had a hundred people watching. Here, with the small factories closed for the day, the drug dealers not yet open for trade, the air too cold and windy for the sensible Berkeleyan, we'd attracted only a couple and their stroller-bound child.

It took the mongrel crane forty-five minutes to extricate the Cushman, battered, muddy, and with something resembling bullrushes sticking out the front where the windshield used to be. Misco found the cut in the brake line in less time than it had taken the perp to make it. And Raksen was poised to point out the glue under the gas pedal. "There's glue and glue, Smith," he said. "Paper glue and airplane glue. I'm not talking model airplanes, I mean the stuff they use in seven-forty-sevens. I can't be sure, and don't quote me, but I'd bet that if Tiress had eased his foot off the pedal after the first push he'd have been okay. But, clearly he didn't."

"He wouldn't," I said. "No one ever accused Tiress of restraint."

"Yeah, it's hard to picture him backing off to consider the options."

"So, what you're saying, Raksen, is that if he panicked and pressed down on the gas pedal, then it'd have stuck?"

"With the brake line cut, and the gas pedal jammed," Misco said, "old Tight Ass was on his way to the moon."

"Lucky there was no one down here sitting on the grass in his way," Heling said.

"There wouldn't have been, not after five," Howard put in. "That could have been part of the plan."

I felt a shiver in my solar plexus. The cleverness of it shouted: Madeleine Riordan. But it couldn't have been her plan, not the Madeleine Riordan who refused to drive antiwar bombers over the border because she hated violence. I shook my head. "He had to cross intersections at rush hour. He could have caused crack-ups in both directions. And if there'd been pedestrians . . ."

Howard nodded slowly, the lines of his face pulled in confusion and distress. He looked as if he'd been abandoned, as if Madeleine Riordan had abandoned him.

I took a step back away from Heling and lowered my voice. "Maybe, Howard, she just got fed up worrying about what was right. Maybe she figured she'd played by the rules all her life and what had it gotten her? Why shouldn't she go ahead with her elegant sting and leave Tiress and the pedestrians to take their chances? Whatever their fate, it wasn't likely to be as bad as hers. Why not?" I could almost hear Herman Ott speaking through my mouth: *You barge in here making up rules, then you carry on like I should follow them. Well, Smith, I'm not a cop; I don't play by your rules.* Ott was like Madeleine.

I wanted Howard to come up with an unassailable argument, but he just shrugged.

Leaving Heling in charge, I headed back to the car. Howard had caught a ride down here with Raksen. He slid into my patrol car for the trip back. "If it was her plan, Jill, why wasn't it in the metal box with the rest of them?"

"I don't know." I started the car.

"Wait." He jumped out.

"Where are you going?" But he was already halfway across the road. I turned the car off and raced after him, catching up just as he reached Heling.

"Tell me about Tiress here," he demanded. This was Heling's district and she had certainly seen enough of Tiress to know his habits. "Was there any spot Tiress stopped at around here? Did he get out of the Cushman, take a leak, or get a doughnut?"

Heling laughed. "Tiress eat a doughnut? He'd choke before he'd put something sweet in that sour mouth of his."

"Did he stop for anything?" Howard asked.

Without shifting her feet Heling seemed to move away from Howard. "Well, yeah, now that you mention it, sometimes he did pull over a couple blocks up from here just before the espresso truck left. He had a friend, if you can imagine that, and the two of them got espressos there. They'd sit and drink them and probably talk about what scum the rest of humanity is."

"So, if someone knew that, they could plan to use that time to insert some glue—"

"They couldn't count on it, Howard. Tiress didn't always stop there, just maybe half the time, but not regularly, like maybe he'd go a week without stopping. And he never sat down to drink his coffee out of sight of the Cushman."

"Was the Cushman in his line of vision while he was getting the coffee?" I asked.

"Not usually."

"But when he did stop, it was around five P.M.?" Howard insisted.

"Right."

"O—kay," Howard said like a coach applauding the winning point after. "Thanks, Heling." Before she could ask for more of an explanation, he was loping back to the car.

"So?" I said as I climbed back behind the wheel.

"So, what we've got here is most likely an aborted plan, but one too elegant to keep quiet about. I mean, Jill, there are magnificent stings no decent person can orchestrate—too dangerous. But they're still magnificent. You can't do 'em, you can't get 'em out of your mind. You sate the urge by talking about 'em."

I recalled a few of Howard's. In a city that is self-insured, every taxpayer would have been relieved to hear of Howard sating himself verbally.

"My guess is it was Madeleine's plan, but done by someone without her standards. If I'm right, Madeleine's plan would have called for adding the glue two blocks up from here, not six."

"So Tiress couldn't get up too much speed, couldn't really endanger anyone, and wouldn't land out far enough in the lake to do anything more than look foolish." I started the engine.

"But, the thing is, Jill, adding the glue at the last moment when Tiress stopped for coffee was the tricky part. Our perp couldn't be sure he'd stop today, tomorrow, or even this week. He didn't have Madeleine's control; couldn't bring himself to wait for the right conditions."

"So he took the easy way out and added the glue earlier, farther away, right?"

Howard shifted his knees against the dashboard. There was no comfortable way for him to stow those forty or so inches of leg when I had the seat pulled forward. "If the parking perp is one of the irresponsibles, I guess that lets out Timms."

"The irresponsibles? As opposed to the responsibles?"

"Not exactly." He sighed. I knew that sigh well. He'd have liked to lean back in his chair, stretch out those long legs, and begin making professorial pronouncements on male psychology. Here all he could do was tap a finger on the microphone as I headed toward University Avenue and declare, "You know the theory that men view women as either madonnas or whores."

"Easy choices for simple minds," I said, taking a right too fast.

"So, Jill, how do women view men?"

"How, O latter-day Freud?"

"As Dads and Cads. Men who are expected to be responsible and guys who are prized for their free spirits."

"Dads and Brats, you mean?"

"It doesn't rhyme. What's pop psychology without rhyme or alliteration?" Howard laughed. Pop psychology took a beating from Howard. "Anyway, Jill, the point is that women give the brats a lot of slack. They love their playfulness, the way they flip the bird to rules; they excuse them when they're late or forget dates altogether. But if the guys they expect to be responsible do any one of those things, they rake them over the coals."

I nodded. The theory annoyed me, but I couldn't disagree. And the more I thought of it, the more it seemed that Madeleine Riordan was exactly the sort of woman Howard was describing. "So in the Dads camp we've got Herbert Timms and Michael Wennerhaver."

Howard nodded.

"She really did pick well, Howard. Herbert Timms she chose to take care of her dog. And Michael . . . Michael must have been a mainstay of the responsible camp from the moment of birth. She devoted a lot of time to him. He benefited from her perception of him. Being a doctor, a caretaker for the elderly, and ignored, what a perfect profession for a Dad.

Michael was her final gift, a memorial to her mother—the caring doctor who could have saved her."

"But, Jill, the chief Brat was Coco Arnero, canine and human. If any other client of hers had talked about out-of-body experiences at a review commission hearing, he'd have been looking for another lawyer."

"But coming from him it was okay," I said with growing excitement. "And there was Coco, the dog, on the bed, never denied access to a room even if the inhabitant didn't want him in, carrying around that meter wand." I pictured Coco with that taperlike dowel. It would have been so easy to bite through. Easy for anyone to cut in half. "Oh, my God, Howard."

"What?"

I stopped at the light by an Indian grocery and a sari shop. "That Brat has got the meter wands displayed in his living room. He cut them in half and made a coatrack out of them. I looked right at them and at his shirts and jackets on the floor underneath. And all I thought was what a slob he was!"

CHAPTER 24

□

I raced back to the station.

But in order to nail Champion I had to run a check on his mother, Lucia Champion. I took the station stairs two at a time and ran through the meeting room that doubled as interview space the rest of the day. Uniformed officers looked up in mild curiosity—need of speed is not an earthshaking occurrence here. The suspects seated across from them stared as if I were carrying pardons from the governor. I ran on through files, ignoring the cries of the phones, past the reception desk, and nearly smacked head-on into Inspector Doyle.

"Jesus have mercy, Smith. It's about time you're here," he said as I skidded to a stop. "Two parking incidents in one day! Phone's been ringing off the hook. The press. The mayor. Every member of the city council. The city manager. Everyone but God the Father, and probably He can't get a line through!" Doyle reached inside reception and snagged a doughnut from this morning's box, then glanced from the box to me questioningly. I shook my head; I was too wired to eat.

"So, Smith, what did your search of files turn up?"

"I haven't gotten to it."

His face flushed red. "Haven't—"

"I'm ready to collar the perp."

Momentarily he stopped, then picked up his pace, veered into his office, plopped the stale doughnut on the desk, and propped himself behind his big green desk chair, arms on its back. "What do you have?"

I brought him up to date on the case, ending with a description of Champion's ersatz coatrack. "He must have laughed his head off after I left." I could feel my face flushing. Doyle's, already red, darkened. No cop takes well to perps mocking his authority, or his subordinate's. There's an imaginary collar, a metal dog collar, that hangs around the neck of all suspects and leashes them into our investigation. Champion's just tightened a link. "It's easy, Inspector, to picture Champion on that ten-speed swooping down and grabbing the meter wands."

"You saying he ran this string of capers just for the fun of it?" Doyle looked ready to pull the chain another link tighter.

"No. We checked Champion through every file known to computer. Zip for means or motive. But the man inherited from his parents. I need to run a check on the mother. I'm betting that'll turn up plenty."

Doyle handed me the phone. I passed the word to the clerk and hung up.

He was still leaning on the back of his chair, his arms crossed, fingers tapping on arm flesh. "So where does Madeleine Riordan fit into it all? She devise all these capers?"

"I found plans for the one by Telegraph in her box. But there was nothing about the hostage incident or the explosion. They're not her style— too violent."

"You got any evidence for that opinion?"

"Nothing to take to court. Champion can tell me."

His fingers snapped into a fist, as if he were jerking the chain. "Smith, we talking about the guy who's starred in 'Make Monkeys of the Police'? You think now he's going to sit down and lay it all out for us?"

"Not for *us*. For *me*."

Doyle didn't say anything. But his silence said, "Are you smug, or crazy?"

I propped a foot on his visitor's chair. "Look, there were only two people who knew what went on with these capers. Madeleine's dead. That leaves me Champion. Here's a guy who's slid through life never mastering anything, and all of a sudden he makes himself a folk hero. Clearly, he revels in it. Then along comes Madeleine, takes over, and adds a panache he never dreamed of. In her eyes she's doing him a favor. In his, she's deposed him. He can't take it. He kills her."

"That a speculation or a theory?" *Smug or crazy* still hung in the air.

Ignoring that, I went on. "Maybe she told him she asked me to come back the next night. Maybe he figured she was going to confess and turn him in, too."

"Why would she tell him?" The air cleared of insinuation.

"Maybe she didn't. The staff at Canyonview knew I was coming back. Maybe he heard it from them."

"Maybe, maybe, Smith. You're going to have to come up with a whole lot more than maybes."

"I will. You can count on that." Even I was surprised by the tightness of my throat. I sounded as if the suspect's choke collar was around my neck.

"Your make on Lucia Champion, Smith." The clerk handed in the report. I read over the sheet and for the first time tonight I smiled. Champion had mentioned inheriting "what little she had" after her death a year ago in Arizona. But it wasn't her money that interested me now. It was *her* car and the possibility of Champion collecting O–Tows (out-of-state tows) with it. After five or more citations an out-of-state vehicle will be towed, impounded, and held till the owner can show proof of payment to both BPD and the towing company. In the last six months a Buick registered to her at a Scottsdale address had been towed, impounded, and held four times. It was still in impound.

I passed the report to Doyle. "So Champion's left with a grudge against Parking Enforcement, and a bicycle for transportation." No wonder he hadn't driven around the city looking for Tiress before he pulled his parking pranks.

It took Doyle and me only three minutes to agree that the best scenario would be to capture the parking perp with lights, camera, action, in front of every reporter in the Bay Area. The worst would be to let him slip through our lines—lights, camera, media, and civilians wandering through our lines. Outside it was already dark, and with the fog it looked like someone pulled a giant comforter over Berkeley's head. If Victor Champion wanted to disappear down into the canyon tonight, we'd have as much luck rooting him out as the neighbors there did the skunks and deer.

"If we could wait till morning . . ." Doyle said with resignation. But we both knew that wasn't an option, not when the perp could have other booby traps set to blow in the canyon—ones we missed or ones he set after we left. "We'll go with a forward force: you and four patrol officers, and a secondary to surround Champion's house and the outlets around the canyon." Glancing at his watch, he added thoughtfully, "It should take an hour to put together."

"Too long! I can't wait. Madeleine Riordan told me to come back at eight thirty. There had to be some reason for that."

"Some reason, Smith? It could be whim. Maybe that was when she finished dinner, or her favorite TV show was over. We can't organize this entire operation around whim."

"Maybe what happened at eight thirty was something she spotted through her binoculars, looking at Champion."

Doyle leaned on the chair back, clearly unimpressed.

"Inspector, we're talking about Madeleine Riordan. Madeleine Riordan didn't have whims. But if she had, it wouldn't have been to chat with a police officer. She knew what we thought of her. Inspector, she'd heard about her picture on the locker room bulletin board."

Doyle flushed brick-red. It made me wonder if he'd tossed one of those darts that pierced her cheek or eye. Or perhaps he just didn't object. Whatever, I could tell the balance had shifted toward Madeleine, and me, and my plan. "Okay, Smith," he said slowly, "take the forward unit. Put a man on each exit. Keep Champion inside. Don't bring him out until we turn on the lights."

It said something about how long we'd worked together that he didn't bother to remind me how bad things would be if I blew it.

It was already after seven. But I hadn't gotten a report back from Kensington P.D. on Champion's guns. From my office I called the Kensington station. Downey, the officer who'd questioned Champion, was still there.

"So, Downey, does he have weaponry?"

"Believe it, Smith. We're just lucky he didn't turn them in when we had the amnesty program. At fifty bucks a gun he could have bankrupted the city. But Champion's not a guy who thinks ahead."

"How so?"

"The guy's got an M-1, a Thompson machine gun that's virtually a collector's item, so many German weapons his father must have done nothing in the second world war but strip the dead. Champion told me about watching the colonel clean them, like it was a religious ceremony. Champion could have sold them for a bundle. But you know what he did with them?"

"No."

"Real Berkeley move. I'll tell you, Smith, this guy's on the wrong side of the county line."

"What did he do with the weapons, Downey?" I said, failing to mask my impatience. I'm not as amused by Berkeley bashing when it comes from the other side of the line.

"He stuck them out in the yard, in the wood bin! They're rusted all the hell up."

I shook my head. Destroying weapons of death would have been a Berkeley move, but this was the reaction of a Brat—a brat who could have used the money from selling the collection, but chose to spite his father instead. His *dead* father. Victor Champion was sounding more unhinged than I'd thought. A bitter loner with guns. "Was all the weaponry unusable?"

"That's the bad part, Smith. He doesn't know. He can't remember what was supposed to be there."

"So anything could be missing."

"You got it."

"Did you search his house?"

"Nope. All of a sudden he got uptight and started carrying on about a warrant. You know how that is."

"Indeed. Thanks, Downey."

Things were clear to me, but I didn't have enough for a warrant, either. As Downey could have told me, too frequently a judge can't see as clearly as a police officer. A judge would need a confession in order to see the truth here.

I called the Evening Watch commander. The officers he gave me for backup would come off patrol in one or two sectors of the city—places where suspicious vehicles or people might now go unnoticed, where victims of robberies or muggings would get slower police response, where the perpetrators of those crimes would stand a better chance of walking free. Those were also districts where the remaining officers would be working harder while my backups were assisting me and, later, writing up reports on the assist. And if anything came down in those districts because they were short, I would hear about it.

The backup units would be waiting at the Kensington Circle. The dispatcher would notify the CoCo County sheriff that I'd be conducting an operation in Kensington. I headed out to the lot for a patrol car.

Sometimes you drive up into the hills and emerge out of the fog. Not tonight. At Kensington Circle above Cerrito Canyon the fog was thicker than at ground level. I slowed the car; I was outdriving the headlights. The lamps on the street poles gave off fake-looking vanilla glows that disappeared long before they fell to the street. It was the worst possible night to confront a suspect like Victor Champion. If I spooked him, he could hop on his bicycle and disappear in two seconds.

Backup—two cars, one bike, total of four patrol officers—was waiting at the Circle. I assigned Nguyen, Stovall, and Patterson to surround Champion's house. The fourth, Megan Williams, the hotshot of bike patrol, would stay near the cars, handy to the radio and the top of the stairs, and to her bike. If we needed her, it meant we'd blown it and we were in trouble.

On the canyon rim road, we parked facing opposite directions—the better to chase if we had to. Though it was only seven fifteen, it was dark as midnight. If there were lights in living room windows, they were hidden behind drapes and the fog. No cars pulled up; no dogs barked; no cats scurried across the deserted road. We started carefully down the hundred stairs to Champion's. The dirt steps, covered with dead leaves and pine needles, were almost invisible in the fog, and their irregular wooden braces threatened to catch my heel and send me headfirst into the canyon. As I made my way down between the houses, the air became clearer, but when I descended beyond them, the fog closed around me like a thick knitted scarf pulled over my face. The light from my flash barely made it to the step below. I stopped and whispered to Patterson, "Champion's back door is at the east side. When we get to the bottom of the stairs, you go west, all the way around the building till you see it. Keep an eye on the windows, too. Living room window doesn't open, but there's a kitchen and bathroom."

"No bedroom?"

"That's on the far side of the companionway. If he gets that far, Stovall and Nguyen will see him." I waited a moment and said, "Any other questions? Okay, no talk beyond here."

As I moved down, the fog thickened as if its very weight was condensing the layers below. I turned off the flash—not a great loss—and felt with my feet for the edge of the stairs. Fog coated my face, iced my skin. Every few yards the smell changed, odors stronger in the night: dirt, wet fur, bay tree, skunk. I could barely hear Nguyen, Stovall, and Patterson behind me. Champion's house couldn't have been more than ten feet below, but it was entirely hidden. No light pierced the fog. Champion was lucky we were police officers. Anyone could have come down here, slit his throat, and tiptoed back up. And Claire Wellington across the canyon, how easily could she be raped, killed? Sitting in the main building, Delia and Michael would never notice. Like Madeleine's, Claire's room didn't even have a window on that side. It was a dangerous, stupid arrangement, crimes just inviting perpetrators: *Come, pillage, slaughter! It's easy! It's safe! It's confidential!*

Suddenly Champion's house was three feet away. I stopped and held my arms out to warn Nguyen and Stovall. Walking across the companionway would announce our numbers. Patterson I motioned around the house. Stovall and Nguyen backed up a step. I counted to three hundred—enough time for Patterson to get all the way around the building to the kitchen door —then walked normally down the last steps, onto the companionway, and knocked on the living room door. It was 7:20 P.M. Under my jacket I was sweating. I listened for music, or a radio. Champion didn't seem the television type. The only sounds were of faint rustling—Nguyen, or possum, or deer. Maybe Champion wasn't the home type. He could be down at the meter cart garage sabotaging every Cushman in the city. I pounded on the door, four times, the police knock. "Pion! Open up!"

It took a third pounding before I heard footsteps, then the familiar voice and familiar words. "Keep your shirt on, I was in the darkroom."

When he opened the door his hair was still wet, his clothes fresh, like he'd just showered. Dumping Elgin Tiress in Aquatic Lake was just the thing to work up a sweat. Looking at me, he shifted expression: annoyance to surprise to wariness. Was he worried I would expose him as the caper artist or as a murderer?

CHAPTER 25

□

You don't mind if I come in out of the cold?" I said, before Champion could consider whether to let me into his living room.

"Yeah, fine."

I still wasn't sure how I'd play him; I had to get a confession about the meter pranks, but I couldn't lose him before he told me about Madeleine. I hurried into the living room. A burst of warm air hit me and I caught the vague smell of photographic chemicals. Only two small lamps lit the room, but the place seemed glowing bright. Piles of clothes were still splattered around the floor and over the canvas chairs. On the wall by the door, the coatrack was bare. There, painted the same white as the wall, it seemed only to underline Champion's poor housekeeping.

Looking at that arrangement of the meter wands I said, "You deserve applause for hiding your trophies on display."

Champion hesitated. I could almost see the gears of his mind clicking one after another. Should he accept my praise? Could he deny his guilt? Should he? Now that Madeleine was dead, who would applaud his cleverness? He'd cut Eckey's brake line, made his escape on a bicycle—and there was no one to tell.

"You are responsible for the parking enforcement capers," I said matter-of-factly. "Tell me about them." Deliberately I stayed out of his path to the door. If he tried to bolt, I'd stop him. But if he succeeded, I wanted him to head out this door, not through the kitchen into the dark canyon, past just Patterson. Champion knew the canyon; we didn't. If he got out there, we might as well give him bus fare.

"So, Pion," I said, smiling. "You finally got Tiress. Did you know that?"

He tried to control his mouth but a little smile crept on.

"There's no point denying it. Sit down. Tell me about the purple paint, the glue."

His small smile stayed in place. So did mine.

"You should have seen the crowd around the Cushman when the meter maid smacked that bag and the paint exploded in her face. Everyone in Peet's raced out for a look."

He pressed his lips together hard, but he wasn't good at controlling his face. He knew I was jerking him around, but I was giving him a payoff he'd get nowhere else. He was tempted, really tempted, I could tell that. But he still wasn't talking. I had to get a confession. Without a confession I had nothing. That imaginary choke collar around his neck was dangling too damned loose; I couldn't get a grip on the chain.

"Pion," I said, trying to keep the tension from my voice, "when it's all over, we'll show you the reports."

He hesitated.

I let go of the smile. And pulled the chain. "Look, we know you pulled those capers. We've got the proof right here on your wall. Either you tell me about them now and we get this cleared up by tomorrow morning in time for you to greet the press—the Hero of the Parking Meter—or, Pion, we take you in and we keep up the investigation. We tell the press we have a suspect, but we don't think the case is closed. We just let the public interest dribble away. Either way we get you; it's just a question of whether you want to be a hero or an afterthought. Which will it be?"

His face stayed absolutely still for so long that I wondered if he'd stopped breathing. Then he shrugged, padded across the room and sprawled in one of those miserable canvas chairs. He was grinning ear to ear.

I remembered when I first interviewed him, thinking there was a reason flattery existed. Victor Champion wasn't about to do without it.

I opened the door, called Nguyen in, and pointed to a chair out of Champion's line of sight where I hoped he'd soon be out of Champion's mind.

I read Champion his rights. He seemed to think that was a joke. He could think whatever he liked, even that this warning referred mainly to the parking enforcement assaults rather than Madeleine Riordan's murder. I could have come on strong here, or taken Champion to the station and leaned on him there, but with him the light flattering approach worked so well. A lot of guys on the force had a hard time with that one, but women, trained to it from childhood, can run it without blinking. I used to choke at the thought of it, but now it pleases me in a perverse way to make use of the tool of the underclass. "Pion," I said, "the escalation was so slow, so subtle we don't even know when you started picking off the Cushmans."

He allowed a small smile of acknowledgment to settle on his angular face as he leaned back in his canvas chair, rested ankle on knee, and lifted a hand to illustrate his story. Moving him as quickly as possible, I led him through the mechanics of the assaults: swooping down on his ten-speed to snatch marking wands left in Cushmans as meter maids wrote out tickets, the release of a brake uphill of a newly delivered pile of manure, the theft of a Cushman and the drive up a ramp into a Dumpster. (According to Champion the hard part of that maneuver had been "borrowing" the portable ramp from a construction project down the street and returning it unseen.) He took full credit for every one of the assaults down to the Aquatic Park incident, glorying in the tidbits of meter maid frustration and humiliation I passed on to him. To hear Champion tell it, he was a sort of pop-psych Robin Hood of oppressed motorists, stealing esteem from the ticket-giving oppressors and bestowing it on the downtrodden drivers. Not once did he mention Madeleine's contribution.

It was already eight twelve. Madeleine had wanted me to come at eight-thirty. Tonight I *would* be over there at eight-thirty. I had to move Champion faster. "What set you off to begin with? Lots of people see parking wands, but no one else snatched them up."

"Assholes ruined my career."

I let my eyes open wide. "How so?"

He propped his forearms on his legs and gave a great, disgusted sigh. "You can't cart your photographs around to galleries on a bicycle, not if they're printed poster-size and mounted. One good wind and you're sailing into the next block. Or you've been blown off the bike, onto your ass and them, and your still life looks like 'After the Earthquake.' "

Police work has given me ample experience listening to perpetual "victims." In the eyes of much of our clientele, the tilt of the earth's axis was away from them, all of life was an uphill climb, and nothing was ever their fault. In Champion's eyes, the towing and impounding of his mother's/ his car would have been acts of a vengeful god. I said, "So, you got some tickets with your mother's car."

"Some!" he exclaimed, all signs of humor gone from his face. "What kind of idiot created twenty-minute parking zones? Who can do business in twenty minutes? Hell, you spend longer than that in the grocery express line. I saw that asshole Tiress. He'd spot my car and if there was five minutes on the meter he'd circle around the block and come back—and just wait for that big red EXPIRED to pop up. He was like a lion who smells a dying wildebeest. He kept coming back to nip me till I dropped."

"And so—?" Eight-fifteen.

"I was riding along Shattuck one day and I spotted the wand." He leaned back and grinned, triumphantly.

Before he could bask, I tightened my grip on his choke collar and pulled. "And after that Madeleine took over the planning?"

"Right," he said, unabashed.

I stared. I'd expected sputtering protests, territorial protections. I'd assumed the Cushman capers were the trophies on his shelf, but if he didn't care about admitting Madeleine planned them, then where was the payoff for him? Had it been merely getting Tiress?

Eight-seventeen. "So the capers were all aimed at Tiress?"

"Yeah, but Madeleine decided it was better to spread them around. Less obvious. Madeleine was a great planner. There was a fine art to her plans. She told me she was brighter than the guys she worked with, brighter than the doggy dentist." He shrugged. "She was right. She probably told people she was brighter than me, and she'd have been right about that, too."

"But—" I prompted. Now I saw what he'd gotten from Madeleine that made these admissions unimportant to him. He'd played for higher stakes, for the only thing she had left to give. I had suspected she had taken *the* thing of value from him. Wrong. He took it from her.

A satisfied smile settled on his face. "Madeleine was as hooked as I was on the capers. She needed me more than I needed her."

I could feel my skin tightening. I was right; and the thought of his bullying made me furious. "For that you made her leave her curtains open."

I hadn't controlled my voice. Or my face. Champion stared at me, the skin by his eyes creased in confusion. Behind him Nguyen had a similar expression. *What are you angry about?* their expressions demanded. Champion said, "It wasn't like she was undressed. That wasn't part of the bargain. You saw the pictures, they weren't smut. She was just sitting there, doing whatever she would have been if I'd ridden over there to visit her. What's the matter?"

My throat had clenched closed. I closed my eyes and swallowed until I was sure I could speak clearly. Then I looked Victor Champion in the eye and said, "If you'd gone there, she would have had the option of saying No. Victor, it is demeaning to have someone watch you as if you were a bear at the zoo."

"It wasn't like that."

I tried again. Somehow it seemed important that he understand how ultimate his theft was. "She had so little left—Coco, of course, and the knowledge that Michael would become a doctor who really cared about people like her mother. But every day she lost more control of her body. All she had left were her privacy and the meter maid pranks that provided her escape from an unrelentingly grim reality. Her privacy and her escape, Victor. And you forced her to choose between them. You forced her to sell you her privacy."

Champion gave no response. It didn't surprise me. But what did was that Madeleine Riordan had had to choose between privacy—control—and escape and that she had opted for the latter. Madeleine, the planner. Had she changed so much? But no; I saw her after she made her choice. She hadn't changed; she still controlled what she could. Then, why did she allow herself to be put in the position where she was killed? Dammit, I could feel the answer, just out of reach. It was already eight twenty. I took a deep breath and forced myself to say calmly, "Pion, it is a very unusual thing for two law-abiding strangers to join together in a basically useless and illegal activity. If the capers had been planned by old friends who'd decided their lives were dull and they needed a fling, it would be more understandable. Or two teenagers who were strangers wouldn't raise any eyebrows. But you and Madeleine are a very unlikely combination."

Champion smiled, a more relaxed, warmer look than the grins he'd had earlier. His eyes were a little dreamy and I had the sense that he was picturing Madeleine. "Maybe it was because I'd already seen her through the lens; I felt like I knew her. I wanted to know her. That meant something." He stopped utterly still as if holding that "something" to himself a last time. Then he focused on me. "If you think the capers were out of character for Madeleine, it just means you didn't know her. She loved it. She loved poring over the plans. She'd do that till I was just about out of my gourd. I mean, I just wanted to get in, do it, get out, and stick my wand on the wall."

I pressed my lips together to keep from laughing.

"But Madeleine, she had to consider the terrain, think about who would be at the scene, what the traffic patterns would be, what about the meter maid rotation, where could I leave my bike, would it be a slow news day. I mean, I had the feeling if there hadn't been enough variables, she would have made them up," he said, flinging his hands to the sides. "And then when it was over, she wanted to know moment by moment, not just did I drive the Cushman into the Dumpster, but who was around, was there much traffic, how far did the cart sink in the Dumpster, what happened when I climbed out. To make her happy, I would have been talking about the caper longer than it took to do it."

I thought about Madeleine in the seventies planning the runs across the border. Champion's description of her wasn't surprising. But I didn't let on to him. "Despite those differences, you two got along."

"Yeah, she loved the thrill of it. She told me once that it was like being on vacation, not just going someplace and being Madeleine Riordan there, but signing into the hotel with a made-up name, speaking French, picking up men, being someone with no similarity to Madeleine Riordan, and knowing that when she came home that vacation person would simply disappear."

"She did that?"

Champion shrugged. "I don't know. Maybe she made it up. She did say she'd had the same giddy feeling the few times she'd had more to drink than she could handle, and that now, in her condition when she'd really like to do that she couldn't."

"And the capers were the only thing that gave her that freedom now."

"Right," he muttered. For the first time he looked like he glimpsed what he had threatened to deny her.

"She showed you the plans for gluing Tiress's pants to the Cushman seat, she talked about her ideas of the Aquatic Lake run, but she never gave you the plans. Why?"

"I didn't need them," he said, but he'd let a beat too much pass before dredging up that rationale. "I made that clear to her."

"You disagreed, didn't you? Her plans were capers, yours were vendettas. She wasn't going to be a part of someone getting hurt, was she?" That was my Madeleine.

"All of a sudden she got so finicky about a little danger," he said giving his head a little angry shake. His gray ponytail wavered in response. In that moment he looked nowhere near fifty years old, in fact much younger than I could imagine Timms or Michael ever appearing. "No one was going to get killed. It was only the meter maids who were in the way. And if we didn't take chances we'd never hit that asshole Tiress where it mattered."

For Champion it was a personal vendetta; for Madeleine Tiress was merely an annoyance allowed to flourish by a system that had to be changed. She would have enjoyed seeing Tiress get justice, but for her, it was the parking enforcement regulations that mattered. For her the principle always superseded the individual—except when the individuals were her mother or her dog. "You disagreed, and Madeleine was ready to pull out, right?"

"She thought she was indispensable. But I managed without her," he said defiantly. "I . . ."

He was on the verge of telling me something. I prodded, "You had her plans. She'd scoped out the scene at Haste and Telegraph. She'd given you the name of the glue. You cannibalized her plan for Aquatic Lake."

"So?"

"So, Pion, you haven't done anything on your own more than grab a wand a meter maid left in her cart. Hardly world-class creativity. Madeleine was the planner, the woman who managed all the details. Without her these pranks would just trail off, no newspaper coverage, no applause. You might as well not do them at all."

He opened his mouth. I almost had him. But he caught himself before the words came out.

I leaned forward, locking his eyes with mine. "You couldn't plan anything. You know and Madeleine knew it! Didn't she?"

"No, dammit! I showed her. She could have seen the best caper of the whole operation if she'd only looked out her window. I gave her a whole goddamned hostage operation right here in the canyon. All she needed to do was point her binoculars, and she would have seen a maneuver that would have amazed even the colonel." He looked so distraught anyone who hadn't spent hours wild-goosing in the canyon and more hours making and tracking down reports would have felt sorry for the man. And as outraged as I was, I felt a twinge of pity for the fifty-year-old still trying to impress his father, trying to impress Madeleine, and maybe offering her a gift of entertainment. A very small and exceedingly short-lived twinge. "And the explosion yesterday, why did you set that up?"

"I didn't! Hey, not me. Why would I do that? Madeleine was already dead." He was halfway out of his chair. "And besides, an explosion wasn't something she'd have liked. I mean, hell, she didn't even watch the hostage thing."

"We found a parking enforcement wand down there."

"*I* didn't put it there. It must have been one of Madeleine's. I gave her two, one for the dog, and one for her. She kept hers in the bushes at the top of the path. You check; it must be gone now."

I believed him. There was no reason for him to set the explosion, and much more for someone wanting to keep the focus in the canyon on the meter maid perp. "Why didn't Madeleine see the hostage operation? Didn't you call her?"

"I tried, but she was over in goddamn Claire's room. I didn't have the number there. I must have called Madeleine's room ten times, let the phone ring half an hour. She never budged, just kept sitting there staring at Claire."

"And that's when you took the picture of her?" Sitting in the chair at the end of Claire's bed, with the screen next to her. Or was it in front of her?

"Yeah. You think she was angry; it was nothing to how I felt."

"And when she came back to her room, did you talk to her then?" I asked with growing excitement.

"Yeah," he snapped, giving me a clear picture of the tone of that conversation.

"What did she say?"

"I don't remember," he muttered to his knees.

"You remember. What?"

Silence.

"It's too late to play dumb. You are in a lot of trouble. You've broken enough laws to keep a court tied up for months. Grand theft, auto theft, felony assault, and depending on the extent of Tiress's injuries, attempted murder."

He looked up, startled.

"We're not talking county jail here."

"Hey, I—"

"But," I said, "how a judge looks at this will depend a whole lot on how he or she perceives your character. How much *I* tell them you've cooperated. Get it?"

It took only a moment for him to take in the picture and nod his acquiescence.

"Now, tell me what she said."

The startled look returned in watered-down form. He wondered why I was concentrating on that, but he was in no position to ask. He rubbed his right hand between the fingers of his left, moving from palm to little finger as if preparing to count the topics he divulged. "Well, we argued. She couldn't appreciate the canyon operation. Christ, I did it for her! You'd think she would have cared! But no. She hadn't even noticed it, and when I told her, it was as if she wasn't even paying attention. She carried on about violence and danger to innocent people. And"—he shifted to the ring finger —"she went on about my betraying her trust. And the thing about not letting people decide which moments of life are important."

My breath caught. Madeleine's statement from the Coco Arnero hearing: "We can't have people choosing which moments of our lives are important enough to deserve respect." She had brought it up to me and to Champion. "This was when she was talking about the meter capers?" I demanded. These weren't the reactions I'd expected. She should have been accusing Champion of grabbing power, or being too unreliable to follow directions, of blunting the point of the caper, or more likely *missing* the point. She should have used terms of indignation, anger, desperation. "Betraying a trust" was a reflective phrase, one used more in disappointment than anger.

"I don't know what she was talking about. She wasn't making sense. It was like she was thinking about something else."

"What else?"

"I don't know. I didn't talk to her about other things. Since she came back to Canyonview, it was hard to talk to her at all; she was in Claire's room all the time. When she was at Canyonview before she never bothered with Claire. Now, after she got so finicky, all of a sudden, she's over in Claire's room in the afternoon and back there again this time of night. I couldn't call her till she got back to her own room. And that'd be ten o'clock at night."

"And that was when she talked about betrayal and which moments of life people deem worthy of consideration?"

"Yeah. I get up early. At ten at night I don't want to be figuring out puzzles."

I shook my head. "Champion, you peer in on a dying woman. You telephone her at ten P.M. And then you have the nerve to complain that her conversation was unsatisfactory."

He started to speak, but I put my hand up. "She was sitting in Claire's room at the end of the bed. Did she mention the screen?"

"Yeah, I guess. Why?"

"Was she sitting next to it, or behind it? Think."

He stood up and walked to the table and picked up the photo and stared, shaking his head, and put it down. The photo didn't answer my question. It hadn't Monday, it wouldn't now. "Pion, think about what she said."

He sank back into his chair, let his eyes close. It was a full minute before he shook his head. "She never mentioned the screen. There's no reason she would. The only time we talked about her being in Claire's . . . I was pissed off about it. She laughed and said I could get in line behind that dog of hers. She said she had to close him in her own room because she could never keep him quiet enough. Just his breathing was too loud."

The only reason Madeleine would have needed—not quiet, but silence—was so someone wouldn't know she was there—*behind* the screen.

Eight twenty-six. I left Champion with Nguyen and Patterson, and ran up the dirt stairs. By the time I got to the top I'd tripped twice, skinned both arms, and was panting so hard I could barely call out to Williams to come with me.

I kept one hand on the horn, and drove like crazy through the fog toward the Arlington Code 2 (lights flashing). It wasn't till I was nearly to Canyonview that I turned off the flasher.

Madeleine had been behind the screen in Claire's room at this hour two nights running. I could already be too late.

CHAPTER 26

□

adeleine?" Claire turned her head slowly toward the door as I crept in. I moved past the head of the bed, next to the door, and stopped beside her where she could see me better. I didn't think she'd been asleep; she looked as if she had been given medication that left her eyes floating in their sockets. Or she was drifting out of time as she had been occasionally yesterday. I expected her to recognize me now, but she said nothing more. Was she so spacey that she really thought I was Madeleine? Dark hair, medium height, chiseled features—Madeleine and I were the same general type. But no one would mistake me for her. And the Madeleine Claire had seen lately had lost all her hair.

The dry flowery scent of Claire's powder mixed unevenly with the acrid smell of the old cigarettes and ash in the tray on the bedside table. The shade was pulled over the canyon window, as it had been last night. It fluttered dangerously close to the side of the bed. But it didn't pierce Claire's wall of opacity. She lay, with that unfocused look, the yellow covers pulled up so high on her neck that the sheet pressed up against her chin and throat. Yesterday she sat up in her pink quilted bed jacket. Her makeup still looked fresh well into the evening. Tonight there was no sign she or Delia had bothered with it at all. Her skin was terribly pale. The hazel of her eyes washed out into the white. Under the covers her arms were wrapped around her thin chest. She looked like an old, brittle paper marionette that could be crumpled by a touch.

"Was I in the past?" she'd asked when I was here before. "I write things down so I can remember." But she hadn't remembered me. If she had asked now, I would have told her who I was. She didn't.

With anyone else I would have asked permission or at least given an explanation. Without comment I took her tape recorder off the bedside table, set it on *Record*, and said, "I'm recording what is said here. Present are Claire Wellington, resident, and Jill Smith, detective, Berkeley Police." Then I slipped the machine under the bed. If this maneuver was one Claire did remember, I just hoped she didn't blurt out a comment about it later. "Claire," I said, fingering the screen by the foot of the bed. "I'm going to sit here behind the screen. Don't tell anyone I'm here."

"Like Madeleine," she said in a quivery voice. I hoped it was loud enough for the tape to pick it up.

"Did Madeleine ask you not to tell anyone she was back there?"

She rolled her head toward the window. "When she came without *him.*"

"Without Coco? Without her dog?" That was what Champion had said, too.

Claire wrinkled her nose. "Awful animal." She shrunk back on the bed. "He touched me."

"You're not talking about Coco now, are you?"

But Claire gave no answer. She didn't look like she was asleep, but she wasn't here any longer either.

I stood utterly still, listening for footsteps, as Madeleine must have Saturday night, as Claire must have night after night. I didn't know how much time I had to question Claire—maybe forever. Maybe killing Madeleine had frightened him off. I could be too late. Madeleine was dead; Claire was no witness at all. All he had to do was keep his cool now and he'd be home free. But if he did come, and he spotted me, I'd never get him. I listened harder, willing distant footfalls to resound through the rustle of leaves, the whir of the night wind. Still nothing. I moved closer to Claire and asked, "Who touched you?"

Claire stared vaguely at the window shade. From her fuzzy focal point she might have been looking out into the canyon, or at memories of the Minton Hall demonstrations, or at nothing more than the skin on the inside of her eyelids.

Eight forty-five. It was all I could do to keep from pacing, wondering if I'd come too late. If the tape would run out. Or if there would be nothing to record on it because nothing at all would happen tonight. It would be so easy for him to just wait a few days, till the police presence was gone from the canyon. Then he could walk back in here and take up where he stopped.

The stuffed chair was still behind the screen. I pushed it a few inches toward the window so its empty seat would be visible from the doorway. Even if it had been totally hidden, I couldn't have made myself sit in it.

I moved behind the big three-panel screen to a spot where I could peer through a crack—at the room that looked too pink, too mockingly ruffly, but now with just one "ceramic statue" waiting to be destroyed. I stood, where Madeleine had sat when Champion took that enraged picture. Madeleine the planner—how could she have planned so poorly? Why hadn't she just called us like any other citizen would have?

But Madeleine Riordan wasn't just any citizen; she was the lawyer whose picture on the locker room wall was full of dart holes. She knew about that picture, and what the force thought of her. If she had reported what she'd seen from behind this screen, her fear would have been that a patrol officer would answer her call, but maybe he'd stop to laugh about her on the way here; maybe he'd drag out the investigation for months, insisting with a snicker that he wanted to be sure Madeleine wouldn't haul him before the review commission. Maybe he wouldn't even believe her. Even if we responded pronto, she couldn't shepherd the investigation through. By the time it came to court, she knew she'd be dead. She needed a witness —a witness with authority—someone who would care the way she did. Or, if not the same way, at least one who would care at all.

Madeleine was not a great judge of character (even she would have to admit that now), but she'd been right on the mark picking me for her witness. Madeleine's murder had grabbed me by the throat; I didn't know why; but I wouldn't draw a free breath till I had her killer. Standing behind the screen, I felt my face coated with sweat. I was breathing in nervous gasps and I couldn't believe the noise of my breath wouldn't expose me. How had Madeleine managed to stay hidden back here?

Claire lay utterly still, eyes unfocused. The covers above her breasts barely moved, but the roar of her breath rivaled the ocean. Or did it just sound that way to me? I forced myself to listen to the noises outside—a car door slamming, a dog barking in the distance, branches snapping back and forth—then judge Claire's volume. No, quiet as her breath was, I could still hear it, as Madeleine must have. As Claire must have heard Madeleine's. And as *he* must have heard it, too. Of course, he had. That was what Claire had been alluding to yesterday when she'd said, "He sniffed her out. Not Coco."

I'd made a mistake they warn you of in training—never assume. It's not the hunches you decide to go with that get you in trouble; it's the assumptions that are so integral a part of you you never question them at all. That's what I'd done here.

"He was too close," Claire had whispered to me yesterday.

I had watched her shrink back fearfully, thought of my old Great Pyrenees, and lumped Claire's complaints with those of my dog-fearing aunt.

"He touched me," she had said. "I couldn't keep him away."

I'd assumed she was talking about Coco. I'd asked if Madeleine knew.

"She sat right there where you are," Claire had said. But even Madeleine couldn't keep him away. He had come when she wasn't there. When she was at home, living with Herbert Timms. The reason Madeleine had left there, come back to Canyonview before she physically had to, was because Claire called. Claire must have said to her what she told me: "I can't keep him out."

There was a scratch on the window. I jumped. It was just the palm branch, that same palm branch that framed Champion's picture of Madeleine staring in outrage—the outrage that led to her telling Champion about not letting anyone choose the moments of life that are worthy of consideration. Claire had put it differently: "They think I'm too old, too dizzy to bother with. They've all packed me away like a summer carpet." They—Delia, Michael, and even Madeleine—had laughed at Claire's prissiness, the modesty as outdated as summer carpets. We'd dismissed her as ridiculous. We had tossed her out, too. Discarded these moments of her life.

I recalled Coco Arnero and his demand that the police guard his body when he was out of it. Madeleine hadn't dismissed him.

And now, watching Claire clutching her arms to her breasts—I realized that Madeleine had not rolled her up and stuck her in the attic like a summer carpet.

Madeleine didn't like Claire, but she would have protected Claire and the rest of the "dizzy" ladies whose "worthy" moments of life were long past. Maybe it was her way of telling her mother she was sorry she hadn't gotten anyone to her bedside in time to help; maybe it was atonement; maybe defending the principle of fairness was enough in itself.

The palm frond scraped again, louder. I thought of the explosion; it was such a clever diversion from this crime in here. The frond scraped once more. This time it sounded different. This time it wasn't the frond at all, but footsteps on the path.

I couldn't stay behind the screen where Madeleine had been—had been *found!* There was nowhere else but the bathroom. I slid behind the door, and with my left hand on the knob, held it half open so I could see through the crack. It was a terrible spot, but I had no choice. If he needed anything from in here, he'd smack the door into my ribs. Then he'd smile and walk free. There wouldn't be a damned thing I could do.

The outside door opened—no easing open warily, not that much care was needed. He pushed it open proprietorially.

"Ready for bed, Claire," Michael said. His voice sounded utterly normal. A smile spread across his wide flat cheeks. In fresh oxford-cloth shirt, clean jeans, his short, dark hair newly combed, he looked like the attractive young doctor all the old patients love. Anyone would have wondered why Claire was cringing.

I had glanced in here the night I'd come to sit in Madeleine's room. Claire had that same look then. I'd taken it for embarrassment at Michael's abruptness to me. I had dismissed it as an old woman's foolish aberration, the teacher's reaction to a student's poor manners.

Now I stood, barely breathing, hoping Claire had forgotten I was here, hoping Michael was sure he'd taken care of any danger when he killed Madeleine.

He moved almost as if in slow motion, his wide face tense, focused, like a spoiled child about to snatch a forbidden candy and plop it in his mouth. He stepped toward the bed, brushing it with his leg before turning to the bedside table and lifting the cigarettes and ashtray and carrying them across the room. His running shoes squeaked on the wood floor, and the smell of dead ash cut one last time through the air as he emptied the ashtray into the garbage. He walked back to the bedside table, this time ignoring Claire, and slowly poured a glass of water. He looked down at Claire, put the glass to his mouth, ran his tongue around the rim, then took a long swallow of water.

Claire watched, transfixed with disgust and dread. The symbolism was clear.

I wanted to smack Michael Wennerhaver so hard his head spun and the moisture flew off his lips. I wanted to knock that smug look off his face. All my muscles ached, pulling back against the overwhelming need to strike. But I couldn't move, couldn't even get my revolver free.

Michael rolled a pill from its container into his palm and let it lie there half a minute before moving it to a paper cup and placing it beside the glass. He looked over at Claire, a strained smile on his wide lips, his face pinched, intense, like the child about to throw a tantrum, a toddler who knows he can intimidate into control.

"You ready to sit up, Claire?" he asked.

She pushed back into the pillows, her arms wrapped so tight around her breasts I was surprised she could still breathe. I could smell the remnants of her perfume and intermingled with it the vague, sour strains of sweat and fear and powerlessness.

I held my breath. My heart was thumping so loud I couldn't believe he didn't hear it. I shifted my arm and reached for the zipper of the fanny pack on my stomach, and began inching it open, metal track by track.

"Here, I'll help you up." He ran a hand behind her, under her quilted bedjacket. I could see the opening in the back of her gown, and the mound of his hand inside it. She was whimpering. He lifted her to a sitting position. With one hand he untied the pink ribbons of her bed jacket, and slowly pulled her thin, pale arms away from her breasts. I shuddered, and clenched my teeth so tight my jaw throbbed. He wasn't looking at her body; he was staring into her eyes, sucking in her fear. He wasn't after sex per se, he wanted power. Like Victor Champion with Madeleine, what Michael was doing to Claire was all about control.

Claire let out a cry.

Michael's hand tightened on her arm. "Don't you pull away from me." He stood, staring down at her, his face inches from hers. *His breath smelled bad*, she'd said to me. How many nights had he exhaled his tense, excited, assaulting breath? He shifted his hands and slid her bed jacket off.

I wasn't breathing at all. My face was scalding; my fingers squeezed the doorknob so tight the indentations cut into my hand. I wanted to kill him.

And I couldn't even stop him. I had to wait, to watch. To get enough evidence so he didn't walk out of here free, to work in another nursing home, to abuse other elderly women whom no one would believe. So he wouldn't go on to medical school, on the scholarship for which Madeleine had championed him.

He slid his hand under her nightgown strap on her far shoulder. With excruciating slowness, he slid it down her arm till the fabric fell loose beneath her wrinkled breast.

Her face went deadly white, her body was rigid. She lay there helpless, exposed.

I slid the zipper to the end and reached into the pack for my revolver.

Michael released her arm and for a moment I thought he was going to pull down the other nightgown strap. But, instead, he glanced nervously at the screen. With a sheepish grin he walked over and looked behind it.

As he turned back to Claire, his grin broadened, "Madeleine's not there anymore, is she? No one to save you now!" He reached down and unzipped his fly.

I waited till he had penis in hand and reached for her, before I yelled, "Freeze!"

The color drained from his face. He stared, unbelieving. Then he pulled a pocket knife from his pants and put the blade to Claire's neck. Her mouth opened, but she didn't make a sound. He pulled her back against him so she was half off the bed, then he glared at me. "Now who's in charge, bitch?"

My hand was still on the revolver, still in my fanny pack on my stomach. I didn't move it. I took one look at Claire, hanging in Michael's grasp: limp, withered, lifelessly pale. She could have been the dummy in the canyon. My whole body shook with rage. I wanted to grab Michael and slam him into the wall again and again until there was no more left of him than that dummy.

I swallowed hard. What I had here was a hostage situation. Forcing myself to think as a negotiator, I said a whole lot more calmly than I felt: "Michael, we have a situation that's gotten out of hand."

"Bullshit! I'm in charge here, for a change. No *woman* tells me what to do now, not my mother, my goddamned aunts, not the nuns at school, not Madeleine." He ran the point of the knife across Claire's throat.

Claire let out an anemic shriek, then called out plaintively, "Madeleine!"

I jammed my teeth together to keep from reacting. I couldn't let Michael see my fear for Claire. God, I wanted to shoot him, to wipe that smirk off his bland, wide face. I wanted to send him to a hell run by Amazons. Taking a breath to control my voice I said, "Madeleine saw you in here."

He smirked. "Big deal. Madeleine thought she was smarter than anyone. So smart she sat behind that screen like she was invisible. A third grader knows better than that. I yanked that screen back and there she was, like a chicken sitting on an egg." He shifted Claire's weight, but his attention was still on Madeleine. "What'd she think she was going to do, run for the cops? She could barely walk without help."

Keep the hostage taker talking. "What did she do?"

"Went back to her room. I *took* her there. She went where I decided."

"But she warned you never to do this again, didn't she?"

Michael shrugged, jostling Claire. "Big deal. She was dying, what could she do?" Standing behind the old woman, his firm body, moist skin, his shiny dark hair screamed youth, power, freedom.

Entice the hostage taker to bond with the negotiator, the instructions say. But there was no time for that. Claire was too fragile. And the tape recorder could snap off at any minute. I had to go create a diversion—get him angry, defensive, off-balance—and then go for him. "Madeleine canceled your scholarship, right?" It was a guess, but a sure one. "You'll never be a doctor now, Michael. You'll spend the rest of your life emptying bedpans. You'll jump to it when the nurse tells you."

He flushed. "I don't need her fucking scholarship," he insisted, but his voice betrayed him. "I told her that."

"When?"

"Right after I tossed her in bed."

I jammed my teeth together; my jaws throbbed. I watched for the smirk that would tell me he had assaulted Madeleine that night as he had Claire. But his stiff, self-righteous expression didn't change. He hadn't touched her; he wouldn't have dared.

"But you didn't kill her then. Why? Because you were afraid?"

"No!"

"Sure!" I taunted.

"Stupid bitch. Just like Madeleine, think you know it all. Madeleine thought she could make me do what she wanted, like I was some tame pet."

"She could have called the police."

"She tried that. She asked you to come back. She would have told you then. But I was too smart. I didn't let her." He jerked Claire against him.

She cried out. I didn't look at her. I kept staring at his face, and goaded, "*You* didn't let her? I don't believe that."

"I was there Sunday night, right outside her door, remember? Then you left. I could have killed her right then."

"But you were too much of a wimp."

"I was too smart. I chose my time."

There hadn't been any defensive wounds only light bruises. She hadn't put up any real struggle. I knew what he had done but I needed to hear it in his words. "What time?"

"She went back on her word. I didn't owe her anything. But I was decent with her. I put the pillow over her face, so it'd be easy for her."

"Easy! Hardly!" I took a breath, pushing down my fury. "Okay, Michael, now put Claire down slowly."

"No way." He gripped her arm so hard she screamed. *The hostage taker knows the value of his hostage.*

Still, I didn't look at her, only at him, like we were the only two people in the world. My throat was so tight I could barely swallow. Willing it to relax, to let me sound calm, I said, "Michael, you have no choice. You're not going anywhere but to jail. Your only decision now is how you'll be treated there. You want to know what they do to guys like you in jail? You want me to spell it out for you?"

For the first time he looked scared. He pressed the point of the blade into Claire's skin.

She screamed but no sound came out.

I kept my eyes on Michael. "In prison, Michael, you can face the lifers on your own, or I can see that you get special treatment. Your choice, Michael. You want a room of your own, nights alone, then you do exactly what I tell you." Textbook hostage negotiation—promise them anything.

The tape recorder clicked off.

Michael jerked backward. He poked the knife in Claire's throat. Blood spurted. She screamed. I lunged for his arm. He thrust her into me. Shrieking, she slid to the floor.

Michael was out the door and gone.

CHAPTER 27

☐

Claire lay on the floor, curled into a fetal position. I yelled for Williams as I ran across the dirt path after Michael Wennerhaver. The fog was pudding-thick; the flashlight beam barely made it to the ground. At the jade plant where Madeleine had hidden the metal box and her Parking Enforcement wand, I flashed the light toward the steep dirt path into the canyon. I couldn't see more than a yard ahead. I doused the light, and leaped onto the downward path, skidding with both feet, leaning back to keep from somersaulting, hands in front of my face batting away leaves and twigs. Dirt flew up, clogging my nose, coating my teeth and tongue with grit. The rocky ground scraped my butt, the revolver banged my ribs, and the flashlight I was still clutching kept jarring my wrist.

At the bottom of the path I slid to a halt and looked around. The air was clearer down here; the fog was held back by the trees. But Michael wasn't in sight. He couldn't be far ahead. I pulled the revolver out of the pack and stood listening. My heart thumped against my ribs; my breath was coming in gasps. Leaves rustled, the creek gurgled loud as the Mississippi, paws scampered: everything made noise; nothing stood out.

I squinted, willing him to come into view. Dammit, he would not get away!

The whole place smelled of wet dirt, eucalyptus, and bay leaves. The damp air slid under my jacket, iced my back. I shivered but the movement didn't warm me.

I stepped across the creek and moved under the thick branches on the far side. He could be scrambling up the canyon wall into the dark of Kensington. There was no way to stop him. It was too late to go back and call for backup. Maybe the patrol units around Champion's were still there. Maybe Michael would run headlong into them. Maybe not.

I stood stone-still, squinting into the darkness, listening. Nothing moved. It was a blind stare-down in the dark, just the two of us. One of us would flinch. When Michael moved, I'd get him. I braced the gun and waited.

In her room I hadn't let myself look at Claire, but I'd seen her out of the corner of my eye. I could see her now, held there in front of Michael with his knife piercing her neck. Terrified, her naked breasts exposed, she hung there as limp as the dummy, and as powerless.

I wanted to kill him.

I "saw" Madeleine begging me to come back . . . because of him. Madeleine Riordan, the woman who terrified the whole police department, reduced to . . . reduced to nothing. I was sweating and shivering. Blood pounded in my ears. I could barely hear the leaves rustling around me.

I pushed the pictures out of my mind and squinted into the darkness. What was Michael thinking? Was he still down here? I couldn't wait forever. But *he'd* be thinking that, too. That's what the stare-down was.

Movement. In the bushes just off the path, five feet to my right. "Freeze!" I yelled.

There was no sound, as if every creature in the canyon had stopped to listen. I could make out the outline of his body. I could have flicked on the flashlight. I didn't. "Lift your hands over your head."

He didn't move. He was bent over, crouched just like he'd been over Claire's bed. My head pounded with rage. I wanted to burst through restraint, decency, responsibility—all those so-female traits—and shoot his balls off.

In the distance came the coo of an owl. Michael stood up.

"Raise those hands! Now!" Time stopped. Every atom of my body screamed at him: *Ignore the command! Lunge forward! Come on, give me an excuse to shoot!*

He didn't move. I didn't have to give him another chance. No one would know. It would be revenge for all the Claires in places much worse than Canyonview, all the hostages of life.

I could see him clearly now. He didn't have a weapon, none visible. But he *could* have one—I could say that—if he had stolen Champion's weapons, he could be reaching for one, even the review commission would believe that. The air swelled thicker in my nostrils; I could barely breathe. My heart was pounding in my throat. "I can kill you right now, Michael. I'll squeeze this trigger and blast your head all over the canyon. Your choice." I wasn't yelling anymore. My voice was low; it sounded utterly calm. I cocked the revolver.

His arms flew up. Leaves fluttered, animals moved, the wind rustled the grasses.

"Keep those hands up, drop to your knees. Now! Do it!" I yelled. "Facedown on the ground. Spread your arms and legs. Do it! Do it now!"

It wasn't till I'd cuffed his right hand to his left foot behind him that he said, petulantly, "So why didn't you just shoot me?"

I was shaking now, thinking how close I'd come, how easy it would have been—how utterly righteous and good I would have felt.

But I hadn't shot him. I had stopped. I stared down at him lying on the muddy path. I didn't have an answer for his question. When I realized my reason, I knew he wouldn't understand it. But I said it out loud anyway. "You can consider this Madeleine's legacy. She would have insisted on justice, even for you."

I shone the light on him. He didn't understand. But there was something here he would remember. I flashed the light around till I found a spread of poison oak. "Crawl over to your right, Michael. That's it, three feet to your right."

It wasn't the same as shooting him, but you take what you can.

CHAPTER 28

□

I was relieved when Michael refused to speak without his lawyer. No matter how depraved an action, there is some cause. Michael Wennerhaver doubtless had suffered himself. But I didn't want to know about that. Not yet.

By the time I finished herding him through processing, the lobby was packed with the press. I could have let Doyle handle them alone; it was the first upbeat press conference he'd had in days. But I'm never going to make chief by shirking the limelight. And when the public read about Michael abusing old women, I wanted them to see the woman who nailed him.

For years when people asked why I became a police officer, I told them I took a bunch of civil service tests, passed some, and when I finished the oral exam for the police I realized I'd be good at the job. That was *how* I got the job. Only now did I see *why* I wanted it. It's not something I'm comfortable admitting here in laid-back Berkeley. I like to think of myself as able to go with the flow, a woman who is not hostage to things, or places, or people. I drive a car built before some of the perps I collar were born. I've lived on a back porch, I've house-sat for months, and my room in Howard's house I see as temporary. I have a superficial freedom. But ask me to leave Berkeley, to live without Howard, and that's a different story. Then I don't want to be caught up in a flow that washes me away from them. There are things in my life I need to control. As a police detective I have more power than Madeleine Riordan ever had. It scares the shit out of me to think I could lose it as entirely as she did. Maybe that press conference was to assure myself I couldn't.

When I finished with the paperwork, it was after two A.M. Usually when you get a big collar there are other officers to share the celebration. But one of Howard's substance abuse perps had been spotted transacting business in west Berkeley; Howard would be there for hours. Eckey would be delighted about Champion, of course. But Madeleine Riordan's murder had been too personal a case for anyone else to understand the flatness of what I felt now. There was nothing to celebrate. I was too wired and still too much in Madeleine's head to go home. And there was only one place to go, only one person who would understand.

I called the pizza takeout. The delivery boy was at Herman Ott's door when I arrived. Ott opened at the first knock. He had heard about the collar, of course. He looked as drawn as if he'd watched the whole operation from the sidelines, unable to help or even holler.

I told him about Michael, gave him a moment to ponder what other seamy scenes Michael might have orchestrated in nursing homes before, and to realize what he would never do in places like that again. Then I said, "I don't know how much Madeleine was motivated by memories of her mother, but she more than evened the balance—for both of you."

I can't swear that I saw Ott's eyes water, he turned away too fast. But he did pay for the pizzas, both of them. Then we ate them, every bit, and talked about Madeleine. I think it was a wake she'd have liked.